SILVER
BULLETS

Classic Werewolf Stories

For Imogen and Joshua Blake,
in honour of 'The Bloodening'

SILVER BULLETS

Classic Werewolf Stories

Selected by
ELEANOR DOBSON

First published 2017 by
The British Library
96 Euston Road
London NW1 2DB

Introduction and notes copyright © 2017 Eleanor Dobson

'Running Wolf' by Algernon Blackwood reprinted by permission
of United Agents LLP on behalf of Susan Reeves-Jones.

Cataloguing in Publication Data

A catalogue record for this book is available
from the British Library

ISBN 978 0 7123 5220 8

Typeset by Tetragon, London
Printed in England by TJ International

CONTENTS

INTRODUCTION

Eleanor Dobson

T HE FIGURE OF THE WEREWOLF STRETCHES BACK TO THE mythological tales of antiquity. One individual, Lycaon (from whom lycanthropy, the metamorphosis from human to wolf, takes its name), was transformed as a punishment, after serving the flesh of one of his sons to the god Zeus. Another man was changed into a wolf by the gods after eating the entrails of a child. In both of these cases, becoming a wolf is a penalty for committing or inciting acts of cannibalism, violating the laws of human (and divine) morality. With the rise of Christianity, werewolf imagery became associated with the devil. Broadly speaking, in the Middle Ages, folkloric traditions differed between French- and German-speaking countries, and Hungary, Romania and the Balkans. Werewolves in these cultures were connected to witchcraft and revenants, respectively. In some rare cases, werewolves in medieval romances were relatively benevolent, aiding knights on their quests, a far cry from the animalistic creature with which we are familiar today.

The werewolf fiction of the nineteenth century onwards can be seen to draw heavily upon these earlier influences. With the rise of Gothic fiction came an increase in demand for stories featuring supernatural creatures: the ghost, the vampire, and even the reanimated Egyptian mummy. The werewolf is a cousin of these aforementioned monsters, a vessel for society's concerns, increasingly appearing in novels, short stories, and poetry over the course of the Victorian period and beyond. Werewolves and vampires have a particularly close affinity: in Bram Stoker's famous novel

Dracula (1897), for example, the count can control wolves, and at one point transforms into a large black dog. Literary greats did not shy away from these sensational or Gothic themes; included in this volume are works by two winners of the Nobel Prize in Literature: Rudyard Kipling and William Butler Yeats.

This collection brings together short stories and two poems spanning from 1831 to 1920, from one of the very first werewolf stories appearing in Britain—Leitch Ritchie's 'The Man-Wolf' (1831)—through to a werewolf tale published after the conclusion of the First World War—Algernon Blackwood's 'Running Wolf' (1920). As Bourgault du Coudray Chantal notes in her excellent study *Curse of the Werewolf: Fantasy, Horror and the Beast Within* (2006), "Werewolves" was the name adopted by the German soldiers who declined to disperse after the conclusion of the First World War. These men had witnessed horrors, and their inner beast had come to the fore. Blackwood's tale is remarkably peaceful given its historical context; perhaps to him, after the horrors of war, the werewolf no longer seemed a creature to be feared, but one which should be met with sympathy. There may be a beast in all of us if exposed to the right stimuli, but the beast is not necessarily a monster.

The werewolf is incredibly versatile in its identity: it can be man or woman, young or old, and of a variety of racial identities. They are often mysterious strangers, but can also be people known to those who interact with them, even family members. Frequently, the werewolf is a threatening figure, but they can also be victims, manipulated by those who seek to destroy them or trap them permanently in their animal forms. They can also be figures of empowerment: it is noteworthy that two of the three female authors in this collection—Rosamund Marriott Watson and Clemence Housman—depict female werewolves, and the remaining female writer, Catherine Crowe, describes a woman accused of being a werewolf. The werewolf almost always raises questions of identity, transforming between two states, and often attempting to keep their lycanthropy secret. It is tempting to read werewolves in the works of Saki, for example, as connected to his homosexuality, part of his identity which had to be concealed during the time when he lived. His story 'Gabriel-Ernest' (1909) appears in this collection. Some of the werewolves that appear here also indicate the xenophobia for which the Victorians are renowned: in Rudyard Kipling's 'The Mark of the Beast' (1890) the transformation of a British man into a werewolf is effected by an Indian leper at a Hindu temple. Native American culture is also associated with human-to-animal metamorphosis: in Henry Beaugrand's 'The Werewolves' (1898), one cannot help but detect prejudice in his insistence that Native American werewolves are particularly dangerous. Blackwood's tale offers a welcome counter-point in which Native American wolf and Canadian man work together peacefully. Werewolves often, as Janine Hatter notes in her essay 'Lycanthropic Landscapes: An EcoGothic Reading of Nineteenth-Century Werewolf Short Stories', show that the wealth of characters who undergo these transformations are united by their sympathy with nature and the environment. This is just one way in which we might "read" the werewolf in a more favourable light: they are creatures which often inhabit a mythological or folkloric past, a "once upon a time" rather than the modern world.

Just as werewolves themselves vary, methods for dispatching werewolves differ from tale to tale. In Beaugrand's 'The Werewolves' (1898), Christian rituals and holy items can alleviate lycanthropy or kill the afflicted: the sign of the cross is cut into bullets or the victim's forehead. Holy water, rosary beads, and four-leafed clover are all effective against werewolves. In other tales, such as Gilbert Campbell's 'The White Wolf of Kostopchin' (1889), werewolves can be killed with ordinary bullets, and after death a permanent transformation back into human form takes place. Many werewolves are never dispatched or cured, giving certain works that appear here a chilling sense of inconclusiveness.

In amassing stories for this collection, I have had, by necessity, to omit many tales, though I have attempted to direct the reader to other stories of interest by the same author in the introductory notes to each work. Algernon Blackwood and Saki, for example, wrote a number of other stories featuring wolves or werewolves. I have favoured short stories in their entirety over excerpts from novel-length works so that a whole story can be enjoyed from start to finish in a single sitting. I have also selected tales which I think best represent the variety of werewolf tales across this period, which spans nearly a century.

Before I let these tales speak for themselves, I would like to thank Robert Davies, Managing Editor of British Library Publishing, for supporting this project from its formation through to its fruition. And I hope that readers with an appetite for tales of danger, seduction and monstrosity are left suitably thrilled.

ELEANOR DOBSON
University of Birmingham

FURTHER READING

Chantal Bourgault du Coudray, *The Curse of the Werewolf: Fantasy, Horror and the Beast Within* (London: I. B. Tauris, 2006).

Janine Hatter, 'Lycanthropic Landscapes: An EcoGothic Reading of Nineteenth-Century Werewolf Short Stories' in *Revenant*, Vol. 2, pp. 6–21.

THE MAN-WOLF

Leitch Ritchie

Published in *The Romance of History: France* (1831)

Leitch Ritchie (1800–1865) was a Scottish journalist, novelist, and travel writer. He worked as editor of a variety of periodicals across his career. While highly regarded in his time, today he is most often remembered as the author of 'The Man-Wolf'.

'The Man-Wolf' was one of the first British werewolf stories, appearing in the first of a two-volume collection of historical fiction entitled *The Romance of History: France* (1831). The tale focuses on a married knight and his unwed lover, with whom he seeks to elope. But talk of such transgressions is accompanied by the howling of wolves outside, and the lovers speak of the possibility that they might be transformed for their sins. Leaving for his home, the knight encounters a series of supernatural creatures, subjecting him to increasing psychological torment. Ultimately, this is a tale where relationships and loyalty are tested; we, as readers, are invited to question: which of the characters is the real monster?

Oh, flesh, flesh, how art thou fishified!

SHAKSPEARE

*Je me souviens, en effet, qu'à la table du sénéschal était un
seigneur qui faisait rire les convives par la manière gauche avec
laquelle il maniait la fourchette et les couteaux; mais comment
me serais-je imaginé que je soupais avec un ancien loup?*

TRISTAN LE VOYAGEUR

IT WAS THE THIRD DAY, AFTER THE GRAND PROCESSION IN
honour of Saint Ursula and the other virgin martyrs, and yet
the town of Josselin was far from having returned to its wonted
repose. The bells of Notre Dame du Roncier still rang out every
now and then, as if forgetting that the fête was over; crowds were
seen rolling, and meeting, and breaking in the streets; banners
floated from the windows, and flowers and branches tapestried the
walls. The representatives, indeed, of the eleven thousand Virgins
had begun to disappear from the gaze of an equivocal worship,
like the flowers at the close of summer. Every hour some glittering fragment was seen detaching itself from the mass, and as the
beautiful pensionnaire, in her litter, or on her palfrey, raised her
head sidelong to listen to the discourse of some wandering knight,
whom chance, or our Lady of the Bramble-bush, had bestowed on
her for an escort, she might have been observed to throw forwards
into the distance a glance of fear, or at least distaste, to where the

bars of her monastic cage seemed to gape for their accustomed prisoner. The ladies of the neighbourhood too, and the high-born cameristes of the nobility, as they floated homewards, surrounded by the chivalry of their province, sighed heavily when the towers of the chateau of the house of Porhoet melted away in the golden sky; and the humbler damsels of the villages, to whom a part in the procession had been accorded, from the difficulty of finding so many virgins of high rank, waved mournfully their chaplets of bluebells in token of adieu, and as the evening drew in, looked round in terror for the wandering fires of the sotray, and the dwarfs who dance at night round the peulvan.

A sufficient number still remained, however, to give an appearance of bustle and animation to the town; and it was thought that so great a concourse had never before been known to grace the annual ceremony of ducking the fishermen, which took place on the day when this history commences. The crowd which lined the river-side was immense. Ladies, knights, and squires, chatelains of the neighbourhood, priests, bourgeois and villeins—all were jumbled together with as little distinction as it was possible for the feudal pact to sanction. Minstrels, trouveres, and jongleurs mingled in the crowd, some singing, some striking the cymbals, and some reciting stories. Tables were spread in the midst where savoury viands were eagerly bought by the spectators—for it was now more than two hours since dinner, being past midday. Instead of tablecloths, the ancient economical substitute of flowers and leaves was tastefully arranged upon the board, and streams of wine and hippocras played from naked statues, in a manner which in our time would be reckoned less delicate than ingenious.

The bells at last began to ring, and the trumpets to bray; and the judges of the place, surrounded with banners, and all the pride, pomp, and circumstance of authority, entered upon the scene. Having taken their station, a solemn proclamation was made, calling upon all the persons who had sold, during Lent, fish taken in the river, to compeer then and there, either personally or by proxy, and for the satisfaction of the lieges, and in token of fealty and submission to the lord of the fief, to throw a somerset in the said river, under pain of a fine of three livres and four sous.

A simultaneous shout arose from the multitude when the crier finished, and the air was shaken for many minutes by a burst of laughter like the neighing of a whole nation of Houyhnhnms. One by one, the fish-merchants answered to the summons; some defying the ridicule of their situation by an air of good-humoured audacity; some looking solemn and sulky; and some casting a glance of marked hostility upon the turbulent and rapid waters before them. These feudal victims, generally speaking, were stout young fellows; but a few among them were evidently quiet towns-folk, who had nothing to do with the catching of the fish they had had the misfortune to sell. Two or three appeared to be the rustic retainers of gentlemen who had not scrupled to make profitable use of the river where it watered their estates, but who were altogether disinclined to do homage in their own persons; and these *locum tenentes* more especially looked with extreme disgust upon an element with which they were connected nei-ther by habit nor interest. Owing to the late rains, indeed, the stream on this day presented an appearance not very inviting to the unpractised bather. The black and swollen waters came down with a sullen turbulence, and an eddy whirling violently in the deep pool chosen for the scene of the divers' exploits, was somewhat startling to the imagination. Some were followed to the water's edge by the elder women of their families visiting and encouraging them, and others were egged on to the adventure by the sheathed swords of their masters, who seemed to enter into the joke with great gusto, shouting and clapping their hands at every deeper plunge.

The sport at length suffered some interruption from the backwardness of a country fellow, whose master in vain endeavoured, partly by fair words and partly by punches with the hilt of his sword, to drive him into the river.

"For the love of the Virgin," said the recusant, "only look at these black and muddy waters! It was on this very spot I saw last Easter the Leader of Wolves step grimly upon the bank in the moonlight, followed by his hellish pack; and, now I think on't, if he did not look at me fixedly with his dead eye, I am no Christian man, but a heathen Turk!"

"Thou shalt tell me the story again—thou shalt indeed," said the master, a man in the prime of life, and a knight by his golden spurs—"but in with thee now, good Hugues—in with thee, for the honour of the house! 'Tis but a step—a jump—a plunge; thou wilt float, I'll warrant thee, like a duck. Now, shut thy mouth, wink thine eyes, and leap, in the name of Saint Gildas!"

"Saint Gildas, indeed!" said the man—"I am neither a duck nor a saint, I trow. I cannot roost upon the waters, not I, with my legs gathered up into my doublet. Were it a league to the bottom, I should down. Neither can I tuck the waves under me like a garment, and sail away in the fashion of the Abbot of Rhuys, as light as a fly in a cockle-shell, singing, *Deus, in adjutorium*."

"Want of faith, good Hugues," returned the knight, repressing his vexation—"nothing save want of faith." But as the crowd began to murmur aloud, his choler awoke, and with a vigorous arm he dragged the victim to the water's edge.

"Beast that thou art!" he exclaimed, "shall the honour of the house of Keridreux be stained by a blot like thee? In with thee, rebellious cur, or I will pitch thee into the middle of the stream like a clod!"

"I will then," said the man, with a gasp, "I will indeed. Holy Saints, I had ever such an aversion to water! For the love of the Virgin, just give me a push, as if by accident, for my legs feel as if they were growing from the bank. Stay—only one moment! Wait till I have shut my eyes and my mouth. I will make as if I was looking into the river, and the bystanders will think we have been discoursing of the fish." The knight clenched his hand in a fury, as the murmurs of the crowd rose into a shout; and while Hugues was running over the names of as many saints as he could remember in so trying a moment—Notre Dame du Roncier, Saint Yves, Saint Brieuc, Saint Gildas—he lent him a blow that would assuredly have sent him beyond the middle of the stream, had not the victim, moved either by a presentiment of danger, or by some sudden qualm of cowardice, sprung round at the same instant, and caught, as if with a death-grip, by his master's doublet. The force which he had exerted almost sufficed of itself to overbalance the knight, and it is no wonder, therefore, that the next moment both master and man were floundering in the river.

A rush took place to the water's edge at this novel exhibition. The bourgeois clapped their hands and shouted to the depth of their throats; the ladies screamed; and those who had handsome knights near them fainted; all was noise and confusion among the crowd.

The knight, in the mean time, being tall, had gained a footing, although up to his neck in water; where he stood tugging at his sword, and casting round a bloodthirsty glance, resolving to sacrifice the caitiff who had so villainously compromised the dignity of the house of Keridreux, before emerging from the river. Hugues was carried out of his reach by the current, and dragged on shore amid the jeers of the bystanders; and the stout knight, as soon as he had become aware of this fact, rejecting indignantly the assistance that was offered him, climbed up on the bank, and clearing a space with a single circle of his sword, strode up to his intended victim. Another instant would have decided the fate of Hugues, who, having escaped a watery death, seemed to view with composure the perils of the land; but a lady, breaking through the circle of spectators, stepped in between him and his master.

"A boon! A boon! Sir Knight," she exclaimed; "give me the villain's life, for the honour of chivalry!" The Sire of Keridreux started back as if at the sight of a spectre; his sword fell from his hand; the flush of anger died on his cheek; and he stood for some moments mute and motionless, like an apparition of the drowned.

"The boon," said he, at length recovering his self-possession, "is too worthless for thy asking. I would I had been commanded to fetch thee the head of the King of the Mohammedans, or to do some other service worthy of thy beauty, fair Beatrix, and of my loyalty!"

"Loyalty!" repeated the lady, half in scorn, half in anger. The knight sighed heavily; and after losing some moments in the purgatory of painful remembrance, his thoughts, reverting to the circumstances of his present situation, fixed eagerly upon the object apparently best qualified to afford them ostensible employment.

"How, dog!" he cried, striding up to the still dripping vassal, "hast thou not the grace even to thank the condescension which stoops to care for thy base and worthless life? Down on thy knees, false cur—crouch!" and catching Hugues by the throat, he hurled him to the feet of his patroness.

"Enough, enough," said the lady; "get thee gone, thou naughty fish-seller; St Gildas be thy speed, and teach thee another time to have more faith in the water, when the need of thy lord requires

thee to represent the worthy person of the Sire of Keridreux!"
Hugues kissed the hem of the mantle of his fair preserver, and
coasting distantly round his master, dived into the crowd and
disappeared.

While with the grave pace and solemn countenance of a Breton
knight, the Sire of Keridreux strode stately along in the townward
direction by the side of the lady, his lank hair and dripping garments
seemed to afford considerable amusement to the spectators. The
bourgeois concealed their merriment only till he had passed to a
distance at which it would be safe to laugh; and the nobles, partly
from politeness and partly from prudence, were fain to put their
gloves upon their mouths. The knight, however, seemed to have
forgotten his late disaster and present plight, in considerations of
more moment. He turned his head neither to the right nor to the
left, but stalked mutely and majestically along, till on arriving at
the house where his fair companion resided, the bubbling sound
that attended his plunging into an armchair recalled his wandering thoughts.

"The beast!" he muttered, "the outcast dog! To serve me such a
trick, and in her presence; after I had arrayed myself in all respects
befitting the dignity of the spurs, and journeyed hither on purpose
to get speech of her! Beatrix," he continued aloud, and seizing hold
of her hand with his wet gloves—"fairest Beatrix, deign to regard
with compassion the most miserable of the slaves of thy beauty!"

"Indeed I do," said Beatrix, with grave simplicity—"the weather
begins now to get cold, and these wet clothes must be both unpleasant and dangerous. I think I hear the cry of 'cupping!' in the street;
allow me to persuade thee to lose a little blood."

"An ocean in a cause of thine!" replied the Knight, "but by a
lance, fair Beatrix, not a lancet; I had ever a horror of losing blood
otherwise than in a fair field."

"Then at least a draught of wine will fortify thy bowels against the cold; and here stands a flask of the true Paris brewing, to which our wines of Brittany are mere cider." She then decanted about a modern quart into a huge silver cup, which she presented to the knight.

"Let it receive virtue from thy lip," said the knight, hesitatingly, "or I shall find none."

"Nay, nay, fair sir," replied Beatrix, "those days are past and gone. We *have* eaten, it is true, out of the same dish, and drunken out of the same cup, but what was only folly then would be sin and shame now." The knight raised the goblet gloomily to his mouth.

"I trust," said Beatrix, while she stooped, as if to look for something among the rushes on the floor—"I trust that the worthy Dame of Keridreux is in good health?" The knight started at the question, and was seized with a fit of coughing which spoiled his draught.

"Confusion upon the name!" he cried, dashing the remainder of the wine upon the floor. "Would to Heaven she were in the health I wish her! And it is thou, cruel as thou art, and fair as thou art cruel, who hast bound me to a stake as doleful as the cross—who hast leagued me, I verily believe, with an incarnate fiend!"

"I have heard," said Beatrix, demurely, but with sparkling eyes, "that the Dame of Keridreux is of somewhat a peculiar temper; but, for my part, I was, as I am, only a simple maiden, and no liege sovereign to give in marriage my vassals at my pleasure."

"Oh, would thou hadst been less my liege sovereign—or more! I loved thee, Beatrix, as a man and a soldier; I knew nothing, not I, of the idle affectation which plays with a true servant even as an angler tickles a trout; I received thy seeming slight as a purposed insult—and straightway went home, and married another in pure fury and despite."

"Alas, alas!" said Beatrix, weeping, "thou wert ever of a fierce and sudden temper! Thou knewest not of the modern fashion of noble and knightly love. Having plighted thy troth, and drunk with me of the cup of faith and unity, thou dreamedst not of aught save holy wedlock after the manner of our ancestors. It entered not into thy brain to imagine that the lays of the minstrel were to be verified in the history of private life, and that thou wert to enter into human happiness, as the soul attains to Heaven, through the portals of doubt, fear, sorrow, suffering, yea, even despair. Alack-a-day! Peradventure I was myself to blame; peradventure I disguised the too great softness of my heart by too stony a hardness of the face, and looked to thee, alas! for more patience and forbearance in the conduct than there was constancy in the soul. But God's will be done!" continued she, drying her eyes. "Time and Our Lady's benevolence will straighten all things, even the crooked temper—if crooked it be—of the Dame of Keridreux."

"Serpent!" exclaimed the knight, bitterly, "thou knowest not what she is. Oh, if I could find but one leper spot on her body for twenty on her soul!"

"Hush! hush!" interrupted the lady, hastily, "thou forgettest that although the laws of man are silent, those of God still speak with a voice of thunder to the transgressor!"

"But thou knowest her not," repeated the knight. "Oh, I could tell thee what would turn thy young blood cold but to hear!"

"Then tell me," said Beatrix, "for I love to have my blood run cold."

"Alas, alas!" ejaculated the sorrowful husband, "she understands Latin!"

"Latin! Holy Virgin, how I pity thee! Out on the false heart! It could not be without a price she bought that knowledge. It was

but last Easter that one of those learned dames in the neighbourhood of the convent where I board, sat upon a viper's eggs, and
produced a winged serpent with three heads, whose nourishment
to this hour, as all men relate, is human blood." The gallant knight
grew pale at this anecdote; but after swallowing down another
goblet-full of wine at a draught, he hemmed stoutly, and again
seizing the hand of his sometime love—

"Beatrix," said he, suddenly, "I am weary of my life; I have come
to the determination of abandoning my inheritance, and passing
over into Italy. Fly with me! I will either beg or buy a dispensation
from the Pope, and make thee my wife in Rome." Beatrix opened
her eyes in astonishment mingled with horror. Turning away her
head in aversion, she looked towards the window. The shades of
evening were beginning to fall, and at that moment the distant
howl of a wolf in the neighbouring forest struck upon her ear.
The maiden shuddered at the ominous sound. Spitting in sign of
abhorrence, while she crossed herself devoutly—

"Alas!" she exclaimed—"unhappy wretch! Knowest thou not
that in Italy—ay, even in Spain, or England, thou wouldst still be
under the jurisdiction of the laws of Heaven? Are we not assured
that such a transgressor shuts upon himself the gates of Paradise—
and with a wife like thine, couldst thou expect them to re-open?
Would the vixen Dame of Keridreux, beseeching the permission
of Saint Peter, come to thee at thy cry, and exclaim through the
bars, 'I forgive thee!'" The knight groaned, and applied again to
the wine-goblet.

"Art thou not afraid," resumed the lady, "to go home to thy
lonely abode, and at so late an hour, with a mortal sin in thy
thoughts? Perchance the howl of that prowling wolf was an omen
sent by Our Lady herself to warn thee; and now, while I recall
it—Holy Saints—methought the voice sounded like thine own!"

"Saint Yves, and Saint Brieuc!" cried the knight, starting suddenly upon his legs—"thou dost not mean it! No longer ago than last night I dreamed that I was myself transformed into a loup-garou; and at Easter the misbegotten cur who dragged me today into the river saw with his own eyes the Leader of Wolves coming out of the very pool where I plunged!"

Beatrix changed colour at this intelligence, and as the room became darker and darker, began to wish her unhallowed lover away.

"Repent," said she—"repent while there is yet time; I will myself beseech Our Lady du Roncier in thy behalf. Good-night, good-night—and Heaven hold thee from turning into a loup-garou!" The knight, true to the Breton custom, having first ascertained that there was no more wine in the jar, made his obeisance with a heavy sigh, and left the house without uttering another word.

His conversation with Beatrix having been greatly fuller than it has been thought necessary to report, it was now late in the evening, being past eight o'clock. The streets were deserted, and the houses shut up; and most of the inhabitants, having supped two hours ago, were beginning to think of retiring to bed. On emerging from the dark and lonely street, where the rows of tall houses inclined their heads to each other in gossip fashion, the knight, with unsteady step, and head bewildered both by love and wine, took the way to the bridge. While walking cautiously over the creaking planks, a hum of distant voices rose upon his ear, and presently a small solitary light appeared dancing wildly upon the troubled waters. He stood still in awe and curiosity, till at length the light was suddenly extinguished, and the voices ceased; and muttering a prayer for the drowned, whose corpse was thus sought for, and miraculously pointed out, he resumed his journey.

The shades of evening fell more thickly around every moment, and the sire began to regret his bootless journey, and to look sharply about at the solitary tree or tall stone which stood here and there with an unpleasant perpendicularity near the road-side. In those days, trees and stones were not the only objects of curiosity which presented themselves to the gaze of the night traveller. Men, housed in their towers, and castles, and cottages, were accustomed piously to leave the kingdom of literal darkness to those whom it more concerned; and when accident compelled some luckless way-farer to encroach upon forbidden hours, he looked upon himself as an intruder where he had no business, and where he was exceed-ingly likely to meet with the chastisement he deserved. Like most persons in a similar situation, the knight experienced a marvellous increase in piety as he went along. He repeated an *Ave* at every step; and on arriving at the different confluences of little village paths, where crosses were raised to serve as direction-posts to the dead who might be disposed to revisit their relations, he stood still, and prayed aloud, with perfect sincerity, for the repose of their souls.

Further on, having reached a stream which, leaping out of a wood, crossed the road, he paused in doubt as to the depth—for, in truth, his brain was somewhat confused with the wine he had drunk. On raising his head he was startled to see a lady standing among the trees at the water's edge. She was dressed in white, and, as well as he could distinguish, very elegantly formed; but her face was concealed from him, as she bent over the stream busily engaged in wringing a garment which she had apparently just washed. An unpleasant sensation swept across the mind of the Sire of Keridreux; and although a man of distinguished courage, and devotedly attached to the fair sex (for all his wife belonged to it), he plunged suddenly knee-deep into the water, and made for the opposite bank. Attracted by the sound, the lady raised her head.

"Sir Knight," she exclaimed, in a voice of touching sweetness— "tarry, I pray thee, for the love of honour, and help me to wring this garment, which is all too heavy for my slender fingers!" The knight, half alarmed and half ashamed, turned back, and leaping into the wood, seized hold of the dripping garment which she presented to him. He twisted to the right; but the lady was twisting the same way.

"We are wrong," said she, with good-humour. The knight tried again, but with the same effect—again—and again; and as at last he perceived with whom he had to deal, his hair bristled upon his head, and cold drops of sweat trickled down his brow. But still he continued the bootless labour, twisting, straining, praying, and perspiring, till at length the garment fell into the water, and danced away like a bubble on the stream; and the false washerwoman, breaking into shrieks of wild laughter, disappeared among the trees.

The knight made but one leap across the river, and regaining the firm road, recommenced his journey with as much speed as could well be exerted by legs which would not be said to run. His brain, unsettled before, was turned completely topsy-turvy by this adventure; the air was thick with shadows; his ears were fitted with strange voices; and at length, as the substantial howl of a wolf arose from the neighbouring thicket, it was echoed by a cry as wild and dismal from his own lips. His dream of the loup-garou—the warning of Beatrix—the horrible similarity she had detected in the voices of the wolf and the man—all rushed upon his heart like a deluge.

At the instant, a sound resembling a human cry floated upon the sluggish wind: it approached nearer and nearer, seeming one moment a shout of menace, the next a call for aid, and the next a moan of agony. Sometimes it appeared to melt away in the distance, and sometimes the heart of the traveller died within him as it crept close to his very heels. In vain he tugged with unstrung fingers at his sword—in vain he essayed to produce one pious ejaculation

from his dry lips; and at length, fairly subdued by the horrors of
his situation, he betook himself to open flight.

The voice of the Crieuses de Nuit pursued him—his brain
began to wander. His rapid steps sounded to his ears like the galloping of a four-footed animal; he rubbed his sleeve upon his face,
and was convinced for the moment that he wore a coat of fur,
forgetting that his own beard produced the peculiarity of friction:
but at length, somewhat relieved by the rattling of his sword, and
the jingling of his spurs, he thanked Our Lady du Roncier that he
was still no loup-garou.

The night in the mean time was getting darker and darker; the
road, where it crossed a plain, became less distinguishable from the
bare and level soil at the sides; and at length the traveller, deviating
by little and little, lost the track altogether. Still, however, he continued to run on—for in mortal fear one cares not about the whither,
contented with escape, even if it should be to a worse danger. And
so it happened with the Sire of Keridreux; for in flying from what,
after all, was but perhaps a mere sound—*vox et praeterea nihil*—he
stumbled upon a substantial misadventure.

On diving down a sudden declivity, with even more velocity
than he had calculated on, he found himself all at once in the midst
of at least a dozen men, dressed from head to foot in white robes.
The abrupt visitor paused in astonishment and dismay, as a shout
of welcome rang in his ears.

"Hail, Sire of Keridreux!" cried one.

"Hail, husband of the dame who understands Latin!" another.

"Hail, guilty lover of Beatrix!" a third.

"Hail, magnanimous ducker in the fisherman's well!" a fourth;
and so on, till the whole had spoken; each speaker, when he had
finished, whirling swiftly round on one foot like a vaulter at a
merry-meeting. When every man had thus given his welcome,

the strange group continued their revolutions in silence for some
minutes, their white garments floating round them like vapour
agitated by the wind. They at length stopped suddenly, and shouted
with one voice, "Hail, *Loup-garou!*" and presently there began so
surprising a din of baying and howling that a whole forest of wolves
could not have produced the like.

The knight listened at first in terror, but by degrees he began to
howl himself as if in emulation. The louder he howled, however,
the louder rose the voices of his companions; and he threw away
his head gear, and spread back his beard to give his voice play.
Thus, by degrees, he tore off his clothes, piece by piece, till at last
he found himself howling *in cuerpo*. His comrades then caught him
by the hand, and joining hands also with one another, they formed
a ring, and began to dance round a great stone standing on end
in the midst. Round and round danced the trees, and the rocks,
and the hills, and the whole world, in the eyes of the knight; and
to his stunned ears every stone had a voice, every leaf and clod its
individual howl. Round flew the dancers—faster, and faster, and
faster; till the Sire of Keridreux sank gasping upon the ground, and
the White Men, springing into the air with a "whirr!" disappeared
from his sight.

When his recollection returned, he found himself lying upon
the same spot, stark naked. It was now daylight, and he heard
the sunrise horn sounding from a watch-tower in the neighbourhood. Gathering himself up, stiff, bruised, and exhausted, he
looked round, and discovered with no small satisfaction that he
stood upon his own ground. The castle of Keridreux was close at
hand, and the scene of his adventure was the corner of a belt of
wood which on one side protected the fortress. Having collected
his scattered garments, he dressed as well as he could, and went
straight home.

The Dame of Keridreux was in bed when her lord arrived, and as he entered the apartment, she raised herself on her elbow, and prepared, with eyes glowing like two live coals, to discharge upon his devoted head the wrath she had been nursing for him the whole night. There was something, however, peculiar in his appearance this morning. In his jaded and haggard air she could discern few of the accusing witnesses of debauchery she had so often produced against him; and his scared look, she saw at a glance, was wholly unconnected with conjugal awe. The lady, therefore, suffered her husband to undress without a single remark, and to throw himself into bed at an hour when more sprightly spouses were sallying forth to the chase.

Altering her usual plan of operations, she crept close to where he lay, and throwing her arm round him, heaved a deep sigh. The knight sprang with a suppressed oath from her embrace, and took refuge in a more distant part of the bed; a thing which it was not difficult to do at a period when such articles of household furniture were usually twelve feet long, and of a proportionate breadth.

"Alas!" sighed the lady, in a tender tone, "how dreary are the hours of night that are passed in the absence of a beloved husband!" The knight groaned.

"Where hast thou been, thou runaway?" continued she— "where hast thou been, my baron?"

"I have been," said the knight—"Oh!" and he groaned again.

"Alack-a-day!" sighed the dame, once more—"I slept not a wink the live-long night. I feared that some mischance had befallen thee; and the wolves in the forest kept such a howling—"

"It was I who howled!" said the knight, suddenly.

"Thou! Nay, now thou art mocking me; the merry wine still dances in thy brain—thou who howled?"

"By the Holy Virgin!" said the knight, "it was none other than my comrades and I!"

"Thou art mad to say it; thou art deepen in the wine-cups than I thought. Where hast thou been?" continued she, sharply—"where wert thou all night?"

"I was dancing in the wood," said the knight, sleepily and sulkily—"and I howled,"—yawning.

"*Why* didst thou howl?" inquired the lady, with fierce curiosity.

"I howled because I was a wolf, and could not choose!"

"O ho!" said she, as the knight dropped asleep—"O ho!" Then stirring him gently, and placing her lips to his ear—

"What part of the wood," she whispered, "my own baron?"

"At the corner," replied the half-unconscious knight, "where stands the great stone—cursed be its generation!" and he slept aloud.

The day was far advanced before the Sire of Keridreux awoke. He found, as usual, at his bedside his vassal Hugues; who indeed, besides his numerous other capacities, was a sort of body squire, or feudal valet (in the modern sense of the word), and superintended more particularly the dress and toilet of his master. Hugues on this occasion had much of the air of one of the class of quadru-peds we have mentioned, when his tail, technically speaking, is between his legs: he stood edgewise to his master, with his face in such a position as to give him the advantage of eyeing with equal perspicuousness the lord on the one hand and the open door on the other, while his feet were so planted upon the rushes that at a word or a look he could have vanished, in the manner vulgarly called "a bolt".

The knight, however, seemed to have been sweated out of his Celtic irascibility; for, although conscious that to the villainous trick of his dependant he owed all his misfortunes, he turned upon him a look more in sorrow than in anger.

"Alas!" said he, with a heavy sigh, "that he who has eaten of my bread, and drunk of my cup, with all his uncles and grand-mothers before him, should at last have served me so unrighteous a turn!"

"I could not help it," replied Hugues, whimpering, yet deriv-ing courage from the placid grief of his master—"St Gildas is my judge, I could not help it! Yet what, my master! It was but a ducking at the best; only fancy it rain water, and it will be dry before thou hast time to take off thy morning's draught."

"Out on thee, false knave!" said the knight—"thinkest thou I care for a wet doublet? It was not the water, alas! but the wine—"

"Holy Saints! and what have I to do with that?" ejaculated Hugues. "If it was not water—ay, and right foul and muddy water too—that thou and I played our gambols in, may I never taste another drop of wine in my life!"

"It was the wine, Hugues—and yet it was the water; for thou shalt know that a superabundance of the one can only be cured by a like quantity of the other. And yet, alas! it was not the wine, but the lateness of the hour; although this being the consequence of the lapse of time, and that of the action of drinking, which again was caused by water, thou, beast that thou art! art at the bottom of all.—Well, well, what is passed and gone may not now be helped; it behooves a wise man to enjoy the present and prepare for the future: hand me therefore my morning's draught, and let us consider of what is to he done; for I vow and protest that I do perspire from my very inmost marrow at the thoughts of the approaching night!"

The sire then raising himself up in bed, with the assistance of Hugues, applied to his lips, at short intervals, a capacious silver flagon filled with hippocras, and between whiles narrated at full length to the confidant the story of his mishaps.

In the consultation which followed it was determined that Hugues should start off incontinent on a fleet steed with a letter to Father Etienne of Ploërmel, the knight's confessor, imploring his immediate presence at the castle of Keridreux; and it was fondly hoped that, by virtue of the prayers and anathemas of that holy man, the evil hour of twilight, when the sire might otherwise expect to be driven forth to resume the nightly character of a loup-garou, would pass over in peace.

"Hie thee away, good Hugues—hie thee away!" said the knight; "ride for life and death, if thou lovest me; and as the holy monk is somewhat of the slowest in equestrian matters, even fix a pillion to thy own horse, and fetch him hither behind thee."

It was not the custom of the Dame of Keridreux to permit egress from the castle without knowing all the whys and where-fores of the matter; and Hugues, who had been trained to turn and double like a hare in such cases, hesitated as to the plan he should adopt to smuggle himself out. Recollecting, however, that in whatever manner he might manage for himself, it would be difficult to compel his steed to crawl upon knees and haunches, or even to repress the joyful neigh with which he was wont to enter upon a journey—and moreover, bethinking himself that, in reality, there was nothing detrimental to the power and dignity of the dame in her husband's desiring to see his confessor in circumstances so criti-cal, he went boldly to the stable and saddled his horse, only taking care to conceal the pillion with an old cloak, for fear of raising the Devil in the jealous mind of his mistress.

"And whither away, good Hugues?" asked the lady, popping in her head just at the moment when man and horse were about to dart from the stable—"whither away so fast, and whither away so late?"

"To Ploërmel," answered Hugues, "with the permission of God."

"And thine errand, if it be not a secret?"

"To order a mass to be said for the deliverance of my master from the power of evil spirits."

"A right holy errand! Our Lady speed thee, amen!"

"Amen!" repeated Hugues; and scarcely conscious that he had told a lie, so much was he in the habit of that figure of speech when in conversation with the dame, he was in the act of clapping his heels to his horse's sides.

"Stay!" said the lady; "I bethink me that I have here a memorandum for my own confessor at Ploërmel; and truly it is the duty of a good wife to seek assistance from holy church, in circumstances so strange and trying. Deliver this with commendations to Father Bonaventure; thou wilt distinguish it from thy master's, if he have given a written order for the mass, by its want both of seal and address; for the thoughts of the innocent require no protection from the curiosity either of men or spirits."

When Hugues, who loved a good gallop with all his heart, arrived at the oak of Mivoie, he bethought himself of his despatches, and slackening his pace, pulled them forth from his breast, to assure himself of their safety.

"This is my lady's," thought he; "for although I cannot read a single letter, yet I have learning enough to know that here there is neither seal nor address; while the other—Holy Mary! What hath come to pass?" and turning it round in consternation, he discovered that the second letter was in precisely the same predicament. The knight, in his anxiety and confusion had forgotten the customary forms; and the two letters, to the unpractised eyes of Hugues, were as indistinguishable as two peas. Although sorely afraid, however, of the consequences of a blunder where the vixen dame of Keridreux was concerned, he determined stoutly to be in the right on his master's side, and to try Father Etienne with both, should the first prove to be the wrong one. Fortifying himself with this resolution, he resumed his gallop, and speedily came within sight of the town of Ploërmel.

The avenues to this town were nothing more than the tracks from the neighbouring huts and castles; no great road appeared in its vicinity, like an artery, spreading wealth abroad into its dependencies; and no navigable river or canal supplied the want of a highway on terra firma. For this reason Ploërmel, although a considerable place, had something singularly melancholy and solitary in its aspect; the houses too were old and black; and the convent, now visible on the brow of a hill, seemed to guard with sullen austerity the strange quiet of the scene. Hugues crossed himself mechanically as he entered the town, and mentally resolved that nothing short of sorcery should detain him beyond sunset within its precincts.

Father Etienne was a precise and somewhat sour-looking elderly man, and Hugues was rejoiced to find, on delivery of the letter, that he had committed no mistake. The priest's countenance expressed both the grief and surprise that were natural on such an occasion; and after a moment's deliberation he told the messenger that he should be ready to accompany him to Keridreux in a few minutes. He then retired to read over again without witnesses the singular epistle he had received, which ran as follows:—

"I fear thy ingratitude for my preference; yet nevertheless, I would confer with thee in private this evening on matters which may concern us both. My husband, it seems, is translated into a loup-garou! I would inquire whether there be not force enough in thy prayers to restore him to his human form, and deprive him of the power of getting into mischief again. If thou understand me not, stay where thou art; but if thou be what I take thee for, and would fain find thee, come to me in the dusk, ascend the private stair, for fear of interruption, and I will meet thee in the closet?"

"Oh, woman, woman!" exclaimed the priest; "and will nothing less than a monk content thee? And a monk of my standing in the convent, and of my sanctity of character? But, nevertheless, I will go—yea, I will attend the rendezvous, and inquire into the real situation of my poor son in the spirit, the Knight of Keridreux. Peradventure the dame will not offer violence; but if she does, I will struggle in prayer and invocation—no saint will I leave unsummoned, and no martyred virgin unsolicited. But, in the mean time, it is necessary to beware of Brother Bonaventure, the dame's former confessor, whose eyes, as sharp at all times as those of a lynx, will now be made ten times more so by jealousy and wounded vanity. Let me first see that the coast is clear, and then steal out to—what may betide."

Father Bonaventure, to whom Hugues delivered the other letter, was a sleek, plump, oily monk of thirty-five, with an appearance of great good-humour in his countenance, belied at second sight by a sinister cast in one eye.

"Hum!" said he, reading the epistle of the afflicted knight; "this is well; the influence of the dame must have gone far indeed, when the Sire of Keridreux sends to *me* for a shrift or a benison! But can there be no blunder?—Hark thee, fellow, from whom hadst thou this letter?"

"From the Dame of Keridreux."

"Right, right; why, this is as it should be; but as for the loup-garou, and the midnight howling—Hark thee again, fellow—how didst thou leave thy master?"

"Queerish, may it please your holiness—a little queerish."

"Drunk—I thought so. I'faith, she is a clever woman, that Dame of Keridreux. To make her very husband send for me! But

we must have a care of brother Etienne, the knight's confessor;
the rogue half suspects me already; and when he knows that I
have supplanted him with the husband, there will be no keeping
his jealous eyes from my affair with the wife. In the mean time,
let us see that the coast is clear, and then hie we to inquire into the
malady of our loup-garou."

Hugues, being at length dismissed by Father Bonaventure, ran
anxiously to Father Etienne, to entreat him to mount and away;
but the latter encountering his brother monk on his road to the
stable-door, where the horse waited, pretended to have forgotten something, and hastily re-entered the convent. As for Father
Bonaventure, he started back with the same confusion, and from
the same cause, so that neither perceived the perplexity of the
other; and thus the two rivals kept playing at bo-peep till Hugues
was ready to tear his beard for very vexation. The sun at length set,
and the warder's horn sounding from tower to tower, struck upon
the heart of the faithful squire like a voice of despair.

"A curse on that monk," cried he, "and on all his grandfathers!
Does he mean to transport the relicks of the convent, one by one,
to our castle, that he thus goes and comes, and fetches and carries,
without beginning or end? My poor master will be out in the forest,
and stripped to the buff, long before we reach Keridreux; and at
every howl we hear on that lonely road, I am sure my heart will
leap higher in my mouth than it did when I plunged head foremost
into the fisherman's well."

Father Etienne, at this moment, approached to within a single
pace of the expectant horse; and while he stopped to look cautiously about him, Hugues, at the last grain of patience, and in the
fear of his life that the monk meant to turn tail again, whipped him
up in his arms, and clapping him upon the saddle, sprang himself
upon the pillion behind, and made off with his prize at full gallop.

The terrified ecclesiastic, seizing fast hold of the horse's mane with one hand, and of Hugues' uncombed beard with the other, kept his seat with admirable firmness, the motion of the animal jolting out sometimes a prayer and sometimes a curse, as they happened to come uppermost; while the venturous squire, looking pertinaciously to the quarter of their destination, already beginning to be covered with the shades of evening, and laying it stoutly into the horse with whip, spur, and tongue, all at one moment, had no time to think of the sacrilege he committed in stealing a churchman.

In the mean time, Father Bonaventure, perceiving the absence of his rival, although without imagining the cause, led his own palfrey in an instant out of the stable, and leaping nimbly on his back, scoured off in the same direction. The first monk no sooner observed the pursuit, than in the confused consciousness of intended secrecy, and perhaps of not overly virtuous intention, he uttered a cry of alarm, and forgetting his dread of equestrian exercises, began to belabour the beast with his heels, and shower upon him the verbal insults which all over the world have so powerful an effect on the exertions of the sensitive and intelligent horse. Hugues, terrified at this exhibition of terror, did not dare to look round for the cause, but gripped the monk still closer in his arms, and whipped, and spurred, and prayed with all his might; while Father Bonaventure, seeing a double-loaded steed maintain the *pas* so bravely, began to fear that his own nag was only trifling with him, and putting heel, and whip, and voice into furious requisition, dashed helter-skelter, neck or nothing, after.

On went the horsemen as if a whole legion of devils were at their heels; and it would have been an even bet which should gain the race, had not Father Bonaventure's palfrey suddenly stumbled in leaping a ditch. When Father Etienne saw his pursuer disappear all at once from the face of the earth, he was struck dumb with amazement; but soon, attributing the appearance to what seemed its probable cause, he wiped the sweat from his brow, and anathematised the phantom horseman with the bitterest curses of the Church.

In a few minutes more he was set down at his destination; and Hugues, without even waiting to receive a blessing for his safe conduct, dragged his horse abruptly and sulkily to the stable, swearing to himself, by every saint he could remember, that he would never ride double with a priest again in his life.

Although it was only dusk out of doors, when Father Etienne gained the secret stair he found himself in utter darkness. He had not groped his way long, however, till he heard a "Hist!" sounding along the corridor; and presently the Dame of Keridreux, encountering his hand, very unceremoniously threw her arm round his neck.

"And at last, my ghostly father!" said she, in a whisper. "What in the name of all the devils has detained thee? Another moment would have ruined all; for out of very madness, I would either have sworn a conspiracy against thee to the knight, or poniarded myself, where I stood here, by turns shivering and burning, in this cold, dark corridor."

Father Etienne blessed himself secretly that he was as yet only on the threshold of an intrigue with such a firebrand; and feeling his heart beat strongly, nay almost audibly, with virtuous resolution, he began to cast about for some means of edging himself out of the adventure.

"Thou knowest," continued the dame, with a sort of chuckle which made her confidant's blood run cold, "that the only way to deprive a loup-garou of the faculty of resuming his human shape in the morning, is to take away the clothes which he strips off on his conversion into a wolf. Ha! Ha! I cannot choose but laugh to think of my dear baron coming smelling, and smelling in vain, for his doublet. How he would glare and snort—Ha! Ha!—and howl— hoo-oo-oo!" Father Etienne's hair stood on end as the malicious dame, with impressible gaiety, began to howl in imitation of a wolf; nor was his horror lessened when, shortly after, a sound resembling an echo appeared to come from the direction of the knight's chamber.

"As I live," cried the lady, "he is at it already! Now will he forth presently into the wood to turn a loup-garou; and what we have to do must be done at once. Stay where thou art; stir not; speak not for thy life, till I come again!" and the dame glided along the corridor towards the chamber of her lord.

Father Etienne was no sooner left alone than, throwing himself upon his hands and knees, for fear of doing himself a mischief upon the steep dark stairs, he crept down like a cat, and with stealthy pace betook himself to the stable, determined to saddle the first horse he could lay hands upon, and ride full speed home to his convent, were it at the hazard of a hundred necks. It was now, however, quite dark; and although he could hear the panting of a steed, there was either no saddle in the stable, or it was hung out of his reach. In this predicament he lay down upon the straw, and waited in great agitation for the coming of some of the servants. A considerable time elapsed, and the meditations of the holy man became more confused every moment; till at length Hugues, bearing in one hand a lantern, and with the other dragging a large bundle, made his appearance at the stable-door.

"Oh heavens!" said he, holding up his lantern, "and is it thou after all? Well, I thought my lady must have been wrong when she talked of a monk and his palfrey, for here be no monks but thou, and no palfreys but my own precious Dapple."

"I pray thee, son," said the Father, "tell me no more of thy lady, but take me incontinent to the place thou broughtest me from, if thou settest aught of value on the prayers of a wretched but holy monk."

"Well, did ever mortal hear the like! I take thee, quotha! May the great Dev—No matter. At an hour like this, and my master just turning a loup-garou, and after thou thyself, monk though thou be, didst nothing but screech and sweat with fear all the way hither, although the darkness was no more to be compared to this than Heaven is to Hell! I take thee! I will see thee—nay, I say nothing; there is my precious Dapple, whom I love as my own soul—take *him*, he is thine for this night. Mount, mount, and be thankful, since thou wilt travel at such untimely hours; and if thou dost not pray heartily for the lender, monk though thou be, thou wilt surely go to — Ploërmel by some worse conveyance! There, thou sittest like a knight—On with thee, in the name of Saint Gildas!"

The monk having suffered Hugues, without expostulation, to perch him upon the horse, and fasten the bundle—although wherefore, he was too down-hearted to take the trouble of asking—behind him, set forth upon his dreary road with no other sign of farewell than a heavy sigh.

While wayfaring gently along, with the perfect concurrence of Dapple, on whose spirits the late race had had a sedative effect, his thoughts were busy with the circumstances of this strange journey. It was evident that some traitorous design was on foot against the knight. Who were the conspirators? Why, the Dame of Keridreux, and he himself, Father Etienne! His presence at the castle on the fatal night, if fatal it was to be, could be proved; he had met the lady by special appointment in secrecy and darkness, and she had imparted her evil intentions without a word of disapprobation on his part. Thus it appeared that his own safety was inextricably wound up with that of the lady; and the monk cursed from the bottom of his bowels the unlucky stars which had made him a party perhaps to a murder, or at least to the impiety of condemning an unfortunate gentleman to the forest for life, in the capacity of a wolf.

He arrived at the convent without further adventure; but, when unsaddling the horse, was surprised to observe the bundle, which, in the confusion of his mind, he had taken for a pillion. He carried it notwithstanding to his cell, telling the porter, in reply to his questions, that it contained a cloak and other habits he had received as a gift. Unfortunate falsehood—as true as any truth he could have told! It was in reality the cloak and other everyday habits of the Knight of Keridreux! The monk, thunderstruck at this new calamity, gazed upon the articles in silence. He felt all the horrors of actual guilt, and all the contrition of sincere repentance; he looked upon himself as a convicted criminal in the eyes of God and man, and upon the hose and doublet before him as the true *corpus delicti* of his villainy.

"Cursed be the minute in which I was born," cried he, "and the year and the day thereof! Cursed be the steed that bore me on its back on that nefarious errand! And may its master who seized me, even as a prisoner, in the snares of Hell never see salvation! What misery is this that has come upon me? Cannot people sin without my sanction? If they imagine treason, am I to be drawn into holes and corners to hatch it? If they murder, can nobody else be found to sharpen the dagger? And if they turn their husbands into beasts, is it still I who must hide the old doublet? Begone, evidences of guilt, and snares of perdition! I spurn ye, filthy rags of unrighteousness! Yea, I spurn ye with my foot—" and in a phrensy of rage and fear, he kicked the old clothes about the room, buffeting his breast, and tearing handfuls of hair from his beard.

The next morning he saw Father Bonaventure at Matins as usual, looking as if nothing had happened; and his choler reawoke, as he considered that all the misfortunes of the previous night ought to have fallen by right to him.

"Plague on the wavering fancies of women!" thought he; "of all the days in the year, what made her send for me at that identical time? And I—I would supplant thee! Ah, rogue, I supplanted thee in good season, if thou but knewest it. From the gallop, and the embrace, down to the old doublet, all should else have been thine—all—all—with a murrain to thee!"

But when the reports, as yet vague and mysterious, at length reached the convent of the misfortune which had befallen the Sire of Keridreux, the unhappy monk was ready to go wild with apprehension. In a few hours more, it was known that the knight, for his sins, had been converted into a loup-garou, and that the anxious search instituted by the distracted wife—if we should not rather say widow—had hitherto been productive of no clue either to the man, or to what were of as much importance in such cases, his clothes.

"I will not stand this!" cried Father Etienne, leaping from the bed where he had thrown himself in a fever—"I will not carry off, in a single evening's confessorship, what Brother Bonaventure so richly deserves by the labours of a whole year! By the Holy Virgin, he shall have the old clothes, if I die for it!" and in pursuance of this resolution, the very same evening, he conveyed secretly into his friend's cell the mysterious bundle.

When Father Bonaventure discovered the present, he had not the remotest idea of the real quarter from whence it had come. The dame, on finding her priest absent from the spot where she had directed him to wait, being too far advanced in the business to recede, had sent the bundle by Hugues, merely commanding him to "fix it on the monk's palfrey"; and meeting Father Bonaventure soon after ascending the stairs, the two proceeded to the execution of their plan without explanation, and without being the least aware that a second monk was in the house. On the present occasion, Father Bonaventure, without thinking of any intermediate channel, set down the gift at once as coming from the lady direct; whose fears he imagined, when the reports and surmises began to buzz, had impelled her thus to get rid of the proofs of their mutual guilt.

"Nay, nay," said he; "I will not put up with this. She might have burned them, if she had chosen; she who has opportunity for such things, and there would have been an end. But to send them to me! Why, what can a monk do with the old clothes of a knight? By my faith, I will not be put upon by any dame of them all! She has as good a right to any risk that is going as I; and they shall e'en find their way back as they came, and let her do with them as she lists."

Hugues, who ever since daybreak had ridden from convent to convent, like one distracted, alarming the enemies of the Devil with news of his triumph, and entreating their spiritual aid, arrived at this moment at the religious house of Ploërmel, and presented a fair opportunity to Father Bonaventure to get rid of his bundle. The dependant was easily persuaded to take charge of the precious deposit, which our priest desired him to deliver into the hands of the Dame of Keridreux; and being assured that the ghostly efforts of the monks should be devoted to the cause of his master, he turned his horse's head towards the castle, and began to jog homewards in a melancholy and meditative trot.

He had not journeyed far, ruminating sadly on the transactions of the last two days, when his eye was caught by a projecting corner of the bundle, which was strapped to the rear of his horse. He had not before bestowed much attention on the charge thus committed to his care, nor indeed on the instructions of the monk regarding it; but at this moment some dim associations were suggested to his mind which gradually led his thoughts to the bundle he had fixed on the same place the night before by command of his mistress. The more he gazed, the more his suspicions of its identity were confirmed, and at last, unable to resist the suggestions of that devil (or angel, as it happens) curiosity, he undid the fastenings, and drawing the huge pillion to the front, opened it out. His emotions on discovering the lost suit of his master may be conceived. At first he merely tied it up again, and applying whip and spur with all his might, set forth at headlong speed towards the castle; but in a few moments, as some sudden thought occurred to him, he pulled in the reins with a jerk, which sent the animal back on his haunches.

"Fair and softly!" said he. "Whither, and for what reason, do I haste? If a lady sends a bundle to a monk, and the monk returns the bundle to the lady, it is clear there is some collusion between them. And further, if that bundle be of the clothes of a loup-garou, is it not evident that nothing honest can be meant? Fair and softly, I say again, honest Hugues, and let us consider, as we go along, what is best to be done." The result of this consideration was a string of resolutions highly favourable to Father Bonaventure, but in nowise redounding to the credit either of the Dame of Keridreux or Father Etienne; and in conclusion, Hugues determined to steal quietly round the castle at nightfall, and, in spite of ghosts and men, to betake himself to the corner of the belt of the forest described by his master, and wait there till the dawn with the clothes, let who would come to claim them.

When it was sufficiently dark for his purpose, he advanced towards the castle, and muffling his horse's heels with handfuls of hay, reached the stable unobserved; then shouldering the bundle, he set out with a good heart for the forest.

While passing an angle of the building, however, a sound met his ear which made him pause. It was of so peculiar a nature, that he was uncertain for the moment whether it came from above, or below, or around, and he therefore stood stock still where he was, in the shadow of the wall. Presently the sound waxed louder, and the ground beside him seemed to tremble and give way; and in another moment a part of what appeared to be a subterranean arch fell in, and disclosed an object from which he recoiled in terror. Its form was human; it gleamed in the dark as white as snow; and when it began to ascend, as dumb as a spirit, to the surface of the earth, Hugues, unable any longer to combat his feelings, turned tail without disguise, and fled.

The footsteps of the phantom pursued him for some time, lending preternatural swiftness to his; but at length, conquering what might after all have been but imagination, he arrived alone at the corner of the forest, deposited the bundle upon the perpendicular stone, and sank fainting at its base.

When he opened his eyes again, startled into life by the howling of the wolves, his hairs stood up one by one upon his head, and cold drops of sweat beaded his brow, as he saw his master standing stark naked before him. The phantom (for such it seemed) seized hold of the bundle, and undoing the knots, dressed himself quietly in the clothes, and bestowing a hearty kick upon the squire—

"And thou, too!" he cried—"thou too must needs be in the cabal! Thou must skip, thou must fly, with a murrain on thy heels! As if there was no other place for a Christian knight to dress in than this accursed corner, with its upright stone of detestable memory!"

"As God is my judge," said Hugues, "it was not from thee I fled! I thought thou wert a loup-garou, and I came hither with thy clothes, of which some villainous treason had despoiled thee. But who, in the name of the Virgin, could have dreamed of seeing thee rising from the earth like a spirit—and from thy own ground too—and as naked as thou wert born!"

"When sawest thou the monk Bonaventure?" asked the knight.

"This afternoon," replied Hugues; "but if he said true, he is by this time in the castle consoling thy disconsolate widow." The knight ground his teeth, and tearing down a branch from a tree, walked with huge strides towards the castle. The noise he made at the gate speedily roused the servants, who were by this time asleep; but in their surprise and confusion, and joy, so long a time elapsed before admittance was afforded, that the birds their master sought were flown.

The Dame of Keridreux, as the history relates, betook herself, Latin, monk, and all, to a far country; and the knight, after mourning a reasonable time for his loss, went forth again to the wooing, this time successful, of the fair Beatrix.

Father Etienne, on one pretext and another, declined farther intermeddling in the spiritual concerns of so dangerous a family; and Hugues, who could not get the affair of the bundle out of his head, was not sorry for it.

This faithful factotum waxed daily in the good graces of both master and mistress; and when the knight, after supper, would relate the story of his translation into a loup-garou, Hugues as regularly took up the thread of the relation at the passages where he came in himself as a witness. As for the truth of the stories so related and so confirmed, it is presumed there can be only one opinion. It need not be concealed, however, that some have supposed the supernatural adventures of the knight to have taken place either in his own imagination or by the frolicsome agency of his neighbours; and that his final resumption of his clothes was not really made in the character of a loup-garou, but in that of a self-delivered man who had been incarcerated in the dungeons of his own castle by the fraud and force of a rascally priest and a faithless wife. But these questions are left to the sagacity of the reader.

A STORY OF A WEIR-WOLF

Catherine Crowe

Published in *Hogg's Weekly Instructor* (1846)

Catherine Crowe (1790–1872) was an author, playwright, and writer on the supernatural. After an unhappy marriage and a subsequent divorce, Crowe moved from England to Scotland, integrating herself into Edinburgh's literary circles. She was deeply interested in occultism, attending séances and befriending those who claimed to have mediumistic powers. She is also noteworthy for creating the first female amateur detectives in her debut novel, *The Adventures of Susan Hopley, or, Circumstantial Evidence* (1841).

'A Story of a Weir-Wolf', which first appeared in *Hogg's Weekly Instructor* in 1846, is believed to be the first werewolf story penned by a female author. In 1849 Crowe published a non-fiction article, 'Lycanthropy', which focused upon the then-recent crimes of the French grave-robber Francis Bertrand, nicknamed the "Vampire of Montparnasse". Evidently, Crowe's interest on such subjects extended from the folkloric and fantastical to the modern and the criminal. 'A Story of a Weir-Wolf' centres on female jealousy. Two cousins (one the daughter of an alchemist) fall for the same man. The mutual attraction that emerges between the man and the alchemist's daughter, two people of different social status, is scandalous. The result is a dangerous web of rumour that puts a number of this tale's characters in mortal danger.

I T WAS ON A FINE BRIGHT SUMMER'S MORNING, IN THE YEAR 1596, that two young girls were seen sitting at the door of a pretty cottage, in a small village that lay buried amidst the mountains of Auvergne. The house belonged to Ludovique Thierry, a tolerably prosperous builder; one of the girls was his daughter Manon, and the other his niece, Francoise, the daughter of his brother-in-law, Michael Thilouze, a physician.

The mother of Francoise had been some years dead, and Michael, a strange old man, learned in all the mystical lore of the Middle Ages, had educated his daughter after his own fancy; teaching her some things useless and futile, but others beautiful and true. He not only instructed her to glean information from books, but he led her into the fields, taught her to name each herb and flower, making her acquainted with their properties; and, directing her attention "to the brave o'erhanging firmament", he had told her all that was known of the golden spheres that were rolling above her head.

But Michael was also an alchemist, and he had for years been wasting his health in nightly vigils over crucibles, and his means in expensive experiments; and now, alas! he was nearly seventy years of age, and his lovely Francoise seventeen, and neither the *elixir vitae* nor the philosopher's stone had yet rewarded his labours. It was just at this crisis, when his means were failing and his hopes expiring, that he received a letter from Paris, informing him that the grand secret was at length discovered by an Italian, who had lately arrived there. Upon this intelligence, Michael thought the most prudent thing he could do was to waste no more time and money by groping in the dark himself, but to have recourse to the fountain of light at once; so sending Francoise to spend the interval with her cousin Manon, he himself started for Paris to visit the successful philosopher. Although she sincerely loved her father, the change was by no means unpleasant to Francoise. The village of Loques, in which Manon resided, humble as it was, was yet more cheerful than the lonely dwelling of the physician; and the conversation of the young girl more amusing than the dreamy speculations of the old alchemist. Manon, too, was rather a gainer by her cousin's arrival; for as she held her head a little high, on account of her father being the richest man in the village, she was somewhat nice about admitting the neighbouring damsels to her intimacy; and a visitor so unexceptionable as Francoise was by no means unwelcome. Thus both parties were pleased, and the young girls were anticipating a couple of months of pleasant companionship at the moment we have introduced them to our readers, seated at the front of the cottage.

"The heat of the sun is insupportable, Manon," said Francoise; "I really must go in."

"Do," said Manon.

"But won't you come in too?" asked Francoise.

"No, I don't mind the heat," replied the other.

Francoise took up her work and entered the house, but as Manon still remained without, the desire for conversation soon overcame the fear of the heat, and she approached the door again, where, standing partly in the shade, she could continue to discourse. As nobody appeared disposed to brave the heat but Manon, the little street was both empty and silent, so that the sound of a horse's foot crossing the drawbridge, which stood at the entrance of the village, was heard some time before the animal or his rider were in sight. Francoise put out her head to look in the direction of the sound, and, seeing no one, drew it in again; whilst Manon, after casting an almost imperceptible glance the same way, hung hers over her work, as if very intent on what she was doing; but could Francoise have seen her cousin's face, the blush that first overspread it, and the paleness that succeeded, might have awakened a suspicion that Manon was not exposing her complexion to the sun for nothing.

When the horse drew near, the rider was seen to be a gay and handsome cavalier, attired in the perfection of fashion, whilst the rich embroidery of the small cloak that hung gracefully over his left shoulder, sparkling in the sun, testified no less than his distinguished air to his high rank and condition. Francoise, who had never seen anything so bright and beautiful before, was so entirely absorbed in contemplating the pleasing spectacle, that forgetting to be shy or to hide her own pretty face, she continued to gaze on him as he approached with dilated eyes and lips apart, wholly unconscious that the surprise was mutual. It was not till she saw him lift his bonnet from his head, and, with a reverential bow, do homage to her charms, that her eye fell and the blood rushed to her young cheek. Involuntarily, she made a step backward into the passage; but when the horse and his rider had passed the door, she almost as involuntarily resumed her position, and protruded her head to look after him. He too had turned round on his horse and was "riding with his eyes behind", and the moment he beheld her he lifted his bonnet again, and then rode slowly forward.

"Upon my word, Mam'selle Francoise," said Manon, with flushed cheeks and angry eyes, "this is rather remarkable, I think! I was not aware of your acquaintance with Monsieur de Vardes!"

"With whom?" said Francoise. "Is that Monsieur de Vardes?"

"To be sure it is," replied Manon; "do you pretend to say you did not know it?"

"Indeed, I did not," answered Francoise. "I never saw him in my life before."

"Oh, I dare say," responded Manon, with an incredulous laugh. "Do you suppose I'm such a fool as to believe you!"

"What nonsense, Manon! How should I know Monsieur de Vardes? But do tell me about him? Does he live at the chateau?"

"He has been living there lately," replied Manon, sulkily.

"And where did he live before?" inquired Francois.

"He has been travelling, I believe," said Manon.

This was true. Victor de Vardes had been making the tour of Europe, visiting foreign courts, jousting in tournaments, and winning fair ladies' hearts, and was but now returned to inhabit his father's chateau; who, thinking it high time he should be married, had summoned him home for the purpose of paying his addresses to Clemence de Montmorenci, one of the richest heiresses in France.

Victor, who had left home very young, had been what is commonly called *in love* a dozen times, but his heart had in reality never been touched. His loves had been mere boyish fancies, "dead ere they were born", one putting out the fire of another before it had had time to hurt himself or any body else; so that when he heard that he was to marry Clemence de Montmorenci, he felt no aversion to the match, and prepared himself to obey his father's behest without a murmur. On being introduced to the lady, he was by no means struck with her. She appeared amiable, sensible, and gentle: but she was decidedly plain, and dressed ill. Victor felt no disposition whatever to love her; but, on the other hand, he had no dislike to her; and as his heart was unoccupied, he expressed himself perfectly ready to comply with the wishes of his family and hers, by whom this alliance had been arranged from motives of mutual interest and accommodation.

So he commenced his course of love; which consisted in riding daily to the chateau of his intended father-in-law, where, if there was company, and he found amusement, he frequently remained a great part of the morning. Now it happened that his road lay through the village of Loques, where Manon lived, and happening one day to see her at the door, with the gallantry of a gay cavalier, he had saluted her. Manon, who was fully as vain as she was pretty, liked this homage to her beauty so well that she thereafter never neglected an opportunity of throwing herself in the way of enjoying it; and the salutation thus accidentally begun had, from almost daily repetition, ripened into a sort of silent flirtation. The young count smiled, she blushed and half smiled too; and whilst he in reality thought nothing about her, she had brought herself to believe he was actually in love with her, and that it was for her sake he so often appeared riding past her door.

But, on the present occasion, the sight of Francoise's beautiful face had startled the young man out of his good manners. It is difficult to say why a gentleman, who looks upon the features of one pretty girl with indifference, should be "frightened from his propriety" by the sight of another, in whom the world in general see nothing superior; but such is the case, and so it was with Victor. His heart seemed taken by storm; he could not drive the beautiful features from his brain; and although he laughed at himself for being thus enslaved by a low-born beauty, he could not laugh himself out of the impatience he felt to mount his horse and ride back again in the hope of once more beholding her. But this time Manon alone was visible; and although he lingered, and allowed his eyes to wander over the house and glance in at the windows, no vestige of the lovely vision could he descry.

"Perhaps she did not live there—she was probably but a visitor to the other girl?" He would have given the world to ask the question of Manon; but he had never spoken to her, and to commence with such an interrogation was impossible, at least Victor felt it so, for his consciousness already made him shrink from betraying the motives of the inquiry. So he saluted Manon and rode on; but the wandering anxious eyes, the relaxed pace, and the cold animation, were not lost upon her. Besides, he had returned from the Chateau de Montmorenci before the usual time, and the mortified damsel did not fail to discern the motive of this deviation from his habits.

Manon was such a woman as you might live with well enough as long as you steered clear of her vanity, but once you came in collision with that, the strongest passion of her nature, and you aroused a latent venom that was sure to make you smart. Without having ever "vowed eternal friendship", or pretending to any remarkable affection, the girls had been hitherto very good friends. Manon was aware that Francoise was possessed of a great deal of knowledge of which she was utterly destitute; but as she did not value the knowledge, and had not the slightest conception of what it was worth, she was not mortified by the want of it nor envious of the advantage; she did not consider that it was one. But in the matter of beauty the case was different. She had always persuaded herself that she was much the handsomer of the two. She had black shining hair and dark flashing eyes; and she honestly thought the soft blue eyes and auburn hair of her cousin tame and ineffective.

But the too evident *saisissement* of the young count had shown her a rival where she had not suspected one, and her vexation was as great as her surprise. Then she was so puzzled what to do. If she abstained from sitting at the door herself, she should not see Monsieur de Vardes, but if she did sit there her cousin would assuredly do the same. It was extremely perplexing; but Francoise settled the question by seating herself at the door of her own accord. Seeing this, Manon came too to watch her, but she was sulky and snappish, and when Victor not only distinguished Francoise as before, but took an opportunity of alighting from his horse to tighten his girths, just opposite the door, she could scarcely control her passion.

It would be tedious to detail how, for the two months that ensued, this sort of silent courtship was carried on. Suffice it to say, that by the end of Francoise's visit to Loques she was in complete possession of Victor's heart, and he of hers, although they had never spoken a word to each other; and when she was summoned home to Cabanis to meet her father, she was completely divided betwixt the joy of once more seeing the dear old man and the grief of losing, as she supposed, all chance of beholding again the first love of her young heart.

But here her fears deceived her. Victor's passion had by this time overcome his diffidence, and he had contrived to learn all he required to know about her from the blacksmith of the village, one day when his horse very opportunely lost a shoe; and as Cabanis was not a great way from the Chateau de Montmorenci, he took an early opportunity of calling on the old physician, under pretence of needing his advice. At first he did not succeed in seeing Francoise, but perseverance brought him better success; and when they became acquainted, he was as much charmed and surprised by the cultivation of her mind as he had been by the beauty of her person. It was not difficult for Victor to win the heart of the alchemist, for the young man really felt, without having occasion to feign, an interest and curiosity with respect to the occult

researches so prevalent at that period; and thus, gradually, larger
and larger portions of his time were subtracted from the Chateau
de Montmorenci to be spent at the physician's. Then, in the green
glades of that wide domain which extended many miles around,
Victor and Francoise strolled together arm in arm; he vowing
eternal affection, and declaring that this rich inheritance of the
Montmorenci should never tempt him to forswear his love.

But though thus happy, "the world forgetting", they were not
"by the world forgot". From the day of Victor's first salutation to
Francoise, Manon had become her implacable enemy. Her pride
made her conceal as much as possible the cause of her aversion;
and Francoise, who learned from herself that she had no acquaintance with Victor, hardly knew how to attribute her daily increasing
coldness to jealousy. But by the time they parted the alienation was
complete, and as, after Francoise went home, all communication
ceased between them, it was some time before Manon heard of
Victor's visits to Cabanis. But this blissful ignorance was not destined to continue. There was a young man in the service of the
Montmorenci family called Jacques Renard; he was a great favourite
with the marquis, who had undertaken to provide for him, when
in his early years he was left destitute by the death of his parents,
who were old tenants on the estate. Jacques, now filling the office
of private secretary to his patron, was extremely in love with the
alchemist's daughter; and Francoise, who had seen too little of the
world to have much discrimination, had not wholly discouraged
his advances. Her heart, in fact, was quite untouched; but very
young girls do not know their own hearts; and when Francoise
became acquainted with Victor de Vardes, she first learned what
love is, and made the discovery that she entertained no such senti-
ment for Jacques Renard. The small encouragement she had given
him was therefore withdrawn, to the extreme mortification of

the disappointed suitor, who naturally suspected a rival, and was extremely curious to learn who that rival could be; nor was it long before he obtained the information he desired.

Though Francoise and her lover cautiously kept far away from that part of the estate which was likely to be frequented by the Montmorenci family, and thus avoided any inconvenient encounter with them, they could not with equal success elude the watchfulness of the foresters attached to the domain; and some time before the heiress or Manon suspected how Victor was passing his time, these men were well aware of the hours the young people spent together, either in the woods or at the alchemist's house, which was on their borders. Now the chief forester, Pierre Bloui, was a suitor for Manon's hand. He was an excellent huntsman, but being a weak, ignorant, ill-mannered fellow, she had a great contempt for him, and had repeatedly declined his proposals. But Pierre, whose dullness rendered his sensibilities little acute, had never been reduced to despair. He knew that his situation rendered him, in a pecuniary point of view, an excellent match, and that old Thierry, Manon's father, was his friend; so he persevered in his attentions, and seldom came into Loques without paying her a visit. It was from him she first learned what was going on at Cabanis.

"Ay," said Pierre, who had not the slightest suspicion of the jealous feelings he was exciting; "Ay, there'll be a precious blow-up by and by, when it comes to the ears of the family! What will the marquis and the old Count de Vardes say, when they find that, instead of making love to Mam'selle Clemence, he spends all his time with Francoise Thilouze?"

"But is not Mam'selle Clemence angry already that he is not more with her?" inquired Manon.

"I don't know," replied Pierre; "but that's what I was thinking of asking Jacques Renard, the first time he comes shooting with me."

"I'm sure I would not put up with it if I were she!" exclaimed Manon, with a toss of the head; "and I think you would do very right to mention it to Jacques Renard. Besides, it can come to no good for Francoise; for of course the count would never think of marrying *her*."

"I don't know that," answered Pierre; "Margot, their maid, told me another story."

"You don't mean that the count is going to marry Francoise Thilouze!" exclaimed Manon, with unfeigned astonishment.

"Margot says he is," answered Pierre.

"Well, then, all I can say is," cried Manon, her face crimsoning with passion—"all I can say is, that they must have bewitched him, between them; she and that old conjuror, my uncle!"

"Well, I should not wonder," said Pierre. "I've often thought old Michael knew more than he should do."

Now, Manon in reality entertained no such idea, but under the influence of the evil passions that were raging within her at the moment, she nodded her head as significantly as if she were thoroughly convinced of the fact—in short, as if she knew more than she chose to say; and thus sent away the weak superstitious Pierre possessed with a notion that he lost no time in communicating to his brother huntsmen; nor was it long before Victor's attentions to Francoise were made known to Jacques Renard, accompanied with certain suggestions, that Michael Thilouze and his daughter were perhaps what the Scotch call, *no canny*; a persuasion that the foresters themselves found little difficulty in admitting.

In the meanwhile, Clemence de Montmorenci had not been unconscious of Victor's daily declining attentions. He had certainly never pressed his suit with great earnestness; but now he did not press it at all. Never was so lax a lover! But as the alliance was one planned by the parents of the young people, not by the election of

their own hearts, she contemplated his alienation with more surprise than pain. The elder members of the two families, however,
were far from equally indifferent; and when they learned from the
irritated, jealous Jacques Renard the cause of the dereliction, their
indignation knew no bounds. It was particularly desirable that the
estates of Montmorenci and De Vardes should be united, and that
the lowly Francoise Thilouze, the daughter of a poor physician,
who probably did not know who his grandfather was, should step
in to the place designed for the heiress of a hundred quarterings,
and mingle her blood with the pure stream that flowed through the
veins of the proud De Vardes, was a thing not to be endured. The
strongest expostulations and representations were first tried with
Victor, but in vain. "He was in love, and pleased with ruin." These
failing, other measures must be resorted to; and as in those days,
pride of blood, contempt for the rights of the people, ignorance,
and superstition, were at their climax, there was little scruple as
to the means, so that the end was accomplished.

It is highly probable that these great people themselves believed
in witchcraft; the learned, as well as the ignorant, believed in it at
that period; and so unaccountable a perversion of the senses as
Victor's admiration of Francoise naturally appeared to persons
who could discern no merit unadorned by rank, would seem to
justify the worst suspicions; so that when Jacques hinted the notion
prevailing amongst the foresters with respect to old Michael and
his daughter, the idea was seized on with avidity. Whether Jacques
believed in his own allegation it is difficult to say; most likely not;
but it gratified his spite and served his turn; and his little scrupulous
nature sought no further. The marquis shook his head ominously,
looked very dignified and very grave, said that the thing must be
investigated, and desired that the foresters, and those who had the
best opportunities for observation, should keep an attentive eye

on the alchemist and his daughter, and endeavour to obtain some proof of their malpractices, whilst he considered what was best to be done in such an emergency.

The wishes and opinions of the great have at all times a strange omnipotence; and this influence in 1588 was a great deal more potential than it is now. No sooner was it known that the Marquis de Montmorenci and the Count de Vardes entertained an ill will against Michael and Francoise, than everybody became suddenly aware of their delinquency, and proofs of it poured in from all quarters. Amongst other stories, there was one which sprung from nobody knew where—probably from some hasty word, or slight coincidence, which flew like wildfire amongst the people, and caused an immense sensation. It was asserted that the Montmorenci huntsmen had frequently met Victor and Francoise walking together, in remote parts of the domain; but that when they drew near, she suddenly changed herself into a wolf and ran off. It was a favourite trick of witches to transform themselves into wolves, cats, and hares, and weir-wolves were the terror of the rustics: and as just at that period there happened to be one particularly large wolf, that had almost miraculously escaped the forester's guns, she was fixed upon as the representative of the metamorphosed Francoise.

Whilst this storm had been brewing, the old man, absorbed in his studies, which had received a fresh impetus from his late journey to Paris, and the young girl, wrapt in the entrancing plea-sures of a first love, remained wholly unconscious of the dangers that were gathering around them. Margot, the maid, had indeed not only heard, but had felt the effects of the rising prejudice against her employers. When she went to Loques for her weekly marketings, she found herself coldly received by some of her old familiars; whilst by those more friendly, she was seriously advised to separate her fortunes from that of persons addicted to such unholy arts. But Margot, who had nursed Francoise in her infancy, was deaf to their insinuations. She knew what they said was false; and feeling assured that if the young count married her mistress, the calumny would soon die away, she did not choose to disturb the peace of the family, and the smooth current of the courtship, by communicating those disagreeable rumours.

In the mean time, Pierre Bloui, who potently believed "the mischief that himself had made", was extremely eager to play some distinguished part in the drama of witch-finding. He knew that he should obtain the favour of his employers if he could bring about the conviction of Francoise; and he also thought that he should gratify his mistress. The source of her enmity he did not know, nor care to inquire; but enmity he perceived there was; and he concluded that the destruction of the object of it would be an agreeable sacrifice to the offended Manon. Moreover, he had no compunction, for the conscience of his superiors was his con- science; and Jacques Renard had so entirely confirmed his belief in the witch story, that his superstitious terrors, as well as his interests, prompted him to take an active part in the affair. Still he felt some reluctance to shoot the wolf, even could he succeed in so doing, from the thorough conviction that it was in reality not a wolf, but a human being he would be aiming at; but he thought if he could entrap her, it would not only save his own feelings, but answer the purpose much better; and accordingly he placed numerous snares, well baited, in that part of the domain most frequented by the lovers; and expected every day, when he visited them, to find Francoise, either in one shape or the other, fast by the leg. He was for some time disappointed; but at length he found in one of the traps, not the wolf or Francoise, but a wolf's foot. An animal had evidently been caught, and in the violence of its struggles for

freedom had left its foot behind it. Pierre carried away the foot
and baited his trap again.

About a week had elapsed since the occurrence of this circumstance, when one of the servants of the chateau, having met
with a slight accident, went to the apothecary's at Loques, for the
purpose of purchasing some medicaments: and there met Margot,
who had arrived from Cabanis for the same purpose. Mam'selle
Francoise, it appeared, had so seriously hurt one of her hands,
that her father had been under the necessity of amputating it. As
all gossip about the Thilouze family was just then very acceptable
at home, the man did not fail to relate what he had heard; and the
news, ere long, reached the ears of Pierre Bloui.

It would have been difficult to decide whether horror or triumph prevailed in the countenance of the astonished huntsman
at this communication. His face first flushed with joy, and then
became pale with affright. It was thus all true! The thing was
clear, and he the man destined to produce the proof! It *had* been
Francoise that was caught in the trap; and she had released herself
at the expense of one of her hands, which, divided from herself,
was no longer under the power of her incantations; and had therefore retained the form she had given it, when she resumed her own.

Here was a discovery! Pierre Bloui actually felt himself so
overwhelmed by its magnitude, that he was obliged to swallow a
glass of cognac to restore his equilibrium, before he could present
himself before Jacques Renard to detail this stupendous mystery
and exhibit the wolf's foot.

How much Jacques Renard, or the marquis, when he heard it,
believed of this strange story, can never be known. Certain it is,
however, that within a few hours after this communication had
been made to them, the *commissaire du quartier*, followed by a mob
from Loques, arrived at Cabanis, and straightway carried away

Michael Thilouze and his daughter, on a charge of witchcraft. The influence of their powerful enemies hurried on the judicial process, by courtesy called a trial, where the advantages were all on one side, and the disadvantages all on the other, and poor, terrified, and unaided, the physician and his daughter were, with little delay, found guilty, and condemned to die at the stake. In vain they pleaded their innocence. The wolf's foot was produced in court, and, combined with the circumstance that Francoise Thilouze had really lost her left hand, was considered evidence incontrovertible.

But where was her lover the while? Alas, he was in Paris, where, shortly before these late events, his father had on some pretext sent him; the real object being to remove him from the neighbourhood of Cabanis.

Now, when Manon saw the fruits of her folly and spite, she became extremely sorry for what she had done, for she knew very well that it was with herself the report had originated. But though powerful to harm, she was weak to save. When she found that her uncle and cousin were to lose their lives and die a dreadful death on account of the idle words dropped from her own foolish tongue, her remorse became agonising. But what could she do? Where look for assistance? Nowhere, unless in Victor de Vardes, and he was far away. She had no jealousy now; glad, glad would she have been, to be preparing to witness her cousin's wedding instead of her execution! But those were not the days of fleet posts—if they had been, Manon would have doubtless known how to write. As it was, she could neither write a letter to the count, nor have sent it when written. And yet, in Victor lay her only hope. In this strait she summoned Pierre Bloui, and asked him if he would go to Paris for her, and inform the young count of the impending misfortune. But it was not easy to persuade Pierre to so rash an enterprise. He was afraid of bringing himself into trouble with the Montmorencis.

But Manon's heart was in the cause. She represented to him, that if he lost one employer he would get another, for that the young count would assuredly become his best friend; and when she found that this was not enough to win him to her purpose, she bravely resolved to sacrifice herself to save her friends.

"If you will hasten to Paris," she said, "stopping neither night nor day, and tell Monsieur de Vardes of the danger my uncle and cousin are in, when you come back I will marry you."

The bribe succeeded, and Pierre consented to go, owning that he was the more willing to do so, because he had privately changed his own opinion with respect to the guilt of the accused parties. "For," said he, "I saw the wolf last night under the chestnut trees, and as she was very lame, I could have shot her, but I feared my lord and lady would be displeased."

"Then, how can you be foolish enough to think it's my cousin," said Manon, "when you know she is in prison?"

"That's what I said to Jacques Renard," replied Pierre; "but he bade me not meddle with what did not concern me."

In fine, love and conscience triumphed over fear and servility, and as soon as the sun set behind the hills, Pierre Bloui started for Paris.

How eagerly now did Manon reckon the days and hours that were to elapse before Victor could arrive. She had so imperfect an idea of the distance to be traversed, that after the third day she began hourly to expect him; but sun after sun rose and set, and no Victor appeared; and in the mean time, before the very windows of the house she dwelt in, she beheld preparations making day by day for the fatal ceremony. From early morn to dewy eve, the voices of the workmen, the hammering of the scaffolding, and the hum of the curious and excited spectators, who watched its progress, resounded in the ears of the unhappy Manon; for a witch-burning was a sort of *auto da fe*, like the burning of a heretic, and was anticipated as a grand spectacle, alike pleasing to gods and men, especially in the little town of Loques, where exciting scenes of any kind were very rare.

Thus time crept on, and still no signs of rescue; whilst the anguish and remorse of the repentant sinner became unbearable.

Now, Manon was not only a girl of strong passions but of a fearless spirit. Indeed the latter was somewhat the offspring of the former; for when her feelings were excited, not only justice and charity, as we have seen, were apt to be forgotten, but personal danger and feminine fears were equally overlooked in the tempest that assailed her. On the present occasion, her better feelings were in full activity. Her whole nature was aroused, self was not thought of, and to save the lives she had endangered by her folly, she would have gladly laid down her own. "For why live," thought she, "if my uncle and cousin die? I can never be happy again; besides, I must keep my promise and marry Pierre Bloui; and I had better lose my life in trying to expiate my fault than live to be miserable."

Manon had a brother called Alexis, who was now at the wars; often and often, in this great strait, she had wished him at home; for she knew that he would have undertaken the mission to Paris for her, and so have saved her the sacrifice she had made in order to win Pierre to her purpose. Now, when Alexis lived at home, and the feuds between the king and the grand seigneurs had brought the battle to the very doors of the peasants of Auvergne, Manon had many a time braved danger in order to bring this much-loved brother refreshments on his night watch; and he had, moreover, as an accomplishment which might be some time needed for her own defence, taught her to carry a gun and shoot at a mark. In those days of civil broil and bloodshed, country maidens were not unfrequently adepts in such exercises. This acquirement she now determined to make available; and when the eve of the day appointed for the execution arrived without any tidings from Paris, she prepared to put her plan in practice. This was no other than to shoot the wolf herself, and, by producing it, to prove the falsity of the accusation. For this purpose, she provided herself with a young pig, which she slung in a sack over her shoulder, and with her brother's gun on the other, and disguised in his habiliments, when the shadows of twilight fell upon the earth, the brave girl went forth into the forest on her bold enterprise alone.

She knew that the moon would rise ere she reached her destination, and on this she reckoned for success. With a beating heart she traversed the broad glades, and crept through the narrow paths that intersected the wide woods till she reached the chestnut avenue where Pierre said he had seen the lame wolf. She was aware that old or disabled animals, who are rendered unfit to hunt their prey, will be attracted a long distance by the scent of food; so having hung her sack with the pig in it to the lower branch of a tree, she herself ascended another close to it, and then presenting the muzzle of her gun straight in the direction of the bag, she sat still as a statue; and there, for the present, we must leave her, whilst we take a peep into the prison of Loques, and see how the unfortunate victims of malice and superstition are supporting their captivity and prospect of approaching death.

Poor Michael Thilouze and his daughter had had a rude awakening from the joyous dreams in which they had both been wrapt. The old man's journey to Paris had led to what he believed would prove the most glorious results. It was true that report had as usual exaggerated the success of his fellow-labourer there. The Italian Alascor had not actually found the philosopher's stone but he was on the eve of finding it; one single obstacle stood in his way, and had for a considerable time arrested his progress; and as he was an old man, worn out by anxious thought and unremitting labour, who could scarcely hope to enjoy his own discovery, he consented to disclose to Michael not only all he knew, but also what was the insurmountable difficulty that had delayed his triumph. This precious stone, he had ascertained, which was not only to ensure to the fortunate possessor illimitable wealth, but perennial youth, could not be procured without the aid of a virgin, innocent, perfect, and pure; and, moreover, capable of inviolably keeping the secret which must necessarily be imparted to her.

"Now," said the Italian, "virgins are to be had in plenty; but the second condition I find it impossible to fulfil; for they invariably confide what I tell them to some friend or lover; and thus the whole process becomes vitiated, and I am arrested on the very threshold of success."

Great was the joy of Michael on hearing this; for he well knew that Francoise, his pure, innocent, beautiful Francoise, *could* keep a secret; he had often had occasion to prove her fidelity; so bidding the Italian keep himself alive but for a little space, when he, in gratitude for what he had taught him, would return with the long-sought-for treasure, and restore him to health, wealth, and vigorous youth, the glad old man hurried back to Cabanis, and "set himself about it like the sea".

It was in performing the operation required of her that Francoise had so injured her hand that amputation had become unavoidable; and great as had been the joy of Michael was now his grief. Not only had his beloved daughter lost her hand, but the hopes he had built on her co-operation were for ever annihilated; maimed and dismembered, she was no longer eligible to assist in the sublime process. But how much greater was his despair, when he learned the suspicions to which this strange coincidence had subjected her, and beheld the innocent, and till now happy girl, led by his side to a dungeon. For himself he cared nothing; for her everything. He was old and disappointed, and to die was little to him—but his Francoise, his young and beautiful Francoise, cut off in her bloom of years, and by so cruel and ignominious a death! And here they were in prison alone, helpless and forsaken! Absorbed in his studies, the poor physician had lived a solitary life; and his daughter, holding a rank a little above the peasantry and below the gentry, had had no companion but Manon, and she was now her bitterest foe; this at least they were told.

How sadly and slowly, and yet how much too fleetly, passed the days that were to intervene betwixt the sentence and the execution. And where was Victor? Where were his vows of love and eternal faith? All, all forgotten. So thought Francoise, who, ignorant of his absence from the Chateau de Vardes, supposed him well acquainted with her distress.

Thus believing themselves abandoned by the world, the poor father and daughter, in tears, and prayers, and attempts at mutual consolation, spent this sad interval, till at length the morning dawned that was to witness the accomplishment of their dreadful fate. During the preceding night old Michael had never closed his eyes; but Francoise had fallen asleep shortly before sunrise, and was dreaming that it was her wedding day; and that, followed by the cheers of the villagers, Victor, the still beloved Victor, was leading her to the altar. The cheers awoke her, and with the smile of joy still upon her lips, she turned her face to her father. He was stretched upon the floor, overcome by a burst of uncontrollable anguish at the sounds that had aroused her from her slumbers; for the sounds were real. The voices of the populace, crowding in from the adjacent country and villages to witness the spectacle, had pierced the thick walls of the prison and reached the ears and the hearts of the captives. Whilst the old man threw himself at her

feet, and, pouring blessings on her fair young head, besought her
pardon, Francoise almost forgot her own misery in his; and when
the assistants came to lead them forth to execution, she not only
exhorted him to patience, but supported with her arm the feeble
frame that, wasted by age and grief, could furnish but little fuel
for the flames that awaited them.

Nobody would have imagined that in this thinly peopled neighbourhood so many persons could have been brought together as
were assembled in the market-place of Loques to witness the deaths
of Michael Thilouze and his daughter. A scaffolding had been
erected all round the square for the spectators—that designed for
the gentry being adorned with tapestry and garlands of flowers.
There sat, amongst others, the families of Montmorenci and De
Vardes—all except the Lady Clemence, whose heart recoiled from
beholding the death of her rival; although, no more enlightened
than her age, she did not doubt the justice of the sentence that
had condemned her. In the centre of the area was a pile of faggots,
and near it stood the assistant executioners and several members
of the Church—priests and friars in their robes of black and grey.

The prisoners, accompanied by a procession which was headed
by the judge and terminated by the chief executioner of the law,
were first marched round the square several times, in order that
the whole of the assembly might be gratified with the sight of
them; and then being placed in front of the pile, the bishop of the
district, who attended in his full canonicals, commenced a mass for
the souls of the unhappy persons about to depart this life under
such painful circumstances, after which he pronounced a somewhat
lengthy oration on the enormity of their crime, ending with an
exhortation to confession and repentance.

These, which constituted the whole of the preliminary ceremonies, being concluded, and the judge having read the sentence,

to the effect, that, being found guilty of abominable and devilish magic arts, Michael and Francoise Thilouze were condemned to be burnt, especially for that the said Francoise, by her own arts, and those of her father, had bewitched the Count Victor de Vardes, and had sundry times visibly transformed herself into the shape of a wolf, and being caught in a trap, had thereby lost her hand, &c, the prisoners were delivered to the executioner, who prepared to bind them previously to their being placed on the pile. Then Michael fell upon his knees, and crying aloud to the multitude, besought them to spare his daughter, and to let him die alone; and the hearts of some amongst the people were moved. But from that part of the area where the nobility were seated, there issued a voice of authority, bidding the executioner proceed; so the old man and the young girl were placed upon the pile, and the assistants, with torches in their hands, drew near to set it alight, when a murmur arose from afar, then a hum of voices, a movement in the assembled crowd, which began to sway to and fro like the swing of vast waters. Then there was a cry of "Make way! Make way! Open a path! Let her advance!" and the crowd divided, and a path was opened, and there came forward, slowly and with difficulty, pale, dishevelled, with clothes torn and stained with blood, Manon Thierry, dragging behind her a dead wolf. The crowd closed in as she advanced, and when she reached the centre of the arena, there was straightway a dead silence. She stood for a moment looking around, and when she saw where the persons in authority sat, she fell upon her knees and essayed to speak; but her voice was choked by emotion, no word escaped her lips; she could only point to the wolf, and plead for mercy by her looks; where her present anguish of soul, and the danger and terror she had lately encountered, were legibly engraved.

The appeal was understood, and gradually the voices of the people rose again—there was a reaction. They who had been so eager for the spectacle, were now ready to supplicate for the victims—the young girl's heroism had conquered their sympathies. "Pardon! Pardon!" was the cry, and a hope awoke in the hearts of the captives. But the interest of the Montmorencis was too strong for that of the populace—the nobility stood by their order, and stern voices commanded silence, and that the ceremony should proceed; and once more the assistants brandished their torches and advanced to the pile; and then Manon, exhausted with grief, terror, and loss of blood, fell upon her face to the ground.

But now, again, there is a sound from afar, and all voices are hushed, and all ears are strained—it is the echo of a horse's foot galloping over the drawbridge; it approaches; and again, like the surface of a stormy sea, the dense crowd is in motion; and then a path is opened, and a horse, covered with foam, is seen advancing, and thousands of voices burst forth into "Viva! Viva!" The air rings with acclamations. The rider was Victor de Vardes, bearing in his hand the king's order for arrest of execution.

Pierre Bloui had faithfully performed his embassy; and the brave Henry IV, moved by the prayers and representations of the ardent lover, had hastily furnished him with a mandate commanding respite till further investigation. Kings were all-powerful in those days; and it was no sooner known that Henry was favourable to the lovers, than the harmlessness of Michael and his daughter was generally acknowledged; the production of the wolf wanting a foot being now considered as satisfactory a proof of their innocence, as the production of the foot wanting the wolf had formerly been of their guilt.

Strange human passions, subject to such excesses and to such revulsions! Michael Thilouze and his daughter happily escaped; and under the king's countenance and protection, the young couple were married; but we need not remind such of our readers as are learned in the annals of witchcraft, how many unfortunate persons have died at the stake for crimes imputed to them, on no better evidence than this.

As for the heiress of Montmorenci, she bore her loss with considerable philosophy. She would have married the young Count de Vardes without repugnance, but he had been too cold a lover to touch her heart or occasion regret; but poor Manon was the sacrifice for her own error. What manner of contest she had had with the wolf was never known, for she never sufficiently recovered from the state of exhaustion in which she had fallen to the earth, to be able to describe what had passed. Alone she had vanquished the savage animal, alone dragged it through the forest and the village, to the market square, where every human being able to stir, for miles round, was assembled; so that all other places were wholly deserted. The wolf had been shot, but not mortally; its death had evidently been accelerated by other wounds. Manon herself was much torn and lacerated; and on the spot where the creature had apparently been slain, was found her gun, a knife, and a pool of blood, in which lay several fragments of her dress. Though unable to give any connected account of her own perilous adventure, she was conscious of the happy result of her generous devotion; and before she died received the heartfelt forgiveness and earnest thanks of her uncle and cousin, the former of whom soon followed her to the grave. Despairing now of ever succeeding in his darling object, what was the world to him! He loved his daughter tenderly, but he was possessed with an idea, which it had been the aim and hope of his life to work out. She was safe and happy, and needed him no more; and the hope being dead, life seemed to ooze out with it.

By the loss of that maiden's hand, who can tell what we have missed! For doubtless it is the difficulty of fulfilling the last condition named by the Italian, which has been the real impediment in the way of all philosophers who have been engaged in alchemical pursuits; and we may reasonably hope, that when women shall have learned to hold their tongues, the philosopher's stone will be discovered, and poverty and wrinkles thereafter cease to deform the earth.

For long years after these strange events, over the portcullis of the old chateau of the De Vardes, till it fell into utter ruin, might be discerned the figure of a wolf, carved in stone, wanting one of its fore-feet; and underneath it the following inscription—"*In perpetuara rei memoriam.*"

THE WEREWOLF

Hans Christian Andersen

First published in English in the *New Monthly Magazine* (1867)

Hans Christian Andersen (1805–75) was a Danish writer, best known for his fairy tales, including 'The Little Mermaid', 'Thumbelina', 'The Ugly Duckling', and 'The Emperor's New Clothes'. He did, however, also write an abundance of poetry, as well as plays, travelogues, and novels. His works were particularly popular amongst British audiences once they were translated into English in the Victorian period.

'The Werewolf' is one of Andersen's lesser-known works. This poem, originally titled 'Varulven' in Danish, was translated by Anne Bushby under its English title in the *New Monthly Magazine* in 1867. Opening at midnight in a misty forest, the story has a decidedly Gothic tone. This poem has much in common with Andersen's fairy tales, raising questions of identity, family, and human-to-animal transformation.

'Twas at the middle hour of night;
    And though the moon gave her pale light,
O'er the haunted wood a thick mist hung,
    And the wind was howling its leaves among.
In a cart along that way so wild
    A peasant was driving his wife and child.

"For the fairy folks thou need'st fear not,
    They dance 'neath the moon on yon green spot.
Should the screech-owl cry from yonder marsh,
    Say a prayer, nor heed its voice so harsh.
Whate'er thou seest, be not afraid.
    But clasp the child," the father said.

"Forward, old horse! Behind yon tree
    Our church's steeple I can see.
Get on! But hold, a moment stop—
    The linch-pin is about to drop;
'Tis cracked—I'll cut a stick, my dear;
    Hold fast the child, and have no fear!"

An hour alone she might have sat,
    When a noise she heard—"Oh, what is that?"
Lo, a coal-black hound! she sees and knows
    The werewolf! while his teeth he shows,
And glares upon her child—she flings
    Her apron o'er it as he springs.

His sharp teeth bite it; but she cries
   To God for help—away he flies.
Her arms the helpless babe enfold,
   She sits like a statue, pale and cold.
But soon her husband's by her side,
   And onwards now they safely ride.

Arrived at home, a light is brought;
   She starts as with some horrid thought:
"What, husband! husband! can these be
   Threads hanging from thy teeth I see?
Thou art thyself a werewolf, then!"
   "Thy words," he said, "have set me free again!"

THE GREY WOLF

George MacDonald

Published in *Works of Fantasy and Imagination* (1871)

George MacDonald (1824–1905) was a Scottish minister and writer, whose sermons were known for their emphasis on poetry as much as the Bible. He wrote in a range of literary modes, from religious poetry, to fairy tales, to non-fictional essays.

'The Grey Wolf' was first published in a collection of stories entitled *Works of Fantasy and Imagination* (1871). This is one of a number of MacDonald's tales with lupine themes: his novel *The Princess and Curdie* (1882), for example, features lycanthropic transformations. MacDonald's work influenced some of the most famous fantasy writers of the twentieth century, including C. S. Lewis and J. R. R. Tolkien. In 'The Grey Wolf' a student is offered shelter with a young woman and her mother during a storm. There is something peculiar about the young woman's appearance, however, which he finds unsettling; perhaps he is not as safe staying with these strangers as he might assume.

One evening twilight in spring, a young English student, who had wandered northwards as far as the outlying fragments of Scotland called the Orkney and Shetland Islands, found himself on a small island of the latter group, caught in a storm of wind and hail, which had come on suddenly. It was in vain to look about for any shelter; for not only did the storm entirely obscure the landscape, but there was nothing around him save a desert moss.

At length, however, as he walked on for mere walking's sake, he found himself on the verge of a cliff, and saw, over the brow of it, a few feet below him, a ledge of rock, where he might find some shelter from the blast, which blew from behind. Letting himself down by his hands, he alighted upon something that crunched beneath his tread, and found the bones of many small animals scattered about in front of a little cave in the rock, offering the refuge he sought. He went in, and sat upon a stone. The storm increased in violence, and as the darkness grew he became uneasy, for he did not relish the thought of spending the night in the cave. He had parted from his companions on the opposite side of the island, and it added to his uneasiness that they must be full of apprehension about him. At last there came a lull in the storm, and the same instant he heard a footfall, stealthy and light as that of a wild beast, upon the bones at the mouth of the cave. He started up in some fear, though the least thought might have satisfied him that there could be no very dangerous animals upon the island. Before he had time to think, however, the face of a woman appeared in the opening. Eagerly the wanderer spoke. She started at the sound of his voice. He could not see her well, because she was turned towards the darkness of the cave.

"Will you tell me how to find my way across the moor to Shielness?" he asked.

"You cannot find it tonight," she answered, in a sweet tone, and with a smile that bewitched him, revealing the whitest of teeth.

"What am I to do, then?"

"My mother will give you shelter, but that is all she has to offer."

"And that is far more than I expected a minute ago," he replied. "I shall be most grateful."

She turned in silence and left the cave. The youth followed.

She was barefooted, and her pretty brown feet went catlike over the sharp stones, as she led the way down a rocky path to the shore. Her garments were scanty and torn, and her hair blew tangled in the wind. She seemed about five and twenty, lithe and small. Her long fingers kept clutching and pulling nervously at her skirts as she went. Her face was very grey in complexion, and very worn, but delicately formed, and smooth-skinned. Her thin nostrils were tremulous as eyelids, and her lips, whose curves were faultless, had no colour to give sign of indwelling blood. What her eyes were like he could not see, for she had never lifted the delicate films of her eyelids.

At the foot of the cliff, they came upon a little hut leaning against it, and having for its inner apartment a natural hollow within. Smoke was spreading over the face of the rock, and the grateful odour of food gave hope to the hungry student. His guide opened the door of the cottage; he followed her in, and saw a woman bending over a fire in the middle of the floor. On the fire lay a large fish broiling. The daughter spoke a few words, and the mother turned and welcomed the stranger. She had an old and very wrinkled, but honest face, and looked troubled. She dusted the only chair in the cottage, and placed it for him by the side of the fire, opposite the one window, whence he saw a little patch of yellow sand over which the spent waves spread themselves out listlessly. Under this window there was a bench, upon which the daughter threw herself in an unusual posture, resting her chin upon her hand. A moment after, the youth caught the first glimpse of her blue eyes. They were fixed upon him with a strange look of greed, amounting to craving, but, as if aware that they belied or betrayed her, she dropped them instantly. The moment she veiled them, her face, notwithstanding its colourless complexion, was almost beautiful.

When the fish was ready, the old woman wiped the deal table, steadied it upon the uneven floor, and covered it with a piece of fine table-linen. She then laid the fish on a wooden platter, and invited the guest to help himself. Seeing no other provision, he pulled from his pocket a hunting knife, and divided a portion from the fish, offering it to the mother first,

"Come, my lamb," said the old woman; and the daughter approached the table. But her nostrils and mouth quivered with disgust.

The next moment she turned and hurried from the hut.

"She doesn't like fish," said the old woman, "and I haven't anything else to give her."

"She does not seem in good health," he rejoined.

The woman answered only with a sigh, and they ate their fish with the help of a little rye bread. As they finished their supper, the youth heard the sound as of the pattering of a dog's feet upon the sand close to the door; but ere he had time to look out of the

window, the door opened, and the young woman entered. She
looked better, perhaps from having just washed her face. She
drew a stool to the corner of the fire opposite him. But as she sat
down, to his bewilderment, and even horror, the student spied a
single drop of blood on her white skin within her torn dress. The
woman brought out a jar of whisky, put a rusty old kettle on the
fire, and took her place in front of it. As soon as the water boiled,
she proceeded to make some toddy in a wooden bowl.

Meantime the youth could not take his eyes off the young
woman, so that at length he found himself fascinated, or rather
bewitched. She kept her eyes for the most part veiled with the love-
liest eyelids fringed with darkest lashes, and he gazed entranced;
for the red glow of the little oil-lamp covered all the strangeness
of her complexion. But as soon as he met a stolen glance out of
those eyes unveiled, his soul shuddered within him. Lovely face
and craving eyes alternated fascination and repulsion.

The mother placed the bowl in his hands. He drank sparingly,
and passed it to the girl. She lifted it to her lips, and as she tasted—
only tasted it—looked at him. He thought the drink must have been
drugged and have affected his brain. Her hair smoothed itself back,
and drew her forehead backwards with it; while the lower part of
her face projected towards the bowl, revealing, ere she sipped, her
dazzling teeth in strange prominence. But the same moment the
vision vanished; she returned the vessel to her mother, and rising,
hurried out of the cottage.

Then the old woman pointed to a bed of heather in one corner
with a murmured apology; and the student, wearied both with
the fatigues of the day and the strangeness of the night, threw
himself upon it, wrapped in his cloak. The moment he lay down,
the storm began afresh, and the wind blew so keenly through the
crannies of the hut, that it was only by drawing his cloak over his

head that he could protect himself from its currents. Unable to sleep, he lay listening to the uproar which grew in violence, till the spray was dashing against the window. At length the door opened, and the young woman came in, made up the fire, drew the bench before it, and lay down in the same strange posture, with her chin propped on her hand and elbow, and her face turned towards the youth. He moved a little; she dropped her head, and lay on her face, with her arms crossed beneath her forehead. The mother had disappeared.

Drowsiness crept over him. A movement of the bench roused him, and he fancied he saw some four-footed creature as tall as a large dog trot quietly out of the door. He was sure he felt a rush of cold wind. Gazing fixedly through the darkness, he thought he saw the eyes of the damsel encountering his, but a glow from the falling together of the remnants of the fire revealed clearly enough that the bench was vacant. Wondering what could have made her go out in such a storm, he fell fast asleep.

In the middle of the night he felt a pain in his shoulder, came broad awake, and saw the gleaming eyes and grinning teeth of some animal close to his face. Its claws were in his shoulder, and its mouth in the act of seeking his throat. Before it had fixed its fangs, however, he had its throat in one hand, and sought his knife with the other. A terrible struggle followed; but regardless of the tearing claws, he found and opened his knife. He had made one futile stab, and was drawing it for a surer, when, with a spring of the whole body, and one wildly contorted effort, the creature twisted its neck from his hold, and with something betwixt a scream and a howl, darted from him. Again he heard the door open; again the wind blew in upon him, and it continued blowing; a sheet of spray dashed across the floor, and over his face. He sprung from his couch and bounded to the door.

It was a wild night-dark, but for the flash of whiteness from the waves as they broke within a few yards of the cottage; the wind was raving, and the rain pouring down the air. A gruesome sound as of mingled weeping and howling came from somewhere in the dark. He turned again into the hut and closed the door, but could find no way of securing it.

The lamp was nearly out, and he could not be certain whether the form of the young woman was upon the bench or not. Overcoming a strong repugnance, he approached it, and put out his hands—there was nothing there. He sat down and waited for the daylight: he dared not sleep any more.

When the day dawned at length, he went out yet again, and looked around. The morning was dim and gusty and grey. The wind had fallen, but the waves were tossing wildly. He wandered up and down the little strand, longing for more light.

At length he heard a movement in the cottage. By and by the voice of the old woman called to him from the door.

"You're up early, sir. I doubt you didn't sleep well."

"Not very well," he answered. "But where is your daughter?"

"She's not awake yet," said the mother. "I'm afraid I have but a poor breakfast for you. But you'll take a dram and a bit of fish. It's all I've got."

Unwilling to hurt her, though hardly in good appetite, he sat down at the table. While they were eating, the daughter came in, but turned her face away and went to the farther end of the hut. When she came forward after a minute or two, the youth saw that her hair was drenched, and her face whiter than before. She looked ill and faint, and when she raised her eyes, all their fierceness had vanished, and sadness had taken its place. Her neck was now covered with a cotton handkerchief. She was modestly attentive to him, and no longer shunned his gaze. He was gradually yielding to the temptation of braving another night in the hut, and seeing what would follow, when the old woman spoke.

"The weather will be broken all day, sir," she said. "You had better be going, or your friends will leave without you."

Ere he could answer, he saw such a beseeching glance on the face of the girl, that he hesitated, confused. Glancing at the mother, he saw the flash of wrath in her face. She rose and approached her daughter, with her hand lifted to strike her. The young woman stooped her head with a cry. He darted round the table to interpose between them. But the mother had caught hold of her; the handkerchief had fallen from her neck; and the youth saw five blue bruises on her lovely throat—the marks of the four fingers and the thumb of a left hand. With a cry of horror he darted from the house, but as he reached the door he turned. His hostess was lying motionless on the floor, and a huge grey wolf came bounding after him.

There was no weapon at hand; and if there had been, his inborn chivalry would never have allowed him to harm a woman even under the guise of a wolf. Instinctively, he set himself firm, leaning a little forward, with half outstretched arms, and hands curved ready to clutch again at the throat upon which he had left those pitiful marks. But the creature as she sprung eluded his grasp, and just as he expected to feel her fangs, he found a woman weeping on his bosom, with her arms around his neck. The next instant, the grey wolf broke from him, and bounded howling up the cliff. Recovering himself as he best might, the youth followed, for it was the only way to the moor above, across which he must now make his way to find his companions.

All at once he heard the sound of a crunching of bones—not as if a creature was eating them, but as if they were ground by the teeth of rage and disappointment; looking up, he saw close above him the mouth of the little cavern in which he had taken refuge the day before. Summoning all his resolution, he passed it slowly and softly. From within came the sounds of a mingled moaning and growling.

Having reached the top, he ran at full speed for some distance across the moor before venturing to look behind him. When at length he did so, he saw, against the sky, the girl standing on the edge of the cliff, wringing her hands. One solitary wail crossed the space between. She made no attempt to follow him, and he reached the opposite shore in safety.

THE WHITE WOLF OF KOSTOPCHIN

Gilbert Campbell

Published in *Wild and Weird Tales of Imagination and Mystery* (1889)

Sir Gilbert Campbell (1833–1899) was a British author and translator, who produced a number of collections of short stories with supernatural themes. In 1892 he was given a jail sentence of eighteen months for involvement in a fraudulent literary agency. Once released, he continued to write and publish. Campbell mysteriously vanished in 1899, and was presumed dead.

'The White Wolf of Kostopchin' appeared in Campbell's collection of short stories, *Wild and Weird Tales of Imagination and Mystery: Russian, English, and Italian* (1889). A review appearing in the *Spectator* in 1890 recommended that this tale, among others, "should really not be read by those in the habit of supping late" or "nervous young people". This story shares much in common with Clemence Housman's 'The Werewolf' (also in this collection), published the year after Campbell's offering: rather than plagiarism, these similarities suggest that these authors had come across similar folkloric sources. The white wolf of the tale's title is hunted after a series of attacks on the local Lithuanian people. This coincides with the appearance of an enigmatic woman who wears a coat of white fur.

A WIDE SANDY EXPANSE OF COUNTRY, FLAT AND UNINTEREST-ing in appearance, with a great staring whitewashed house standing in the midst of wide fields of cultivated land; whilst far away were the low sand hills and pine forests to be met with in the district of Lithuania, in Russian Poland. Not far from the great white house was the village in which the serfs dwelt, with the large bakehouse and the public bath which are invariably to be found in all Russian villages, however humble. The fields were negligently cultivated, the hedges broken down and the fences in bad repair, shattered agricultural implements had been carelessly flung aside in remote corners, and the whole estate showed the want of the superintending eye of an energetic master. The great white house was no better looked after, the garden was an utter wilderness, great patches of plaster had fallen from the walls, and many of the Venetian shutters were almost off the hinges. Over all was the dark lowering sky of a Russian autumn, and there were no signs of life to be seen, save a few peasants lounging idly towards the *vodki* shop, and a gaunt half-starved cat creeping stealthily abroad in quest of a meal.

The estate, which was known by the name of Kostopchin, was the property of Paul Sergevitch, a gentleman of means, and the most discontented man in Russian Poland. Like most wealthy Muscovites, he had travelled much, and had spent the gold which had been amassed by serf labour, like water, in all the dissolute revelries of the capitals of Europe. Paul's figure was as well known in the boudoirs of the *demi mondaines* as his face was familiar at the public gaming tables. He appeared to have no thought for the future, but only to live in the excitement of the mad career of dissipation which he was pursuing. His means, enormous as they were, were all forestalled, and he was continually sending to his intendant for fresh supplies of money. His fortune would not have long held out against the constant inroads that were being made upon it, when an unexpected circumstance took place which stopped his career like a flash of lightning. This was a fatal duel, in which a young man of great promise, the son of the prime minister of the country in which he then resided, fell by his hand. Representations were made to the Tsar, and Paul Sergevitch was recalled, and, after receiving a severe reprimand was ordered to return to his estates in Lithuania. Horribly discontented, yet not daring to disobey the Imperial mandate, Paul buried himself at Kostopchin, a place he had not visited since his boyhood. At first he endeavoured to interest himself in the workings of the vast estate; but agriculture had no charm for him, and the only result was that he quarrelled with and dismissed his German intendant, replacing him by an old serf, Michael Vassilitch, who had been his father's valet. Then he took to wandering about the country, gun in hand, and upon his return home would sit moodily drinking brandy and smoking innumerable cigarettes, as he cursed his lord and master, the emperor, for consigning him to such a course of dullness and *ennui*. For a couple of years he led this aimless life, and at last, hardly knowing the reason for so doing, he married the daughter of a neighbouring landed proprietor. The marriage was a most unhappy one; the girl had really never cared for Paul, but had married him in obedience to her father's mandates, and the man, whose temper was always brutal and violent, treated her, after a brief interval of contemptuous indifference, with savage cruelty. After three years the unhappy woman expired, leaving behind her two children—a boy, Alexis, and a girl, Katrina. Paul treated his wife's death with the most perfect indifference; but he did not put anyone in her place. He was very fond of the little Katrina, but did not take much notice of the boy, and resumed his lonely wanderings about the country with dog and gun. Five years had passed since the death of his wife. Alexis was a fine, healthy boy of seven, whilst Katrina was some eighteen months younger. Paul was lighting one of his eternal cigarettes at the door of his house, when the little girl came running up to him.

"You bad, wicked Papa," said she. "How is it that you have never brought me the pretty grey squirrels that you promised I should have the next time you went to the forest?"

"Because I have never yet been able to find any, my treasure," returned her father, taking up his child in his arms and half smothering her with kisses. "Because I have not found them yet, my golden queen; but I am bound to find Ivanovitch, the poacher, smoking about the woods, and if he can't show me where they are, no one can."

"Ah, Little Father," broke in old Michael, using the term of address with which a Russian of humble position usually accosts his superior; "Ah, Little Father, take care; you will go to those woods once too often."

"Do you think I am afraid of Ivanovitch?" returned his master, with a coarse laugh. "Why, he and I are the best of friends; at any rate, if he robs me, he does so openly, and keeps other poachers away from my woods."

"It is not of Ivanovitch that I am thinking," answered the old man. "But oh! Gospodin, do not go into these dark solitudes; there are terrible tales told about them, of witches that dance in the moonlight, of strange, shadowy forms that are seen amongst the trunks of the tall pines, and of whispered voices that tempt the listeners to eternal perdition."

Again the rude laugh of the lord of the manor rang out, as Paul observed, "If you go on addling your brain, old man, with these nearly half-forgotten legends, I shall have to look out for a new intendant."

"But I was not thinking of these fearful creatures only," returned Michael, crossing himself piously. "It was against the wolves that I meant to warn you."

"Oh, Father, dear, I am frightened now," whimpered little Katrina, hiding her head on her father's shoulder. "Wolves are such cruel, wicked things."

"See there, greybearded dotard," cried Paul, furiously, "you have terrified this sweet angel by your farrago of lies; besides, who ever heard of wolves so early as this? You are dreaming, Michael Vassilitch, or have taken your morning dram of *vodki* too strong."

"As I hope for future happiness," answered the old man, solemnly, "as I came through the marsh last night from Kosma the herdsman's cottage—you know, my lord, that he has been bitten by a viper, and is seriously ill—as I came through the marsh, I repeat, I saw something like sparks of fire in the clump of alders on the right-hand side. I was anxious to know what they could be, and cautiously moved a little nearer, recommending my soul to the protection of Saint Vladimir. I had not gone a couple of paces when a wild howl came that chilled the very marrow of my bones, and a pack of some ten or a dozen wolves, gaunt and famished as you see them, my lord, in the winter, rushed out. At their head was a white she-wolf, as big as any of the male ones, with gleaming tusks and a pair of yellow eyes that blazed with lurid fire. I had round my neck a crucifix that had been given me by the priest of

Streletza, and the savage beasts knew this and broke away across the marsh, sending up the mud and water in showers in the air; but the white she-wolf, Little Father, circled round me three times, as though endeavouring to find some place from which to attack me. Three times she did this, and then, with a snap of her teeth and a howl of impotent malice, she galloped away some fifty yards and sat down, watching my every movement with her fiery eyes. I did not delay any longer in so dangerous a spot, as you may well imagine, Gospodin, but walked hurriedly home, crossing myself at every step; but, as I am a living man, that white devil followed me the whole distance, keeping fifty paces in the rear, and every now and then licking her lips with a sound that made my flesh creep. When I got to the last fence before you come to the house I raised up my voice and shouted for the dogs, and soon I heard the deep bay of Troska and Branskoe as they came bounding towards me. The white devil heard it, too, and, giving a high bound into the air, she uttered a loud howl of disappointment, and trotted back leisurely towards the marsh."

"But why did you not set the dogs after her?" asked Paul, interested, in spite of himself, at the old man's narrative. "In the open Troska and Branskoe would run down any wolf that ever set foot to the ground in Lithuania."

"I tried to do so, Little Father," answered the old man, solemnly; "but directly they got up to the spot where the beast had executed her last devilish gambol, they put their tails between their legs and ran back to the house as fast as their legs could carry them."

"Strange," muttered Paul, thoughtfully, "that is, if it is truth and not *vodki* that is speaking."

"My lord," returned the old man, reproachfully, "man and boy, I have served you and my lord your father for fifty years, and no one can say that they ever saw Michael Vassilitch the worse for liquor."

"No one doubts that you are a sly old thief, Michael," returned his master, with his coarse, jarring laugh; "but for all that, your long stories of having been followed by white wolves won't prevent me from going to the forest today. A couple of good buckshot cartridges will break any spell, though I don't think that the she-wolf, if she existed anywhere than in your own imagination, has anything to do with magic. Don't be frightened, Katrina, my pet; you shall have a fine white wolf skin to put your feet on, if what this old fool says is right."

"Michael is not a fool," pouted the child, "and it is very wicked of you to call him so. I don't want any nasty wolf skins, I want the grey squirrels."

"And you shall have them, my precious," returned her father, setting her down upon the ground. "Be a good girl, and I will not be long away."

"Father," said the little Alexis, suddenly, "let me go with you. I should like to see you kill a wolf, and then I should know how to do so, when I grow older and taller."

"Pshaw," returned his father, irritably. "Boys are always in the way. Take the lad away, Michael; don't you see that he is worrying his sweet little sister?"

"No, no, he does not worry me at all," answered the impetuous little lady, as she flew to her brother and covered him with kisses. "Michael, you shan't take him away, do you hear?"

"There, there, leave the children together," returned Paul, as he shouldered his gun, and kissing the tips of his fingers to Katrina, stepped away rapidly in the direction of the dark pine woods. Paul walked on, humming the fragment of an air that he had heard in a very different place many years ago. A strange feeling of elation crept over him, very different to the false excitement which his solitary drinking bouts were wont to produce. A change seemed to have come over his whole life, the skies looked brighter, the *spiculae* of the pine trees of a more vivid green, and the landscape seemed to have lost that dull cloud of depression which had for years appeared to hang over it. And beneath all this exaltation of the mind, beneath all this unlooked-for promise of a more happy future, lurked a heavy, inexplicable feeling of a power to come, a something without form or shape, and yet the more terrible because it was shrouded by that thick veil which conceals from the eyes of the soul the strange fantastic designs of the dwellers beyond the line of earthly influences.

There were no signs of the poacher, and wearied with searching for him, Paul made the woods re-echo with his name. The great dog, Troska, which had followed his master, looked up wistfully into his face, and at a second repetition of the name "Ivanovitch", uttered a long plaintive howl, and then, looking round at Paul as though entreating him to follow, moved slowly ahead towards a denser portion of the forest. A little mystified at the hound's unusual proceedings, Paul followed, keeping his gun ready to fire at the least sign of danger. He thought that he knew the forest well, but the dog led the way to a portion which he never remembered to have visited before. He had got away from the pine trees now, and had entered a dense thicket formed of stunted oaks and hollies. The great dog kept only a yard or so ahead; his lips were drawn back, showing the strong white fangs, the hair upon his neck and back was bristling, and his tail firmly pressed between his hind legs. Evidently the animal was in a state of the most extreme terror, and yet it proceeded bravely forward. Struggling through the dense thicket, Paul suddenly found himself in an open space of some ten or twenty yards in diameter. At one end of it was a slimy pool, into the waters of which several strange-looking reptiles glided as the man and dog made their appearance. Almost in the centre of the opening was a shattered stone cross, and at its base lay a dark heap, close to which Troska stopped, and again raising his head, uttered a long melancholy howl. For an instant or two, Paul gazed hesitatingly at the shapeless heap that lay beneath the cross, and then, mustering up all his courage, he stepped forwards and bent anxiously over it. Once glance was enough, for he recognised the body of Ivanovitch the poacher, hideously mangled. With a cry of surprise, he turned over the body and shuddered as he gazed upon the terrible injuries that had been inflicted. The unfortunate man had evidently been attacked by some savage beast, for there were marks of teeth upon the throat, and the jugular vein had been almost torn out. The breast of the corpse had been torn open, evidently by long sharp claws, and there was a gaping orifice upon the left side, round which the blood had formed in a thick coagulated patch. The only animals to be found in the forests of Russia capable of inflicting such wounds are the bear or the wolf, and the question as to the class of the assailant was easily settled by a glance at the dank ground, which showed the prints of a wolf so entirely different from the plantegrade traces of the bear.

"Savage brutes," muttered Paul. "So, after all, there may have been some truth in Michael's story, and the old idiot may for once in his life have spoken the truth. Well, it is no concern of mine, and if a fellow chooses to wander about the woods at night to kill my game, instead of remaining in his own hovel, he must take his chance. The strange thing is that the brutes have not eaten him, though they have mauled him so terribly."

He turned away as he spoke, intending to return home and send out some of the serfs to bring in the body of the unhappy man, when his eye was caught by a small white object, hanging from a bramble bush near the pond. He made towards the spot, and taking up the object, examined it curiously. It was a tuft of coarse white hair, evidently belonging to some animal.

"A wolfs hair, or I am much mistaken," muttered Paul, pressing the hair between his fingers, and then applying it to his nose. "And from its colour, I should think that it belonged to the white lady who so terribly alarmed old Michael on the occasion of his night walk through the marsh."

Paul found it no easy task to retrace his steps towards those parts of the forest with which he was acquainted, and Troska seemed unable to render him the slightest assistance, but followed moodily behind. Many times Paul found his way blocked by impenetrable thicket or dangerous quagmire, and during his many wanderings he had the ever-present sensation that there was a something close to him, an invisible something, a noiseless something, but for all that a presence which moved as he advanced, and halted as he stopped in vain to listen. The certainty that an impalpable thing of some shape or other was close at hand grew so strong, that as the short autumn day began to close, and darker shadows to fall between the trunks of the lofty trees, it made him hurry on at his utmost speed. At length, when he had grown almost mad with terror, he suddenly came upon a path he knew, and with a feeling of intense relief, he stepped briskly forward in the direction of Kostopchin. As he left the forest and came into the open country, a faint wail seemed to ring through the darkness; but Paul's nerves had been so much shaken that he did not know whether this was an actual fact or only the offspring of his own excited fancy. As he crossed the neglected lawn that lay in front of the house, old Michael came rushing out of the house with terror convulsing every feature.

"Oh, my lord, my lord!" gasped he, "is not this too terrible?"

"Nothing has happened to my Katrina?" cried the father, a sudden sickly feeling of terror passing through his heart.

"No, no, the little lady is quite safe, thanks to the Blessed Virgin and Saint Alexander of Nevskoi," returned Michael; "but oh, my lord, poor Marta, the herd's daughter—"

"Well, what of the slut?" demanded Paul, for now that his momentary fear for the safety of his daughter had passed away, he had but little sympathy to spare for so insignificant a creature as a serf girl.

"I told you that Kosma was dying," answered Michael. "Well, Marta went across the marsh this afternoon to fetch the priest, but alas! she never came back."

"What detained her, then?" asked his master.

"One of the neighbours, going in to see how Kosma was getting on, found the poor old man dead; his face was terribly contorted, and he was half in the bed, and half out, as though he had striven to reach the door. The man ran to the village to give the alarm, and as the men returned to the herdsman's hut, they found the body of Marta in a thicket by the clump of alders on the marsh."

"Her body—she was dead then?" asked Paul.

"Dead, my lord; killed by wolves," answered the old man. "And oh, my lord, it is too horrible, her breast was horribly lacerated, and her heart had been taken out and eaten, for it was nowhere to be found."

Paul started, for the horrible mutilation of the body of Ivanovitch the poacher occurred to his recollection.

"And, my lord," continued the old man, "this is not all; on a bush close by was this tuft of hair," and, as he spoke, he took it from a piece of paper in which it was wrapped and handed it to his master.

Paul took it and recognised a similar tuft of hair to that which he had seen upon the bramble bush beside the shattered cross.

"Surely, my lord," continued Michael, not heeding his master's look of surprise, "you will have out men and dogs to hunt down this terrible creature, or, better still, send for the priest and holy water, for I have my doubts whether the creature belongs to this earth."

Paul shuddered, and, after a short pause, he told Michael of the ghastly end of Ivanovitch the poacher.

The old man listened with the utmost excitement, crossing himself repeatedly, and muttering invocations to the Blessed Virgin and the saints every instant; but his master would no longer listen to him, and, ordering him to place brandy on the table, sat drinking moodily until daylight.

The next day a fresh horror awaited the inhabitants of Kostopchin. An old man, a confirmed drunkard, had staggered out of the *vodki* shop with the intention of returning home; three hours later he was found at a turn of the road, horribly scratched and mutilated, with the same gaping orifice in the left side of the breast, from which the heart had been forcibly torn out.

Three several times in the course of the week the same ghastly tragedy occurred—a little child, an able-bodied labourer, and an old woman, were all found with the same terrible marks of mutilation upon them, and in every case the same tuft of white hair was found in the immediate vicinity of the bodies. A frightful panic ensued, and an excited crowd of serfs surrounded the house at Kostopchin, calling upon their master, Paul Sergevitch, to save them from the fiend that had been let loose upon them, and shouting out various remedies, which they insisted upon being carried into effect at once.

Paul felt a strange disinclination to adopt any active measures. A certain feeling which he could not account for urged him to remain quiescent; but the Russian serf when suffering under an access of superstitious terror is a dangerous person to deal with, and, with extreme reluctance, Paul Sergevitch issued instructions for a thorough search through the estate, and a general *battue* of the pine woods.

The army of beaters convened by Michael was ready with the first dawn of sunrise, and formed a strange and almost grotesque-looking assemblage, armed with rusty old firelocks, heavy bludgeons, and scythes fastened on to the end of long poles. Paul, with his double-barrelled gun thrown across his shoulder and a keen hunting knife thrust into his belt, marched at the head of the serfs, accompanied by the two great hounds, Troska and Branskoe. Every nook and corner of the hedgerows were examined, and the little outlying clumps were thoroughly searched, but without success; and at last a circle was formed round the larger portion of the forest, and with loud shouts, blowing of horns, and beating of copper cooking utensils, the crowd of eager serfs pushed their way through the brushwood. Frightened birds flew up, whirring through the pine branches; hares and rabbits darted from their hiding places behind tufts and hummocks of grass, and scurried away in the utmost terror. Occasionally a roe deer rushed through the thicket, or a wild boar burst through the thin lines of beaters, but no signs of wolves were to be seen. The circle grew narrower and yet more narrow, when all at once a wild shriek and a confused murmur of voices echoed through the pine trees. All rushed to the spot, and a young lad was discovered weltering in his blood and terribly mutilated, though life still lingered in the mangled frame. A few drops of *vodki* were poured down the throat, and he managed to gasp out that the white wolf had sprung upon him suddenly, and, throwing him to the ground, had commenced tearing at the flesh over his heart. He would inevitably have been killed, had not the animal quitted him, alarmed by the approach of the other beaters.

"The beast ran into that thicket," gasped the boy, and then once more relapsed into a state of insensibility.

But the words of the wounded boy had been eagerly passed round, and a hundred different propositions were made.

"Set fire to the thicket," exclaimed one.

"Fire a volley into it," suggested another.

"A bold dash in, and trample the beast's life out," shouted a third.

The first proposal was agreed to, and a hundred eager hands collected dried sticks and leaves, and then a light was kindled. Just as the fire was about to be applied, a soft, sweet voice issued from the centre of the thicket.

"Do not set fire to the forest, my dear friends; give me time to come out. Is it not enough for me to have been frightened to death by that awful creature?"

All started back in amazement, and Paul felt a strange, sudden thrill pass through his heart as those soft musical accents fell upon his ear.

There was a light rustling in the brushwood, and then a vision suddenly appeared, which filled the souls of the beholders with surprise. As the bushes divided, a fair woman, wrapped in a mantle of soft white fur, with a fantastically shaped travelling cap of green velvet upon her head, stood before them. She was exquisitely fair, and her long Titian red hair hung in dishevelled masses over her shoulders.

"My good man," began she, with a certain tinge of aristocratic hauteur in her voice, "is your master here?"

As moved by a spring, Paul stepped forward and mechanically raised his cap.

"I am Paul Sergevitch," said he, "and these woods are on my estate of Kostopchin. A fearful wolf has been committing a series of terrible devastations upon my people, and we have been endeavouring to hunt it down. A boy whom he has just wounded says that he ran into the thicket from which you have just emerged, to the surprise of us all."

"I know," answered the lady, fixing her clear, steel-blue eyes keenly upon Paul's face. "The terrible beast rushed past me, and dived into a large cavity in the earth in the very centre of the thicket. It was a huge white wolf, and I greatly feared that it would devour me."

"Ho, my men," cried Paul, "take spade and mattock, and dig out the monster, for she has come to the end of her tether at last. Madam, I do not know what chance has conducted you to this wild solitude, but the hospitality of Kostopchin is at your disposal, and I will, with your permission, conduct you there as soon as this scourge of the countryside has been dispatched."

He offered his hand with some remains of his former courtesy, but started back with an expression of horror on his face.

"Blood," cried he; "why, madam, your hand and fingers are stained with blood."

A faint colour rose to the lady's cheek, but it died away in an instant as she answered, with a faint smile:—

"The dreadful creature was all covered with blood, and I suppose I must have stained my hands against the bushes through which it had passed, when I parted them in order to escape from the fiery death with which you threatened me."

There was a ring of suppressed irony in her voice, and Paul felt his eyes drop before the glance of those cold steel-blue eyes. Meanwhile, urged to the utmost exertion by their fears, the serfs plied spade and mattock with the utmost vigour. The cavity was speedily enlarged, but, when a depth of eight feet had been attained, it was found to terminate in a little burrow not large enough to admit a rabbit, much less a creature of the white wolf's size. There were none of the tufts of white hair which had hitherto been always found beside the bodies of the victims, nor did that peculiar rank odour which always indicates the presence of wild animals hang about the spot.

The superstitious Muscovites crossed themselves, and scrambled out of the hole with grotesque alacrity. The mysterious disappearance of the monster which had committed such frightful ravages had cast a chill over the hearts of the ignorant peasants, and, unheeding the shouts of their master, they left the forest, which seemed to be overcast with the gloom of some impending calamity.

"Forgive the ignorance of these boors, madam," said Paul, when he found himself alone with the strange lady, "and permit me to escort you to my poor house, for you must have need of rest and refreshment, and—"

Here Paul checked himself abruptly, and a dark flush of embarrassment passed over his face.

"And," said the lady, with the same faint smile, "and you are dying with curiosity to know how I suddenly made my appearance from a thicket in your forest. You say that you are the lord of Kostopchin; then you are Paul Sergevitch, and should surely know how the ruler of Holy Russia takes upon himself to interfere with the doings of his children?"

"You know me, then?" exclaimed Paul, in some surprise.

"Yes, I have lived in foreign lands, as you have, and have heard your name often. Did you not break the bank at Blankburg? Did you not carry off Isola Menuti, the dancer, from a host of competitors; and, as a last instance of my knowledge, shall I recall to your memory a certain morning, on a sandy shore, with two men facing each other pistol in hand, the one young, fair, and boyish-looking, hardly twenty-two years of age, the other—"

"Hush!" exclaimed Paul, hoarsely; "you evidently know me, but who in the fiend's name are you?"

"Simply a woman who once moved in society and read the papers, and who is now a hunted fugitive."

"A fugitive!" returned Paul, hotly; "who dares to persecute you?" The lady moved a little closer to him, and then whispered in his ear:—

"The police!"

"The police!" repeated Paul, stepping back a pace or two. "The police!"

"Yes, Paul Sergevitch, the police," returned the lady, "that body at the mention of which it is said the very emperor trembles as he sits in his gilded chambers in the Winter Palace. Yes, I have had the imprudence to speak my mind too freely, and—well, you know what women have to dread who fall into the hands of the police in Holy Russia. To avoid such infamous degradations I fled, accompanied by a faithful domestic. I fled in hopes of gaining the frontier, but a few *versts* from here a body of mounted police rode up. My poor old servant had the imprudence to resist, and was shot dead. Half wild with terror I fled into the forest, and wandered about until I heard the noise your serfs made in the beating of the woods. I thought it was the police, who had organised a search for me, and I crept into the thicket for the purpose of concealment. The rest you know. And now, Paul Sergevitch, tell me whether you dare give shelter to a proscribed fugitive such as I am."

"Madam," returned Paul, gazing into the clear-cut features before him, glowing with the animation of the recital, "Kostopchin is ever open to misfortune—and beauty," added he, with a bow.

"Ah!" cried the lady, with a laugh in which there was something sinister; "I expect that misfortune would knock at your door for a long time, if it was unaccompanied by beauty. However, I thank you, and will accept your hospitality; but if evil come upon you, remember that I am not to be blamed."

"You will be safe enough at Kostopchin," returned Paul. "The police won't trouble their heads about me; they know that since the emperor drove me to lead this hideous existence, politics have no charm for me, and that the brandy bottle is the only charm of my life."

"Dear me," answered the lady, eyeing him uneasily, "a morbid drunkard, are you? Well, as I am half perished with cold, suppose you take me to Kostopchin; you will be conferring a favour on me, and will get back all the sooner to your favourite brandy."

She placed her hand upon Paul's arm as she spoke, and mechanically he led the way to the great solitary white house. The few servants betrayed no astonishment at the appearance of the lady, for some of the serfs on their way back to the village had spread the report of the sudden appearance of the mysterious stranger; besides, they were not accustomed to question the acts of their somewhat arbitrary master.

Alexis and Katrina had gone to bed, and Paul and his guest sat down to a hastily improvised meal.

"I am no great eater," remarked the lady, as she played with the food before her; and Paul noticed with surprise that scarcely a morsel passed her lips, though she more than once filled and emptied a goblet of the champagne which had been opened in honour of her arrival.

"So it seems," remarked he; "and I do not wonder, for the food in this benighted hole is not what either you or I have been accustomed to."

"Oh, it does well enough," returned the lady, carelessly. "And now, if you have such a thing as a woman in the establishment, you can let her show me to my room, for I am nearly dead for want of sleep."

Paul struck a handbell that stood on the table beside him, and the stranger rose from her seat, and with a brief "Good night", was moving towards the door, when the old man Michael suddenly made his appearance on the threshold. The aged intendant started backwards as though to avoid a heavy blow, and his fingers at once sought for the crucifix which he wore suspended round his neck, and on whose protection he relied to shield him from the powers of darkness.

"Blessed Virgin!" he exclaimed. "Holy Saint Radislas protect me, where have I seen her before?"

The lady took no notice of the old man's evident terror, but passed away down the echoing corridor.

The old man now timidly approached his master, who, after swallowing a glass of brandy, had drawn his chair up to the stove, and was gazing moodily at its polished surface.

"My lord," said Michael, venturing to touch his master's shoulder, "is that the lady that you found in the forest?"

"Yes," returned Paul, a smile breaking out over his face; "she is very beautiful, is she not?"

"Beautiful!" repeated Michael, crossing himself, "she may have beauty, but it is that of a demon. Where have I seen her before?— where have I seen those shining teeth and those cold eyes? She is not like anyone here, and I have never been ten *versts* from Kostopchin in my life. I am utterly bewildered. Ah, I have it, the dying herdsman—save the mark! Gospodin, have a care. I tell you that the strange lady is the image of the white wolf."

"You old fool," returned his master, savagely, "let me ever hear you repeat such nonsense again, and I will have you skinned alive. The lady is highborn, and of good family; beware how you insult her. Nay, I give you further commands: see that during her sojourn here she is treated with the utmost respect. And communicate this to all the servants. Mind, no more tales about the vision that your addled brain conjured up of wolves in the marsh, and above all do not let me hear that you have been alarming little Katrina with your senseless babble."

The old man bowed humbly, and, after a short pause, remarked:—

"The lad that was injured at the hunt today is dead, my lord."

"Oh, dead is he, poor wretch!" returned Paul, to whom the death of a serf lad was not a matter of overweening importance. "But look here, Michael, remember that if any inquiries are made about the lady, that no one knows anything about her; that, in fact, no one has seen her at all."

"Your lordship shall be obeyed," answered the old man; and then, seeing that his master had relapsed into his former moody reverie, he left the room, crossing himself at every step he took.

Late into the night Paul sat up thinking over the occurrences of the day. He had told Michael that his guest was of noble family, but in reality he knew nothing more of her than she had condescended to tell him.

"Why, I don't even know her name," muttered he; "and yet somehow or other it seems as if a new feature of my life was opening before me. However, I have made one step in advance by getting her here, and if she talks about leaving, why, all that I have to do is threaten her with the police."

After his usual custom he smoked cigarette after cigarette, and poured out copious tumblers of brandy. The attendant serf replenished the stove from a small den which opened into the corridor, and after a time Paul slumbered heavily in his armchair. He was aroused by a light touch upon the shoulder, and, starting up, saw the stranger of the forest standing by his side.

"This is indeed kind of you," said she, with her usual mocking smile. "You felt that I should be strange here, and you got up early to see to the horses, or can it really be, those ends of cigarettes, that empty bottle of brandy? Paul Sergevitch, you have not been to bed at all."

Paul muttered a few indistinct words in reply, and then, ringing the bell furiously, ordered the servant to clear away the *débris* of last night's orgy, and lay the table for breakfast; then, with a hasty apology, he left the room to make a fresh toilet, and in about half an hour returned with his appearance sensibly improved by his ablutions and change of dress.

"I dare say," remarked the lady, as they were seated at the morning meal, for which she manifested the same indifference that she had for the dinner of the previous evening, "that you would like to know my name and who I am. Well, I don't mind telling you my name. It is Ravina, but as to my family and who I am, it will perhaps be best for you to remain in ignorance. A matter of policy, my dear Paul Sergevitch, a mere matter of policy, you see. I leave you to judge from my manners and appearance whether I am of sufficiently good form to be invited to the honour of your table—"

"None more worthy," broke in Paul, whose bemuddled brain was fast succumbing to the charms of his guest; "and surely that is a question upon which I may be deemed a competent judge."

"I do not know about that," returned Ravina, "for from all accounts the company that you used to keep was not of the most select character."

"No, but hear me," began Paul, seizing her hand and endeavouring to carry it to his lips. But as he did so an unpleasant chill passed over him, for those slender fingers were icy cold.

"Do not be foolish," said Ravina, drawing away her hand, after she had permitted it to rest for an instant in Paul's grasp, "do you not hear someone coming?"

As she spoke the sound of tiny pattering feet was heard in the corridor, then the door was flung violently open, and with a shrill cry of delight, Katrina rushed into the room, followed more slowly by her brother Alexis.

"And are these your children?" asked Ravina, as Paul took up the little girl and placed her fondly upon his knee, whilst the boy stood a few paces from the door gazing with eyes of wonder upon the strange woman, for whose appearance he was utterly unable to account. "Come here, my little man," continued she; "I suppose you are the heir of Kostopchin, though you do not resemble your father much."

"He takes after his mother, I think," returned Paul carelessly; "and how has my darling Katrina been?" he added, addressing his daughter.

"Quite well, Papa dear," answered the child; "but where is the fine white wolf skin that you promised me?"

"Your father did not find her," answered Ravina, with a little laugh; "the white wolf was not so easy to catch as he fancied."

Alexis had moved a few steps nearer to the lady, and was listening with grave attention to every word she uttered.

"Are white wolves so difficult to kill, then?" asked he.

"It seems so, my little man," returned the lady, "since your father and all the serfs of Kostopchin were unable to do so."

"I have got a pistol, that good old Michael has taught me to fire, and I am sure I could kill her if ever I got sight of her," observed Alexis, boldly.

"There is a brave boy," returned Ravina, with one of her shrill laughs; "and now, won't you come and sit on my knee, for I am very fond of little boys?"

"No, I don't like you," answered Alexis, after a moment's consideration, "for Michael says—"

"Go to your room, you insolent young brat," broke in the father, in a voice of thunder. "You spend so much of your time with Michael and the serfs that you have learned all their boorish habits."

Two tiny tears rolled down the boy's cheeks as in obedience to his father's orders he turned about and quitted the room, whilst Ravina darted a strange look of dislike after him. As soon, however, as the door had closed, the fair woman addressed Katrina.

"Well, perhaps you will not be so unkind to me as your brother," said she. "Come to me," and as she spoke she held out her arms.

The little girl came to her without hesitation, and began to smooth the silken tresses which were coiled and wreathed around Ravina's head.

"Pretty, pretty," she murmured, "beautiful lady."

"You see, Paul Sergevitch, that your little daughter has taken to me at once," remarked Ravina.

"She takes after her father, who was always noted for his good taste," returned Paul, with a bow; "but take care, madam, or the little puss will have your necklace off."

The child had indeed succeeded in unclasping the glittering ornament, and was now inspecting it in high glee.

"That is a curious ornament," said Paul, stepping up to the child and taking the circlet from her hand.

It was indeed a quaintly fashioned ornament, consisting as it did of a number of what were apparently curved pieces of sharp-pointed horn set in gold, and depending from a snake of the same precious metal.

"Why, these are claws," continued he, as he looked at them more carefully.

"Yes, wolves' claws," answered Ravina, taking the necklet from the child and reclasping it round her neck. "It is a family relic which I have always worn."

Katrina at first seemed inclined to cry at her new plaything being taken from her, but by caresses and endearments Ravina soon contrived to lull her once more into a good temper.

"My daughter has certainly taken to you in a most wonderful manner," remarked Paul, with a pleased smile. "You have quite obtained possession of her heart."

"Not yet, whatever I may do later on," answered the woman, with her strange cold smile, as she pressed the child closer towards her and shot a glance at Paul which made him quiver with an emotion that he had never felt before. Presently, however, the child grew tired of her new acquaintance, and sliding down from her knee, crept from the room in search of her brother Alexis.

Paul and Ravina remained silent for a few instants, and then the woman broke the silence.

"All that remains for me now, Paul Sergevitch, is to trespass on your hospitality, and to ask you to lend me some disguise, and assist me to gain the nearest post town, which, I think, is Vitroski."

"And why should you wish to leave this at all," demanded Paul, a deep flush rising to his cheek. "You are perfectly safe in my house, and if you attempt to pursue your journey there is every chance of your being recognised and captured."

"Why do I wish to leave this house?" answered Ravina, rising to her feet and casting a look of surprise upon her interrogator. "Can you ask me such a question? How is it possible for me to remain here?"

"It is perfectly impossible for you to leave; of that I am quite certain," answered the man, doggedly. "All I know is, that if you leave Kostopchin, you will inevitably fall into the hands of the police."

"And Paul Sergevitch will tell them where they can find me?" questioned Ravina, with an ironical inflection in the tone of her voice.

"I never said so," returned Paul.

"Perhaps not," answered the woman, quickly, "but I am not slow in reading thoughts; they are sometimes plainer to read than words. You are saying to yourself, 'Kostopchin is but a dull hole after all; chance has thrown into my hands a woman whose beauty pleases me; she is utterly friendless, and is in fear of the pursuit of the police; why should I not bend her to my will?' That is what you have been thinking—is it not so, Paul Sergevitch?"

"I never thought, that is—" stammered the man.

"No, you never thought that I could read you so plainly," pursued the woman, pitilessly; "but it is the truth that I have told you, and sooner than remain an inmate of your house, I would leave it, even if all the police of Russia stood ready to arrest me on its very threshold."

"Stay, Ravina," exclaimed Paul, as the woman made a step towards the door. "I do not say whether your reading of my thoughts is right or wrong, but before you leave, listen to me. I do not speak to you in the usual strain of a pleading lover—you, who know my past, would laugh at me should I do so; but I tell you plainly that from the first moment that I set eyes upon you, a strange new feeling has risen up in my heart, not the cold thing that society calls love, but a burning resistless flood which flows down like molten lava from the volcano's crater. Stay, Ravina, stay, I implore you, for if you go from here you will take my heart with you."

"You may be speaking more truthfully than you think," returned the fair woman, as, turning back, she came close up to Paul, and placing both her hands upon his shoulders, shot a glance of lurid fire from her eyes. "Still, you have but given me a selfish reason for my staying, only your own self-gratification. Give me one that more nearly affects myself."

Ravina's touch sent a tremor through Paul's whole frame which caused every nerve and sinew to vibrate. Gaze as boldly as he might into those steel-blue eyes, he could not sustain their intensity.

"Be my wife, Ravina," faltered he. "Be my wife. You are safe enough from all pursuit here, and if that does not suit you I can easily convert my estate into a large sum of money, and we can fly to other lands, where you can have nothing to fear from the Russian police."

"And does Paul Sergevitch actually mean to offer his hand to a woman whose name he does not even know, and of whose feelings towards him he is entirely ignorant?" asked the woman, with her customary mocking laugh.

"What do I care for name or birth," returned he, hotly, "I have enough for both, and as for love, my passion would soon kindle some sparks of it in your breast, cold and frozen as it may now be."

"Let me think a little," said Ravina; and throwing herself into an armchair she buried her face in her hands and seemed plunged in deep reflection, whilst Paul paced impatiently up and down the room like a prisoner awaiting the verdict that would restore him to life or doom him to a shameful death.

At length Ravina removed her hands from her face and spoke.

"Listen," said she. "I have thought over your proposal seriously, and upon certain conditions, I will consent to become your wife."

"They are granted in advance," broke in Paul, eagerly.

"Make no bargains blindfold," answered she, "but listen. At the present moment I have no inclination for you, but on the other hand I feel no repugnance for you. I will remain here for a month, and during that time I shall remain in a suite of apartments which you will have prepared for me. Every evening I will visit you here, and upon your making yourself agreeable my ultimate decision will depend."

"And suppose that decision should be an unfavourable one?" asked Paul.

"Then," answered Ravina, with a ringing laugh, "I shall, as you say, leave this and take your heart with me."

"These are hard conditions," remarked Paul. "Why not shorten the time of probation?"

"My conditions are unalterable," answered Ravina, with a little stamp of the foot. "Do you agree to them or not?"

"I have no alternative," answered he, sullenly; "but remember that I am to see you every evening."

"For two hours," said the woman, "so you must try and make yourself as agreeable as you can in that time; and now, if you will give orders regarding my rooms, I will settle myself in them with as little delay as possible."

Paul obeyed her, and in a couple of hours three handsome chambers were got ready for their fair occupant in a distant part of the great rambling house.

THE AWAKENING OF THE WOLF

The days slipped slowly and wearily away, but Ravina showed no signs of relenting. Every evening, according to her bond, she spent two hours with Paul and made herself most agreeable, listening to his far-fetched compliments and asseverations of love and tenderness either with a cold smile or with one of her mocking laughs. She refused to allow Paul to visit her in her own apartments, and the only intruder she permitted there, save the servants, was little Katrina, who had taken a strange fancy to the fair woman. Alexis, on the contrary, avoided her as much as he possibly could, and the pair hardly ever met. Paul, to while away the time, wandered about the farm and the village, the inhabitants of which had recovered from their panic as the white wolf appeared to have entirely desisted from her murderous attacks upon belated peasants. The shades of evening had closed in as Paul was one day returning from his customary round, rejoiced with the idea that the hour for Ravina's visit was drawing near, when he was startled by a gentle touch upon the shoulder, and turning round, saw the old man Michael standing just behind him. The intendant's face was perfectly livid, his eyes gleamed with the lustre of terror, and his fingers kept convulsively clasping and unclasping.

"My lord," exclaimed he, in faltering accents; "oh, my lord, listen to me, for I have terrible news to narrate to you."

"What is the matter?" asked Paul, more impressed than he would have liked to confess by the old man's evident terror.

"The wolf, the white wolf! I have seen it again," whispered Michael.

"You are dreaming," retorted his master, angrily. "You have got the creature on the brain, and have mistaken a white calf or one of the dogs for it."

"I am not mistaken," answered the old man, firmly. "And oh, my lord, do not go into the house, for she is there."

"She—who—what do you mean?" cried Paul.

"The white wolf, my lord. I saw her go in. You know the strange lady's apartments are on the ground floor on the west side of the house. I saw the monster cantering across the lawn, and, as if it knew its way perfectly well, make for the centre window of the reception room; it yielded to a touch of the fore paw, and the beast sprang through. Oh, my lord, do not go in; I tell you that it will never harm the strange woman. Ah! let me—"

But Paul cast off the detaining arm with a force that made the old man reel and fall, and then, catching up an axe, dashed into the house, calling upon the servants to follow him to the strange lady's rooms. He tried the handle, but the door was securely fastened, and then, in all the frenzy of terror, he attacked the panels with heavy blows of his axe. For a few seconds no sound was heard save the ring of metal and the shivering of panels, but then the clear tones of Ravina were heard asking the reason for this outrageous disturbance.

"The wolf, the white wolf," shouted half a dozen voices.

"Stand back and I will open the door," answered the fair woman. "You must be mad, for there is no wolf here."

The door flew open and the crowd rushed tumultuously in; every nook and corner were searched, but no signs of the intruder could be discovered, and with many shamefaced glances Paul and his servants were about to return, when the voice of Ravina arrested their steps.

"Paul Sergevitch," sad she, coldly, "explain the meaning of this daring intrusion on my privacy."

She looked very beautiful as she stood before them; her right arm extended and her bosom heaved violently, but this was doubt-less caused by her anger at the unlooked-for invasion.

Paul briefly repeated.what he had heard from the old serf, and Ravina's scorn was intense.

"And so," cried she, fiercely, "it is to the crotchets of this old dotard that I am indebted for this. Paul, if you ever hope to succeed in winning me, forbid that man ever to enter the house again."

Paul would have sacrificed all his serfs for a whim of the haughty beauty, and Michael was deprived of the office of intendant and exiled to a cabin in the village, with orders never to show his face again near the house. The separation from the children almost broke the old man's heart, but he ventured on no remonstrance and meekly obeyed the mandate which drove him away from all he loved and cherished.

Meanwhile, curious rumours began to be circulated regarding the strange proceedings of the lady who occupied the suite of apartments which had formerly belonged to the wife of the owner of Kostopchin. The servants declared that the food sent up, though hacked about and cut up, was never tasted, but that the raw meat in the larder was frequently missing. Strange sounds were often heard to issue from the rooms as the panic-stricken serfs hurried past the corridor upon which the doors opened, and dwellers in the house were frequently disturbed by the howlings of wolves, the footprints of which were distinctly visible the next morning, and, curiously enough, invariably in the gardens facing the west side of the house in which the lady dwelt. Little Alexis, who found no encouragement to sit with his father, was naturally thrown a great deal amongst the serfs, and heard the subject discussed with many exaggerations. Weird old tales of folklore were often narrated as the servants discussed their evening meal, and the boy's hair would bristle as he listened to the wild and fanciful narratives of wolves, witches, and white ladies with which the superstitious serfs filled his ears. One of his most treasured possessions was an old brass-mounted cavalry pistol, a present from Michael; this he has learned to load, and by using both hands to the cumbrous weapon could contrive to fire it off, as many an ill-starred sparrow could attest. With his mind constantly dwelling upon the terrible tales he had so greedily listened to, this pistol became his daily companion, whether he was wandering about the long echoing corridors of the house or wandering through the neglected shrubberies of the garden. For a fortnight matters went on in this manner, Paul becoming more and more infatuated by the charms of his strange guest, and she every now and then letting drop occasional crumbs of hope which led the unhappy man further and further upon the dangerous course that he was pursuing. A mad, soul-absorbing passion for the fair woman and the deep draughts of brandy with which he consoled himself during her hours of absence were telling upon the brain of the master of Kostopchin, and except during the brief space of Ravina's visit, he would relapse into moods of silent sullenness from which he would occasionally break out into furious bursts of passion for no assignable cause. A shadow seemed to be closing over the house of Kostopchin; it became the abode of grim whispers and undeveloped fears; the men and maidservants went about their work glancing nervously over their shoulders, as though they were apprehensive that some hideous thing was following at their heels.

After three days of exile, poor old Michael could endure the state of suspense regarding the safety of Alexis and Katrina no longer; and, casting aside his superstitious fears, he took to wandering by night about the exterior of the great white house, and peering curiously into such windows as had been left unshuttered. At first he was in continual dread of meeting the terrible white wolf; but his love for the children and his confidence in the crucifix he wore prevailed, and he continued his nocturnal wanderings about Kostopchin and its environs. He kept near the western front of the house, urged on to do so from some vague feeling which he could in no wise account for. One evening as he was making his accustomed tour of inspection, the wail of a child struck upon his ear. He bent down his head and eagerly listened, again he heard the same faint sounds, and in them he fancied he recognised the accents of his dear little Katrina. Hurrying up to one of the ground-floor windows, from which a dim light streamed, he pressed his face against the pane, and looked steadily in. A horrible sight presented itself to his gaze. By the faint light of a shaded lamp, he saw Katrina stretched upon the ground; but her wailing had now ceased, for a shawl had been tied across her little mouth. Over her was bending a hideous shape, which seemed to be clothed in some white and shaggy covering. Katrina lay perfectly motionless, and the hands of the figure were engaged in hastily removing the garments from the child's breast. The task was soon effected; then there was a bright gleam of steel, and the head of the thing bent closely down to the child's bosom.

With a yell of apprehension, the old man dashed in through the window frame, and, drawing the cross from his breast, sprang boldly into the room. The creature sprang to its feet, and the white fur cloak falling from its head and shoulders disclosed the pallid features of Ravina, a short, broad knife in her hand, and her lips discoloured with blood.

"Vile sorceress!" cried Michael, dashing forward and raising Katrina in his arms. "What hellish work are you about?"

Ravina's eyes gleamed fiercely upon the old man, who had interfered between her and her prey. She raised her dagger, and was about to spring in upon him, when she caught sight of the cross in his extended hand. With a low cry, she dropped the knife, and, staggering back a few paces, wailed out: "I could not help it; I liked the child well enough, but I was so hungry."

Michael paid but little heed to her words, for he was busily engaged in examining the fainting child, whose head was resting helplessly on his shoulder. There was a wound over the left breast, from which the blood was flowing; but the injury appeared slight, and not likely to prove fatal. As soon as he had satisfied himself on this point, he turned to the woman, who was crouching before the cross as a wild beast shrinks before the whip of the tamer.

"I am going to remove the child," said he, slowly. "Dare you to mention a word of what I have done or whither she has gone, and I will arouse the village. Do you know what will happen then? Why, every peasant in the place will hurry here with a lighted brand in his hand to consume this accursed house and the unnatural dwellers in it. Keep silence, and I leave you to your unhallowed work. I will no longer seek to preserve Paul Sergevitch, who has given himself over to the powers of darkness by taking a demon to his bosom."

Ravina listened to him as if she scarcely comprehended him; but, as the old man retreated to the window with his helpless burden, she followed him step by step; and as he turned to cast one last glance at the shattered window, he saw the woman's pale face and bloodstained lips glued against an unbroken pane, with a wild look of unsatiated appetite in her eyes.

Next morning the house, of Kostopchin was filled with terror and surprise, for Katrina, the idol of her father's heart, had disappeared, and no signs of her could be discovered. Every effort was made, the woods and fields in the neighbourhood were thoroughly searched; but it was at last concluded that robbers had carried off the child for the sake of the ransom that they might be able to extract from the father. This seemed the more likely as one of the windows in the fair stranger's room bore marks of violence, and she declared that, being alarmed by the sound of crashing glass, she had risen and confronted a man who was endeavouring to enter her apartment, but who, on perceiving her, turned and fled away with the utmost precipitation.

Paul Sergevitch did not display as much anxiety as might have been expected from him, considering the devotion which he had ever evinced for the lost Katrina, for his whole soul was wrapped up in one mad, absorbing passion for the fair woman who had so strangely crossed his life. He certainly directed the search, and gave all the necessary orders; but he did so in a listless and half-hearted manner, and hastened back to Kostopchin as speedily as he could as though fearing to be absent for any length of time from the casket in which his new treasure was enshrined. Not so Alexis; he was almost frantic at the loss of his sister, and accompanied the searchers daily until his little legs grew weary, and he had to be carried on the shoulders of a sturdy *moujik*. His treasured brass-mounted pistol was now more than ever his constant companion; and when he met the fair woman who had cast a spell upon his father, his face would flush, and he would grind his teeth in impotent rage.

The day upon which all search had ceased, Ravina glided into the room where she knew that she would find Paul awaiting her. She was fully an hour before her usual time, and the lord of Kostopchin started to his feet in surprise.

"You are surprised to see me," said she; "but I have only come to pay you a visit for a few minutes. I am convinced that you love me, and could I but relieve a few of the objections that my heart continues to raise, I might be yours."

"Tell me what these scruples are," cried Paul, springing towards her, and seizing her hands in his; "and be sure that I will find means to overcome them."

Even in the midst of all the glow and fervour of anticipated triumph, he could not avoid noticing how icily cold were the fingers that rested in his palm, and how utterly passionless was the pressure with which she slightly returned his enraptured clasp.

"Listen," said she, as she withdrew her hand; "I will take two more hours for consideration. By that time the whole of the house of Kostopchin will be cradled in slumber; then meet me at the old sundial near the yew tree at the bottom of the garden, and I will give you my reply. Nay, not a word," she added, as he seemed about to remonstrate, "for I tell you that I think it will be a favourable one."

"But why not come back here?" urged he; "there is a hard frost tonight, and—"

"Are you so cold a lover," broke in Ravina, with her accustomed laugh, "to dread the changes of the weather? But not another word; I have spoken."

She glided from the room, but uttered a low cry of rage. She had almost fallen over Alexis in the corridor.

"Why is that brat not in his bed?" cried she, angrily; "he gave me quite a turn."

"Go to your room, boy," exclaimed his father, harshly; and with a malignant glance at his enemy, the child slunk away.

Paul Sergevitch paced up and down the room for the two hours that he had to pass before the hour of meeting. His heart was very heavy, and a vague feeling of disquietude began to creep over him. Twenty times he made up his mind not to keep his appointment, and as often the fascination of the fair woman compelled him to rescind his resolution. He remember that he had from childhood disliked that spot by the yew tree, and had always looked upon it as a dreary, uncanny place; and he even now disliked the idea of finding himself here after dark, even with such fair companion-ship as he had been promised. Counting the minutes, he paced backwards and forwards, as though moved by some concealed machinery. Now and again he glanced at the clock, and at last its deep metallic sound, as it struck the quarter, warned him that he had but little time to lose, if he intended to keep his appointment. Throwing on a heavily furred coat and pulling a travelling cap down over his ears, he opened a side door and sallied out into the grounds. The moon was at its full, and shone coldly down upon the leafless trees, which looked white and ghostlike in its beams. The paths and unkept lawns were now covered with hoar frost, and a keen wind every now and then swept by, which, in spite of his wraps, chilled Paul's blood in his veins. The dark shape of the yew tree soon rose up before him, and in another moment he stood beside its dusky boughs. The old grey sundial stood only a few paces off, and by its side was standing a slender figure, wrapped in a white, fleecy-looking cloak. It was perfectly motionless, and again a terror of undefined dread passed through every nerve and muscle of Paul Sergevitch's body.

"Ravina!" said he, in faltering accents. "Ravina!"

"Did you take me for a ghost?" answered the fair woman, with her shrill laugh; "no, no, I have not come to that yet. Well, Paul Sergevitch, I have come to give you my answer; are you anxious about it?"

"How can you ask me such a question?" returned he; "do you not know that my whole soul has been aglow with anticipations of what your reply might be? Do not keep me any longer in suspense. Is it yes, or no?"

"Paul Sergevitch," answered the young woman, coming up to him and laying her hands upon his shoulders, and fixing her eyes upon his with that strange weird expression before which he always quailed; "do you really love me, Paul Sergevitch?" asked she.

"Love you!" repeated the lord of Kostopchin; "have I not told you a thousand times how much my whole soul flows out towards you, how I only live and breathe in your presence, and how death at your feet would be more welcome than life without you?"

"People often talk of death, and yet little know how near it is to them," answered the fair lady, a grim smile appearing upon her face; "but say, do you give me your whole heart?"

"All I have is yours, Ravina," returned Paul, "name, wealth, and the devoted love of a lifetime."

"But your heart," persisted she; "it is your heart that I want; tell me, Paul, that it is mine and mine only."

"Yes, my heart is yours, dearest Ravina," answered Paul, endeavouring to embrace the fair form in his impassioned grasp; but she glided from him, and then with a quick bound sprang upon him and glared in his face with a look that was absolutely appalling. Her eyes gleamed with a lurid fire, her lips were drawn back, showing her sharp, white teeth, whilst her breath came in sharp, quick gasps.

"I am hungry," she murmured, "oh, so hungry; but now, Paul Sergevitch, your heart is mine."

Her movement was so sudden and unexpected that he stumbled and fell heavily to the ground, the fair woman clinging to him and falling upon his breast. It was then that the full horror of his position came upon Paul Sergevitch, and he saw his fate clearly before him; but a terrible numbness prevented him from using his hands to free himself from the hideous embrace which was paralysing all his muscles. The face that was glaring into his seemed to be undergoing some fearful change, and the features to be losing their semblance of humanity. With a sudden, quick movement, she tore open his garments, and in another moment she had perforated his left breast with a ghastly wound, and, plunging in her delicate hands, tore out his heart and bit at it ravenously. Intent upon her hideous banquet she heeded not the convulsive struggles which agitated the dying form of the lord of Kostopchin. She was too much occupied to notice a diminutive form approaching, sheltering itself behind every tree and bush until it had arrived within ten paces of the scene of the terrible tragedy. Then the moonbeams glistened upon the long shining barrel of a pistol, which a boy was levelling with both hands at the murderess. Then quick and sharp rang out the report, and with a wild shriek, in which there was something beastlike, Ravina leaped from the body of the dead man and staggered away to a thick clump of bushes some ten paces distant. The boy Alexis had heard the appointment that had been made, and dogged his father's footsteps to the trysting place. After firing the fatal shot his courage deserted him, and he fled backwards to the house, uttering loud shrieks for help. The startled servants were soon in the presence of their slaughtered master, but aid was of no avail, for the lord of Kostopchin had passed away. With fear and trembling the superstitious peasants searched the clump of bushes, and started back in horror as they perceived a huge white wolf, lying stark and dead, with a half-devoured human heart clasped between its forepaws.

No signs of the fair lady who had occupied the apartments in the western side of the house were ever again seen. She had passed away from Kostopchin like an ugly dream, and as the *moujiks* of the village sat around their stoves at night they whispered strange stories regarding the fair woman of the forest and the white wolf of Kostopchin. By order of the Tsar a surtee was placed in charge of the estate of Kostopchin, and Alexis was ordered to be sent to a military school until he should be old enough to join the army. The meeting between the boy and his sister, whom the faithful Michael, when all danger was at an end, had produced from his hiding place, was most affecting; but it was not until Katrina had been for some time resident at the house of a distant relative at Vitepak, that she ceased to wake at night and cry out in terror as she again dreamed that she was in the clutches of the white wolf.

THE MARK OF THE BEAST

Rudyard Kipling

Published in *Pioneer* magazine (July 1890)

Rudyard Kipling (1865–1936) is one of the most famous authors, poets, and journalists of the nineteenth and twentieth centuries, renowned for such works as *The Jungle Book* (1894) and poetry including the stirring 'If—' (1910). In 1907 he was awarded the Nobel Prize in Literature.

'The Mark of the Beast' was first published across two issues of *Pioneer* in July 1890. As in much of Kipling's writing, this story is set in India, the country of Kipling's birth. The tale details the desecration of a statue of the Hindu god Hanuman, an act which is punished by what is assumed to be the transmission of leprosy to the perpetrator. But the symptoms manifest in unusual and troubling ways, such as an appetite for raw meat and an uncanny ability to frighten animals, all too suggestive that something super-natural might be at work.

Your gods and my gods—do you or I know which are the stronger?
NATIVE PROVERB

E AST OF SUEZ, SOME HOLD, THE DIRECT CONTROL OF
Providence ceases, man being there handed over to the
power of the gods and devils of Asia, and the Church of England
Providence only exercising an occasional and modified supervision
in the case of Englishmen.

This theory accounts for some of the more unnecessary horrors
of life in India; it may be stretched to explain my story.

My friend Strickland of the police, who knows as much of
natives of India as is good for any man, can bear witness to the facts
of the case. Dumoise, our doctor, also saw what Strickland and I
saw. The inference which he drew from the evidence was entirely
incorrect. He is dead now; he died in a rather curious manner,
which has been elsewhere described.

When Fleete came to India he owned a little money and some
land in the Himalayas, near a place called Dharmsala. Both properties had been left him by an uncle, and he came out to finance them.
He was a big, heavy, genial, and inoffensive man. His knowledge
of natives was, of course, limited, and he complained of the dif-
ficulties of the language.

He rode in from his place in the hills to spend New Year in the
station, and he stayed with Strickland. On New Year's Eve there was
a big dinner at the club, and the night was excusably wet. When

men foregather from the uttermost ends of the empire, they have a right to be riotous. The frontier had sent down a contingent o' Catch-'em-Alive-O's who had not seen twenty white faces for a year, and were used to ride fifteen miles to dinner at the next fort at the risk of a Khyberee bullet where their drinks should lie. They profited by their new security, for they tried to play pool with a curled-up hedgehog found in the garden, and one of them carried the marker round the room in his teeth. Half a dozen planters had come in from the south and were talking "horse" to the Biggest Liar in Asia, who was trying to cap all their stories at once. Everybody was there, and there was a general closing up of ranks and taking stock of our losses in dead or disabled that had fallen during the past year. It was a very wet night, and I remember that we sang "Auld Lang Syne" with our feet in the Polo Championship Cup and our heads among the stars, and swore that we were all dear friends. Then some of us went away and annexed Burma, and some tried to open up the Sudan and were opened up by Fuzzies in that cruel scrub outside Suakin, and some found stars and medals, and some were married, which was bad, and some did other things which were worse, and the others of us stayed in our chains and strove to make money on insufficient experiences.

Fleete began the night with sherry and bitters, drank champagne steadily up to dessert, then raw, rasping Capri with all the strength of whisky, took Benedictine with his coffee, four or five whiskies and sodas to improve his pool strokes, beer and bones at half past two, winding up with old brandy. Consequently, when he came out at half past three in the morning into fourteen degrees of frost, he was very angry with his horse for coughing, and tried to leapfrog into the saddle. The horse broke away and went to his stables, so Strickland and I formed a Guard of Dishonour to take Fleete home.

Our road lay through the bazaar, close to a little temple of Hanuman, the monkey-god, who is a leading divinity worthy of respect. All gods have good points, just as have all priests. Personally, I attach much importance to Hanuman, and am kind to his people—the great grey apes of the hills. One never knows when one may want a friend.

There was a light in the temple, and as we passed we could hear voices of men chanting hymns. In a native temple the priests rise at all hours of the night to do honour to their god. Before we could stop him Fleete dashed up the steps, patted two priests on the back, and was gravely grinding the ashes of his cigar-butt into the fore head of the red stone image of Hanuman. Strickland tried to drag him out, but he sat down and said solemnly, "Shee that? Mark of the b-beasht! I made it. Ishn't it fine?"

In half a minute the temple was alive and noisy, and Strickland, who knew what came of polluting gods, said that things might occur. He, by virtue of his official position, long residence in the country, and weakness for going among the natives, was known to the priests, and he felt unhappy. Fleete sat on the ground and refused to move. He said that "good old Hanuman" made a very soft pillow.

Then, without any warning, a silver man came out of a recess behind the image of the god. He was perfectly naked in that bitter, bitter cold, and his body shone like frosted silver, for he was what the Bible calls a "leper as white as snow". Also he had no face, because he was a leper of some years' standing, and his disease was heavy upon him. We two stooped to haul Fleete up, and the temple was filling and filling with folk who seemed to spring from the earth, when the silver man ran in under our arms, making a noise exactly like the mewing of an otter, caught Fleete round the body, and dropped his head on Fleete's breast before we could wrench him away. Then he retired to a corner and sat mewing while the crowd blocked all the doors. The priests were very angry until the silver man touched Fleete. That nuzzling seemed to sober them.

At the end of a few minutes' silence one of the priests came to Strickland and said in perfect English, "Take your friend away. He has done with Hanuman, but Hanuman has not done with him." The crowd gave room and we carried Fleete into the road.

Strickland was very angry. He said that we might all three have been knifed and that Fleete should thank his stars that he had escaped without injury.

Fleete thanked no one. He said that he wanted to go to bed. He was gorgeously drunk. We moved on, Strickland silent and wrathful, until Fleete was taken with violent shivering fits and sweating. He said that the smells of the bazaar were overpowering, and he wondered why slaughter-houses were permitted so near English residences. "Can't you smell the blood?" said Fleete.

We put him to bed at last, just as the dawn was breaking, and Strickland invited me to have another whisky and soda. While we were drinking he talked of the trouble in the temple and admitted that it baffled him completely. Strickland hates being mystified by natives, because his business in life is to overmatch them with their own weapons. He has not yet succeeded in doing this, but in fifteen or twenty years he will have made some small progress.

"They should have mauled us," he said, "instead of mewing at us. I wonder what they meant. I don't like it one little bit."

I said that the Managing Committee of the temple would in all probability bring a criminal action against us for insulting their religion. There was a section of the Indian Penal Code which exactly met Fleete's offence. Strickland said he only hoped and prayed that they would do this. Before I left I looked into Fleete's room and saw him lying on his right side, scratching his left breast.

Then I went to bed, cold, depressed, and unhappy, at seven o'clock in the morning. At one o'clock I rode over to Strickland's house to inquire after Fleete's head. I imagined that it would be a sore one. Fleete was breakfasting and seemed unwell. His temper was gone, for he was abusing the cook for not supplying him with an underdone chop. A man who can eat raw meat after a wet night is a curiosity. I told Fleete this, and he laughed.

"You breed queer mosquitoes in these parts," he said. "I've been bitten to pieces, but only in one place."

"Let's have a look at the bite," said Strickland. "It may have gone down since this morning." While the chops were being cooked, Fleete opened his shirt and showed us, just over his left breast, a mark, the perfect double of the black rosettes—the five or six irregular blotches arranged in a circle—on a leopard's hide. Strickland looked and said, "It was only pink this morning. It's grown black now."

Fleete ran to a glass. "By Jove!" he said. "This is nasty. What is it?" We could not answer. Here the chops came in, all red and juicy, and Fleete bolted three in a most offensive manner. He ate on his right grinders only, and threw his head over his right shoulder as he snapped the meat. When he had finished, it struck him that he had been behaving strangely, for he said apologetically, "I don't think I ever felt so hungry in my life. I've bolted like an ostrich."

After breakfast Strickland said to me, "Don't go. Stay here, and stay for the night." Seeing that my house was not three miles from Strickland's, this request was absurd. But Strickland insisted, and was going to say something when Fleete interrupted by declaring in a shamefaced way that he felt hungry again. Strickland sent a man to my house to fetch over my bedding and a horse, and we three went down to Strickland's stables to pass the hours until it was time to go out for a ride. The man who has a weakness for horses never wearies of inspecting them, and when two men are killing time in this way they gather knowledge and lies the one from the other.

There were five horses in the stables, and I shall never forget the scene as we tried to look them over. They seemed to have gone mad. They reared and screamed and nearly tore up their pickets; they sweated and shivered and lathered and were distraught with fear. Strickland's horses used to know him as well as his dogs, which made the matter more curious. We left the stable for fear of the brutes throwing themselves in their panic. Then Strickland turned back and called me. The horses were still frightened, but they let us "gentle" and make much of them, and put their heads in our bosoms.

"They aren't afraid of us," said Strickland. "D'you know, I'd give three months' pay if Outrage here could talk."

But Outrage was dumb and could only cuddle up to his master and blow out his nostrils, as is the custom of horses when they wish to explain things but can't. Fleete came up when we were in the stalls, and as soon as the horses saw him their fright broke out afresh. It was all that we could do to escape from the place unkicked. Strickland said, "They don't seem to love you, Fleete."

"Nonsense," said Fleete; "my mare will follow me like a dog." He went to her; she was in a loose-box; but as he slipped the bars she plunged, knocked him down, and broke away into the garden. I laughed, but Strickland was not amused. He took his moustache in both fists and pulled at it till it nearly came out. Fleete, instead of going off to chase his property, yawned, saying that he felt sleepy. He went to the house to lie down, which was a foolish way of spending New Year's Day.

Strickland sat with me in the stables and asked if I had noticed anything peculiar in Fleete's manner. I said that he ate his food like a beast but that this might have been the result of living alone in the hills out of the reach of society as refined and elevating as ours, for instance. Strickland was not amused. I do not think that he listened to me, for his next sentence referred to the mark on Fleete's breast, and I said that it might have been caused by blister-flies or that it was possibly a birthmark newly born and now visible for the first time. We both agreed that it was unpleasant to look at, and Strickland found occasion to say that I was a fool. "I can't tell you what I think now," said he, "because you would call me a madman; but you must stay with me for the next few days if you can. I want you to watch Fleete, but don't tell me what you think till I have made up my mind."

"But I am dining out tonight," I said. "So am I," said Strickland, "and so is Fleete. At least if he doesn't change his mind." We walked about the garden smoking but saying nothing—because we were friends, and talking spoils good tobacco—till our pipes were out. Then we went to wake up Fleete. He was wide awake and fidgeting about his room.

"I say, I want some more chops," he said. "Can I get them?" We laughed and said, "Go and change. The ponies will be round in a minute."

"All right," said Fleete. "I'll go when I get the chops—underdone ones, mind." He seemed to be quite in earnest. It was four o'clock, and we had had breakfast at one; still, for a long time he demanded those underdone chops. Then he changed into riding clothes and went out into the veranda. His pony—the mare had not been caught—would not let him come near. All three horses were unmanageable—mad with fear—and finally Fleete said that he would stay at home and get something to eat. Strickland and I rode out wondering. As we passed the temple of Hanuman, the silver man came out and mewed at us.

"He is not one of the regular priests of the temple," said Strickland. "I think I should peculiarly like to lay my hands on him."

There was no spring in our gallop on the race-course that evening. The horses were stale and moved as though they had been ridden out.

"The fright after breakfast has been too much for them," said Strickland. That was the only remark he made through the remainder of the ride. Once or twice I think he swore to himself, but that did not count.

We came back in the dark at seven o'clock and saw that there were no lights in the bungalow. "Careless ruffians my servants are!" said Strickland.

My horse reared at something on the carriage-drive, and Fleete stood up under its nose. "What are you doing, grovelling about the garden?" said Strickland.

But both horses bolted and nearly threw us. We dismounted by the stables and returned to Fleete, who was on his hands and knees under the orange-bushes.

"What the devil's wrong with you?" said Strickland. "Nothing, nothing in the world," said Fleete, speaking very quickly and thickly. "I've been gardening—botanising, you know. The smell of the earth is delightful. I think I'm going for a walk—a long walk all night."

Then I saw that there was something excessively out of order somewhere, and I said to Strickland, "I am not dining out."

"Bless you!" said Strickland. "Here, Fleete, get up. You'll catch fever there. Come in to dinner and let's have the lamps lit. We'll all dine at home."

Fleete stood up unwillingly and said, "No lamps—no lamps. It's much nicer here. Let's dine outside and have some more chops—lots of 'em, and underdone—bloody ones with gristle." Now, a

December evening in northern India is bitterly cold, and Fleete's suggestion was that of a maniac.

"Come in," said Strickland sternly. "Come in at once." Fleete came, and when the lamps were brought, we saw that he was literally plastered with dirt from head to foot. He must have been rolling in the garden. He shrank from the light and went to his room. His eyes were horrible to look at. There was a green light behind them, not in them, if you understand, and the man's lower lip hung down.

Strickland said, "There is going to be trouble—big trouble— tonight. Don't you change your riding things."

We waited and waited for Fleete's reappearance, and ordered dinner in the meantime. We could hear him moving about his own room, but there was no light there. Presently from the room came the long-drawn howl of a wolf.

People write and talk lightly of blood running cold and hair standing up and things of that kind. Both sensations are too horrible to be trifled with. My heart stopped as though a knife had been driven through it, and Strickland turned as white as the table cloth.

The howl was repeated and was answered by another howl far across the fields. That set the gilded roof on the horror. Strickland dashed into Fleete's room. I followed, and we saw Fleete getting out of the window. He made beast noises in the back of his throat. He could not answer us when we shouted at him. He spat.

I don't quite remember what followed, but I think that Strickland must have stunned him with the long bootjack, or else I should never have been able to sit on his chest. Fleete could not speak, he could only snarl, and his snarls were those of a wolf, not of a man. The human spirit must have been giving way all day and have died out with the twilight. We were dealing with a beast that had once been Fleete.

The affair was beyond any human and rational experience. I tried to say "hydrophobia", but the word wouldn't come, because I knew that I was lying.

We bound this beast with leather thongs of the punkah rope, and tied its thumbs and big toes together, and gagged it with a shoe-horn, which makes a very efficient gag if you know how to arrange it. Then we carried it into the dining-room and sent a man to Dumoise, the doctor, telling him to come over at once. After we had dispatched the messenger and were drawing breath, Strickland said, "It's no good. This isn't any doctor's work." I also knew that he spoke the truth. The beast's head was free, and it threw it about from side to side. Anyone entering the room would have believed that we were curing a wolf's pelt. That was the most loathsome accessory of all.

Strickland sat with his chin in the heel of his fist, watching the beast as it wriggled on the ground, but saying nothing. The shirt had been torn open in the scuffle and showed the black rosette mark on the left breast. It stood out like a blister.

In the silence of the watching we heard something without mewing like a she-otter. We both rose to our feet, and I answer for myself, not Strickland, felt sick—actually and physically sick. We told each other, as did the men in Pinafore, that it was the cat.

Dumoise arrived, and I never saw a little man so unprofessionally shocked. He said that it was a heart-rending case of hydrophobia and that nothing could be done. At least any palliative measures would only prolong the agony. The beast was foaming at the mouth. Fleete, as we told Dumoise, had been bitten by dogs once or twice. Any man who keeps half a dozen terriers must expect a nip now and again. Dumoise could offer no help. He could only certify that Fleete was dying of hydrophobia. The beast was then howling, for it had managed to spit out the shoe-horn. Dumoise said that he would be ready to certify to the cause of death and that the end was certain. He was a good little man, and he offered to remain with us, but Strickland refused the kindness. He did not wish to poison Dumoise's New Year. He would only ask him not to give the real cause of Fleete's death to the public.

So Dumoise left, deeply agitated; and as soon as the noise of the cart-wheels had died away, Strickland told me, in a whisper, his suspicions. They were so wildly improbable that he dared not say them out aloud; and I, who entertained all Strickland's beliefs, was so ashamed of owning to them that I pretended to disbelieve.

"Even if the silver man had bewitched Fleete for polluting the image of Hanuman, the punishment could not have fallen so quickly."

As I was whispering this the cry outside the house rose again, and the beast fell into a fresh paroxysm of struggling till we were afraid that the thongs that held it would give way. "Watch!" said Strickland. "If this happens six times I shall take the law into my own hands. I order you to help me."

He went into his room and came out in a few minutes with the barrels of an old shotgun, a piece of fishing-line, some thick cord, and his heavy wooden bedstead. I reported that the convulsions had followed the cry by two seconds in each case, and the beast seemed perceptibly weaker.

Strickland muttered, "But he can't take away the life! He can't take away the life!" I said, though I knew that I was arguing against myself, "It may be a cat. It must be a cat. If the silver man is responsible, why does he dare to come here?"

Strickland arranged the wood on the hearth, put the gun barrels into the glow of the fire, spread the twine on the table, and broke a walking-stick in two. There was one yard of fishing-line, gut lapped with wire, such as is used for mahseer-fishing, and he tied the two ends together in a loop.

Then he said, "How can we catch him? He must be taken alive and unhurt." I said that we must trust in Providence and go out softly with polo-sticks into the shrubbery at the front of the house. The man or animal that made the cry was evidently moving round the house as regularly as a night-watchman. We could wait in the bushes till he came by and knock him over.

Strickland accepted this suggestion, and we slipped out from a bathroom window into the front veranda and then across the carriage-drive into the bushes.

In the moonlight we could see the leper coming round the corner of the house. He was perfectly naked, and from time to time he mewed and stopped to dance with his shadow. It was an unattractive sight, and thinking of poor Fleete, brought to such degradation by so foul a creature, I put away all my doubts and resolved to help Strickland from the heated gun barrels to the loop of twine—from the loins to the head and back again—with all tortures that might be needful.

The leper halted in the front porch for a moment and we jumped out on him with the sticks. He was wonderfully strong, and we were afraid that he might escape or be fatally injured before we caught him. We had an idea that lepers were frail creatures, but this proved to be incorrect. Strickland knocked his legs from under him, and I put my foot on his neck. He mewed hideously, and even through my riding-boots I could feel that his flesh was not the flesh of a clean man. He struck at us with his hand and feet-stumps. We looped the lash of a dog-whip round him, under the armpits, and dragged him backwards into the hall and so into the dining-room, where the beast lay. There we tied him with trunk-straps. He made no attempt to escape, but mewed. When

we confronted him with the beast the scene was beyond description. The beast doubled backwards into a bow, as though he had
been poisoned with strychnine, and moaned in the most pitiable
fashion. Several other things happened also, but they cannot be put
down here. "I think I was right," said Strickland. "Now we will ask
him to cure this case."

But the leper only mewed. Strickland wrapped a towel round his
hand and took the gun barrels out of the fire. I put the half of the
broken walking-stick through the loop of fishing-line and buckled
the leper comfortably to Strickland's bedstead. I understood then
how men and women and little children can endure to see a witch
burnt alive; for the beast was moaning on the floor, and though
the silver man had no face, you could see horrible feelings passing
through the slab that took its place, exactly as waves of heat play
across red-hot iron—gun barrels for instance.

Strickland shaded his eyes with his hands for a moment, and
we got to work. This part is not to be printed.

The dawn was beginning to break when the leper spoke. His
mewings had not been satisfactory up to that point. The beast
had fainted from exhaustion, and the house was very still. We
unstrapped the leper and told him to take away the evil spirit. He
crawled to the beast and laid his hand upon the left breast. That
was all. Then he fell face down and whined, drawing in his breath
as he did so.

We watched the face of the beast and saw the soul of Fleete
coming back into the eyes. Then a sweat broke out on the forehead, and the eyes—they were human eyes—closed. We waited
for an hour, but Fleete still slept. We carried him to his room and
bade the leper go, giving him the bedstead, and the sheet on the
bedstead to cover his nakedness, the gloves and the towels with
which we had touched him, and the whip that had been hooked

round his body. He put the sheet about him and went out into the early morning without speaking or mewing.

Strickland wiped his face and sat down. A night-gong, far away in the city, made seven o'clock.

"Exactly four and twenty hours!" said Strickland. "And I've done enough to ensure my dismissal from the service, besides permanent quarters in a lunatic asylum. Do you believe that we are awake?"

The red-hot gun barrel had fallen on the floor and was singeing the carpet. The smell was entirely real.

That morning at eleven we two together went to wake up Fleete. We looked and saw that the black leopard-rosette on his chest had disappeared. He was very drowsy and tired, but as soon as he saw us he said, "Oh! Confound you fellows. Happy New Year to you. Never mix your liquors. I'm nearly dead."

"Thanks for your kindness, but you're overtime," said Strickland. "Today is the morning of the second. You've slept the clock round with a vengeance."

The door opened, and little Dumoise put his head in. He had come on foot, and fancied that we were laying our Fleete.

"I've brought a nurse," said Dumoise. "I suppose that she can come in for—what is necessary."

"By all means," said Fleete cheerily, sitting up in bed. "Bring on your nurses." Dumoise was dumb. Strickland led him out and explained that there must have been a mistake in the diagnosis.

Dumoise remained dumb and left the house hastily. He considered that his professional reputation had been injured and was inclined to make a personal matter of the recovery. Strickland went out too. When he came back he said that he had been to call on the temple of Hanuman to offer redress for the pollution of the god, and had been solemnly assured that no white man had ever touched the idol and that he was an incarnation of all the virtues labouring under a delusion. "What do you think?" said Strickland.

I said, "There are more things—" But Strickland hates that quotation. He says that I have worn it threadbare.

One other curious thing happened which frightened me as much as anything in all the night's work. When Fleete was dressed he came into the dining-room and sniffed. He had a quaint trick of moving his nose when he sniffed. "Horrid doggy smell here," said he. "You should really keep those terriers of yours in better order. Try sulphur, Strick."

But Strickland did not answer. He caught hold of the back of a chair and without warning went into an amazing fit of hysterics. It is terrible to see a strong man overtaken with hysteria. Then it struck me that we had fought for Fleete's soul with the silver man in that room and had disgraced ourselves as Englishmen forever, and I laughed and gasped and gurgled just as shamefully as Strickland, while Fleete thought that we had both gone mad. We never told him what we had done.

Some years later, when Strickland had married and was a church-going member of society for his wife's sake, we reviewed the incident dispassionately, and Strickland suggested that I should put it before the public.

I cannot myself see that this step is likely to clear up the mystery, because in the first place no one will believe a rather unpleasant story, and in the second, it is well known to every right-minded man that the gods of the heathen are stone and brass, and any attempt to deal with them otherwise is justly condemned.

THE WEREWOLF

Clemence Housman

Published in the magazine *Atalanta* (1890)

Clemence Housman (1861–1955) was an author, illustrator, and suffragette. She worked as a wood-engraver for illustrated newspapers including the *Illustrated London News* and the *Graphic* before the rise of photomechanical engraving methods. Her home was often used by the Suffrage Atelier, a group of creatives seeking female emancipation.

'The Werewolf' was first published in *Atalanta*, a monthly magazine for girls, before appearing in a version illustrated by her brother, Laurence Housman, published by John Lane at the Bodley Head in 1896. Housman wrote this fantastical Christian allegory to entertain her fellow wood-engraving students at the City and Guilds South London Technical Art School. The story begins with the voice of a child at the door, asking to be let in. But the response of the wolfhound inside the house suggests that this voice may not be what it seems. Housman's fight for women's rights takes on new resonances when we read this tale: the creature at the door—a beautiful stranger in white fur—is not the threatening bestial monster that we have come to expect, but a sinister figure of alluring female empowerment.

T HE GREAT FARM HALL WAS ABLAZE WITH THE FIRELIGHT, and noisy with laughter and talk and many-sounding work. None could be idle but the very young and the very old: little Rol, who was hugging a puppy, and old Trella, whose palsied hand fumbled over her knitting. The early evening had closed in, and the farm servants, come from their outdoor work, had assembled in the ample hall, which gave space for a score or more of workers. Several of the men were engaged in carving, and to these were yielded the best place and light; others made or repaired fishing-tackle and harness, and a great seine net occupied three pairs of hands. Of the women most were sorting and mixing eider feathers and chopping straw to add to it. Looms were there, though not in present use, but three wheels whirred emulously, and the finest and swiftest thread of the three ran between the fingers of the house mistress. Near her were some children, busy too, plaiting wicks for candles and lamps. Each group of workers had a lamp in its centre, and those farthest from the fire had live heat from two braziers filled with glowing wood embers, replenished now and again from the generous hearth. But the flicker of the great fire was manifest to the remotest corners, and prevailed beyond the limits of the weaker lights.

Little Rol grew tired of his puppy, dropped it incontinently, and made an onslaught on Tyr, the old wolfhound, who basked dozing, whimpering and twitching in his hunting dreams. Prone went Rol beside Tyr, his young arms round the shaggy neck, his curls against the black jowl. Tyr gave a perfunctory lick, and stretched with a sleepy sigh. Rol growled and rolled and shoved invitingly, but could only gain from the old dog placid toleration and a half-observant blink. "Take that then!" said Rol, indignant at this ignoring of his advances, and sent the puppy sprawling against the dignity that disdained him as playmate. The dog took no notice, and the child wandered off to find amusement elsewhere.

The baskets of white eider feathers caught his eye far off in a distant corner. He slipped under the table, and crept along on all-fours, the ordinary commonplace custom of walking down a room upright not being to his fancy. When close to the women he lay still for a moment watching, with his elbows on the floor and his chin in his palms. One of the women seeing him nodded and smiled, and presently he crept out behind her skirts and passed, hardly noticed, from one to another, till he found opportunity to possess himself of a large handful of feathers. With these he traversed the length of the room, under the table again, and emerged near the spinners. At the feet of the youngest he curled himself round, sheltered by her knees from the observation of the others, and disarmed her of interference by secretly displaying his handful with a confiding smile. A dubious nod satisfied him, and presently he started on the play he had devised. He took a tuft of the white down, and gently shook it free of his fingers close to the whirl of the wheel. The wind of the swift motion took it, spun it round and round in widening circles, till it floated above like a slow white moth. Little Rol's eyes danced, and the row of his small teeth shone in a silent laugh of delight. Another and another of the white tufts was sent whirling round like a winged thing in a spider's web and floating clear at last. Presently the handful failed.

Rol sprawled forward to survey the room, and contemplate another journey under the table. His shoulder, thrusting forward, checked the wheel for an instant; he shifted hastily. The wheel flew on with a jerk, and the thread snapped. "Naughty Rol!" said the girl. The swiftest wheel stopped also, and the house mistress, Rol's aunt, leaned forward, and sighting the low curly head, gave a warning against mischief, and sent him off to old Trella's corner.

Rol obeyed, and after a discreet period of obedience, sidled out again down the length of the room farthest from his aunt's eye. As he slipped in among the men, they looked up to see that their tools might be, as far as possible, out of reach of Rol's hands, and close to their own. Nevertheless, before long he managed to secure a fine chisel and take off its point on the leg of the table. The carver's strong objections to this disconcerted Rol, who for five minutes thereafter effaced himself under the table.

During this seclusion he contemplated the many pairs of legs that surrounded him, and almost shut out the light of the fire. How very odd some of the legs were: some were curved where they should be straight, some were straight where they should be curved, and, as Rol said to himself, "they all seemed screwed on differently". Some were tucked away modestly under the benches, others were thrust far out under the table, encroaching on Rol's own particular domain. He stretched out his own short legs and regarded them critically, and, after comparison, favourably. Why were not all legs made like his, or like *his*?

These legs approved by Rol were a little apart from the rest. He crawled opposite and again made comparison. His face grew quite solemn as he thought of the innumerable days to come before his legs could be as long and strong. He hoped they would be just like those, his models, as straight as to bone, as curved as to muscle.

A few moments later Sweyn of the long legs felt a small hand caressing his foot, and looking down, met the upturned eyes of his little cousin Rol. Lying on his back, still softly patting and stroking the young man's foot, the child was quiet and happy for a good while. He watched the movement of the strong deft hands, and the shifting of the bright tools. Now and then, minute chips of wood, puffed off by Sweyn, fell down upon his face. At last he raised himself, very gently, lest a jog should wake impatience in the carver, and crossing his own legs round Sweyn's ankle, clasping with his arms too, laid his head against the knee. Such act is evidence of a child's most wonderful hero-worship. Quite content when Sweyn paused a minute to joke, and pat his head and pull his curls. Quiet he remained, as long as quiescence is possible to limbs young as his. Sweyn forgot he was near, hardly noticed when his leg was gently released, and never saw the stealthy abstraction of one of his tools.

Ten minutes thereafter was a lamentable wail from low on the floor, rising to the full pitch of Rol's healthy lungs; for his hand was gashed across, and the copious bleeding terrified him. Then was there soothing and comforting, washing and binding, and a modicum of scolding, till the loud outcry sank into occasional sobs, and the child, tear-stained and subdued, was returned to the chimney-corner settle, where Trella nodded.

In the reaction after pain and fright, Rol found that the quiet of that fire-lit corner was to his mind. Tyr, too, disdained him no longer, but, roused by his sobs, showed all the concern and sympathy that a dog can by licking and wistful watching. A little shame weighed also upon his spirits. He wished he had not cried quite so much. He remembered how once Sweyn had come home with his arm torn down from the shoulder, and a dead bear; and how he had never winced nor said a word, though his lips turned white with pain. Poor little Rol gave another sighing sob over his own faint-hearted shortcomings.

The light and motion of the great fire began to tell strange stories to the child, and the wind in the chimney roared a corroborative note now and then. The great black mouth of the chimney, impending high over the hearth, received as into a mysterious gulf murky coils of smoke and brightness of aspiring sparks; and beyond, in the high darkness, were muttering and wailing and strange doings, so that sometimes the smoke rushed back in panic, and curled out and up to the roof, and condensed itself to invisibility among the rafters. And then the wind would rage after its lost prey, and rush round the house, rattling and shrieking at window and door.

In a lull, after one such loud gust, Rol lifted his head in surprise and listened. A lull had also come on the babel of talk, and thus could be heard with strange distinctness a sound outside the door— the sound of a child's voice, a child's hands. "Open, open; let me in!" piped the little voice from low down, lower than the handle, and the latch rattled as though a tiptoe child reached up to it, and soft small knocks were struck. One near the door sprang up and opened it. "No one is here," he said. Tyr lifted his head and gave utterance to a howl, loud, prolonged, most dismal.

Sweyn, not able to believe that his ears had deceived him, got up and went to the door. It was a dark night; the clouds were heavy with snow, that had fallen fitfully when the wind lulled. Untrodden snow lay up to the porch: there was no sight nor sound of any human being. Sweyn strained his eyes far and near, only to see dark sky, pure snow, and a line of black fir trees on a hill brow, bowing down before the wind. "It must have been the wind," he said, and closed the door.

Many faces looked scared. The sound of a child's voice had been so distinct—and the words "Open, open; let me in!" The wind might creak the wood, or rattle the latch, but could not speak with a child's voice, nor knock with the soft plain blows that a plump fist gives. And the strange unusual howl of the wolfhound was an omen to be feared, be the rest what it might. Strange things were said by one and another, till the rebuke of the house mistress quelled them into far-off whispers. For a time after there was uneasiness, constraint, and silence; then the chill fear thawed by degrees, and the babble of talk flowed on again.

Yet half an hour later a very slight noise outside the door sufficed to arrest every hand, every tongue. Every head was raised, every eye fixed in one direction. "It is Christian; he is late," said Sweyn.

No, no: this is a feeble shuffle, not a young man's tread. With the sound of uncertain feet came the hard tap-tap of a stick against the door, and the high-pitched voice of eld, "Open, open; let me in!" Again Tyr flung up his head in a long doleful howl.

Before the echo of the tapping stick and the high voice had fairly died away, Sweyn had sprung across to the door and flung it wide. "No one again," he said in a steady voice, though his eyes looked startled as he stared out. He saw the lonely expanse of snow, the clouds swagging low, and between the two the line of dark fir-trees bowing in the wind. He closed the door without a word of comment, and re-crossed the room.

A score of blanched faces were turned to him as though he must be solver of the enigma. He could not be unconscious of this mute eye-questioning, and it disturbed his resolute air of composure. He hesitated, glanced towards his mother, the house mistress, then back at the frightened folk, and gravely, before them all, made the sign of the cross. There was a flutter of hands as the sign was repeated by all, and the dead silence was stirred as by a huge sigh, for the held breath of many was freed as though the sign gave magic relief.

Even the house mistress was perturbed. She left her wheel and crossed the room to her son, and spoke with him for a moment in a low tone that none could overhear. But a moment later her voice was high-pitched and loud, so that all might benefit by her rebuke of the "heathen chatter" of one of the girls. Perhaps she essayed to silence thus her own misgivings and forebodings.

No other voice dared speak now with its natural fulness. Low tones made intermittent murmurs, and now and then silence drifted over the whole room. The handling of tools was as noiseless as might be, and suspended on the instant if the door rattled in a gust of wind. After a time Sweyn left his work, joined the group nearest the door, and loitered there on the pretence of giving advice and help to the unskilful.

A man's tread was heard outside in the porch. "Christian!" said Sweyn and his mother simultaneously, he confidently, she authoritatively, to set the checked wheels going again. But Tyr flung up his head with an appalling howl.

"Open, open; let me in!"

It was a man's voice, and the door shook and rattled as a man's strength beat against it. Sweyn could feel the planks quivering, as on the instant his hand was upon the door, flinging it open, to face the blank porch, and beyond only snow and sky, and firs aslant in the wind.

He stood for a long minute with the open door in his hand. The bitter wind swept in with its icy chill, but a deadlier chill of fear came swifter, and seemed to freeze the beating of hearts. Sweyn stepped back to snatch up a great bearskin cloak.

"Sweyn, where are you going?"

"No farther than the porch, mother," and he stepped out and closed the door.

He wrapped himself in the heavy fur, and leaning against the most sheltered wall of the porch, steeled his nerves to face the Devil and all his works. No sound of voices came from within; the most distinct sound was the crackle and roar of the fire.

It was bitterly cold. His feet grew numb, but he forbore stamping them into warmth lest the sound should strike panic within; nor would he leave the porch, nor print a footmark on the untrodden white that declared so absolutely how no human voices and hands could have approached the door since snow fell two hours or more ago. "When the wind drops there will be more snow," thought Sweyn.

For the best part of an hour he kept his watch, and saw no living thing—heard no unwonted sound. "I will freeze here no longer," he muttered, and re-entered.

One woman gave a half-suppressed scream as his hand was laid on the latch, and then a gasp of relief as he came in. No one questioned him, only his mother said, in a tone of forced unconcern, "Could you not see Christian coming?" as though she were made anxious only by the absence of her younger son. Hardly had Sweyn stamped near to the fire than clear knocking was heard at the door. Tyr leapt from the hearth, his eyes red as the fire, his fangs showing white in the black jowl, his neck ridged and bristling; and overleaping Rol, ramped at the door, barking furiously.

Outside the door a clear mellow voice was calling. Tyr's bark made the words undistinguishable.

No one offered to stir towards the door before Sweyn.

He stalked down the room resolutely, lifted the latch, and swung back the door.

A white-robed woman glided in.

No wraith! Living—beautiful—young.

Tyr leapt upon her.

Lithely she baulked the sharp fangs with folds of her long fur robe, and snatching from her girdle a small two-edged axe, whirled it up for a blow of defence.

Sweyn caught the dog by the collar, and dragged him off yelling and struggling.

The stranger stood in the doorway motionless, one foot set forward, one arm flung up, till the house mistress hurried down the room; and Sweyn, relinquishing to others the furious Tyr, turned again to close the door, and offer excuse for so fierce a greeting. Then she lowered her arm, slung the axe in its place at her waist, loosened the furs about her face, and shook over her shoulders the long white robe—all as it were with the sway of one movement.

She was a maiden, tall and fair. The fashion of her dress was strange, half masculine, yet not unwomanly. A fine fur tunic, reaching but little below the knee, was all the skirt she wore; below were the cross-bound shoes and leggings that a hunter wears. A white fur cap was set low upon the brows, and from its edge strips of fur fell lappet-wise about her shoulders; two of these at her entrance had been drawn forward and crossed about her throat, but now, loosened and thrust back, left unhidden long plaits of fair hair that lay forward on shoulder and breast, down to the ivory-studded girdle where the axe gleamed.

Sweyn and his mother led the stranger to the hearth without question or sign of curiosity, till she voluntarily told her tale of a long journey to distant kindred, a promised guide unmet, and signals and landmarks mistaken.

"Alone!" exclaimed Sweyn in astonishment. "Have you journeyed thus far, a hundred leagues, alone?"

She answered "Yes" with a little smile.

"Over the hills and the wastes! Why, the folk there are savage and wild as beasts."

She dropped her hand upon her axe with a laugh of some scorn.

"I fear neither man nor beast; some few fear me." And then she told strange tales of fierce attack and defence, and of the bold free huntress life she had led.

Her words came a little slowly and deliberately, as though she spoke in a scarce familiar tongue; now and then she hesitated, and stopped in a phrase, as though for lack of some word.

She became the centre of a group of listeners. The interest she excited dissipated, in some degrees, the dread inspired by the mysterious voices. There was nothing ominous about this young, bright, fair reality, though her aspect was strange.

Little Rol crept near, staring at the stranger with all his might. Unnoticed, he softly stroked and patted a corner of her soft white robe that reached to the floor in ample folds. He laid his cheek against it caressingly, and then edged up close to her knees.

"What is your name?" he asked.

The stranger's smile and ready answer, as she looked down, saved Rol from the rebuke merited by his unmannerly question.

"My real name," she said, "would be uncouth to your ears and tongue. The folk of this country have given me another name, and from this" (she laid her hand on the fur robe) "they call me 'White Fell'."

Little Rol repeated it to himself, stroking and patting as before: "White Fell, White Fell".

The fair face, and soft, beautiful dress pleased Rol. He knelt up, with his eyes on her face and an air of uncertain determination, like a robin's on a doorstep, and plumped his elbows into her lap with a little gasp at his own audacity.

"Rol!" exclaimed his aunt; but, "Oh, let him!" said White Fell, smiling and stroking his head; and Rol stayed.

He advanced farther, and panting at his own adventurousness in the face of his aunt's authority, climbed up on to her knees. Her welcoming arms hindered any protest. He nestled happily, fingering the axe head, the ivory studs in her girdle, the ivory clasp at her throat, the plaits of fair hair; rubbing his head against the softness of her fur-clad shoulder, with a child's full confidence in the kindness of beauty.

White Fell had not uncovered her head, only knotted the pendant fur loosely behind her neck. Rol reached up his hand towards it, whispering her name to himself, "White Fell, White Fell," then slid his arms round her neck, and kissed her—once—twice. She laughed delightedly, and kissed him again.

"The child plagues you?" said Sweyn.

"No, indeed," she answered, with an earnestness so intense as to seem disproportionate to the occasion.

Rol settled himself again on her lap, and began to unwind the bandage bound round his hand. He paused a little when he saw where the blood had soaked through; then went on till his hand was bare and the cut displayed, gaping and long, though only skin deep. He held it up towards White Fell, desirous of her pity and sympathy.

At sight of it, and the blood-stained linen, she drew in her breath suddenly, clasped Rol to her—hard, hard—till he began to struggle. Her face was hidden behind the boy, so that none could see its expression. It had lighted up with a most awful glee.

Afar, beyond the fir grove, beyond the low hill behind, the absent Christian was hastening his return. From daybreak he had been afoot, carrying notice of a bear hunt to all the best hunters of the farms and hamlets that lay within a radius of twelve miles. Nevertheless, having been detained till a late hour, he now broke

into a run, going with a long smooth stride of apparent ease that
fast made the miles diminish.

He entered the midnight blackness of the fir grove with scarcely
slackened pace, though the path was invisible; and passing through
into the open again, sighted the farm lying a furlong off down the
slope. Then he sprang out freely, and almost on the instant gave
one great sideways leap, and stood still. There in the snow was the
track of a great wolf.

His hand went to his knife, his only weapon. He stooped, knelt
down, to bring his eyes to the level of a beast, and peered about; his
teeth set, his heart beat a little harder than the pace of his running
insisted on. A solitary wolf, nearly always savage and of large size,
is a formidable beast that will not hesitate to attack a single man.
This wolf-track was the largest Christian had ever seen, and, so far
as he could judge, recently made. It led from under the fir trees
down the slope. Well for him, he thought, was the delay that had
so vexed him before: well for him that he had not passed through
the dark fir grove when that danger of jaws lurked there. Going
warily, he followed the track.

It led down the slope, across a broad ice-bound stream, along
the level beyond, making towards the farm. A less precise knowledge had doubted, and guessed that here might have come straying
big Tyr or his like; but Christian was sure, knowing better than to
mistake between footmark of dog and wolf.

Straight on—straight on towards the farm.

Surprised and anxious grew Christian, that a prowling wolf
should dare so near. He drew his knife and pressed on, more hastily, more keen-eyed. Oh that Tyr were with him!

Straight on, straight on, even to the very door, where the snow
failed. His heart seemed to give a great leap and then stop. There
the track *ended*.

Nothing lurked in the porch, and there was no sign of return. The firs stood straight against the sky, the clouds lay low; for the wind had fallen and a few snowflakes came drifting down. In a horror of surprise, Christian stood dazed a moment: then he lifted the latch and went in. His glance took in all the old familiar forms and faces, and with them that of the stranger, fur-clad and beautiful. The awful truth flashed upon him: he knew what she was.

Only a few were startled by the rattle of the latch as he entered. The room was filled with bustle and movement, for it was the supper hour, when all tools were laid aside, and trestles and tables shifted. Christian had no knowledge of what he said and did: he moved and spoke mechanically, half thinking that soon he must wake from this horrible dream. Sweyn and his mother supposed him to be cold and dead-tired, and spared all unnecessary questions. And he found himself seated beside the hearth, opposite that dreadful Thing that looked like a beautiful girl; watching her every movement, curdling with horror to see her fondle the child Rol.

Sweyn stood near them both, intent upon White Fell also: but how differently! She seemed unconscious of the gaze of both—neither aware of the chill dread in the eyes of Christian, nor of Sweyn's warm admiration.

These two brothers, who were twins, contrasted greatly, despite their striking likeness. They were alike in regular profile, fair brown hair, and deep blue eyes; but Sweyn's features were perfect as a young god's, while Christian's showed faulty details. Thus, the line of his mouth was set too straight, the eyes shelved too deeply back, and the contour of the face flowed in less generous curves than Sweyn's. Their height was the same, but Christian was too slender for perfect proportion, while Sweyn's well-knit frame, broad shoulders, and muscular arms, made him pre-eminent for manly beauty as well as for strength. As a hunter Sweyn was without rival; as a fisher without rival. All the countryside acknowledged him to be the best wrestler, rider, dancer, singer. Only in speed could he be surpassed, and in that only by his younger brother. All others Sweyn could distance fairly; but Christian could outrun him easily. Ay, he could keep pace with Sweyn's most breathless burst, and laugh and talk the while. Christian took little pride in his fleetness of foot, counting a man's legs to be the least worthy of his members. He had no envy of his brother's athletic superiority, though to several feats he had made a moderate second. He loved as only a twin can love—proud of all that Sweyn did, content with all that Sweyn was; humbly content also that his own great love should not be so exceedingly returned, since he knew himself to be so far less love-worthy.

Christian dared not, in the midst of women and children, launch the horror that he knew into words. He waited to consult his brother; but Sweyn did not, or would not, notice the signal he made, and kept his face always turned towards White Fell. Christian drew away from the hearth, unable to remain passive with that dread upon him.

"Where is Tyr?" he said suddenly. Then, catching sight of the dog in a distant corner, "Why is he chained there?"

"He flew at the stranger," one answered.

Christian's eyes glowed. "Yes?" he said, interrogatively.

"He was within an ace of having his brain knocked out."

"Tyr?"

"Yes; she was nimbly up with that little axe she has at her waist. It was well for old Tyr that his master throttled him off."

Christian went without a word to the corner where Tyr was chained. The dog rose up to meet him, as piteous and indignant as a dumb beast can be. He stroked the black head. "Good Tyr! brave dog!"

They knew, they only; and the man and the dumb dog had comfort of each other.

Christian's eyes turned again towards White Fell: Tyr's also, and he strained against the length of the chain. Christian's hand lay on the dog's neck, and he felt it ridge and bristle with the quivering of impotent fury. Then he began to quiver in like manner with a fury born of reason, not instinct; as impotent morally as was Tyr physically. Oh! the woman's form that he dare not touch! Anything but that, and he with Tyr would be free to kill or be killed.

Then he returned to ask fresh questions.

"How long has the stranger been here?"

"She came about half an hour before you."

"Who opened the door to her?"

"Sweyn: no one else dared."

The tone of the answer was mysterious.

"Why?" queried Christian. "Has anything strange happened? Tell me."

For answer he was told in a low undertone of the summons at the door thrice repeated without human agency; and of Tyr's ominous howls; and of Sweyn's fruitless watch outside.

Christian turned towards his brother in a torment of impatience for a word apart. The board was spread, and Sweyn was leading White Fell to the guest's place. This was more awful: she would break bread with them under the roof tree!

He started forward, and touching Sweyn's arm, whispered an urgent entreaty. Sweyn stared, and shook his head in angry impatience.

Thereupon Christian would take no morsel of food.

His opportunity came at last. White Fell questioned of the landmarks of the country, and of one Cairn Hill, which was an appointed meeting-place at which she was due that night. The house mistress and Sweyn both exclaimed.

"It is three long miles away," said Sweyn; "with no place for shelter but a wretched hut. Stay with us this night, and I will show you the way tomorrow."

White Fell seemed to hesitate. "Three miles," she said; "then I should be able to see or hear a signal."

"I will look out," said Sweyn; "then, if there be no signal, you must not leave us."

He went to the door. Christian rose silently, and followed him out.

"Sweyn, do you know what she is?"

Sweyn, surprised at the vehement grasp, and low hoarse voice, made answer: "She? Who? White Fell?"

"Yes."

"She is the most beautiful girl I have ever seen."

"She is a werewolf."

Sweyn burst out laughing. "Are you mad?" he asked.

"No; here, see for yourself."

Christian drew him out of the porch, pointing to the snow where the footmarks had been. Had been, for now they were not. Snow was falling fast, and every dint was blotted out.

"Well?" asked Sweyn.

"Had you come when I signed to you, you would have seen for yourself."

"Seen what?"

"The footprints of a wolf leading up to the door; none leading away."

It was impossible not to be startled by the tone alone, though it was hardly above a whisper. Sweyn eyed his brother anxiously, but in the darkness could make nothing of his face. Then he laid his hands kindly and reassuringly on Christian's shoulders and felt how he was quivering with excitement and horror.

"One sees strange things," he said, "when the cold has got into the brain behind the eyes; you came in cold and worn out."

"No," interrupted Christian. "I saw the track first on the brow of the slope, and followed it down right here to the door. This is no delusion."

Sweyn in his heart felt positive that it was. Christian was given to day dreams and strange fancies, though never had he been possessed with so mad a notion before.

"Don't you believe me?" said Christian desperately. "You must. I swear it is sane truth. Are you blind? Why, even Tyr knows."

"You will be clearer-headed tomorrow after a night's rest. Then come too, if you will, with White Fell, to the Hill Cairn; and if you have doubts still, watch and follow, and see what footprints she leaves."

Galled by Sweyn's evident contempt, Christian turned abruptly to the door. Sweyn caught him back.

"What now, Christian? What are you going to do?"

"You do not believe me; my mother shall."

Sweyn's grasp tightened. "You shall not tell her," he said authoritatively. Customarily Christian was so docile to his brother's mastery that it was now a surprising thing when he wrenched himself free vigorously, and said as determinedly as Sweyn, "She shall know!" but Sweyn was nearer the door and would not let him pass.

"There has been scare enough for one night already. If this notion of yours will keep, broach it tomorrow." Christian would not yield.

"Women are so easily scared," pursued Sweyn, "and are ready to believe any folly without shadow of proof. Be a man, Christian, and fight this notion of a werewolf by yourself."

"If you would believe me—" began Christian.

"I believe you to be a fool," said Sweyn, losing patience. "Another, who was not your brother, might believe you to be a knave, and guess that you had transformed White Fell into a werewolf because she smiled more readily on me than on you."

The jest was not without foundation, for the grace of White Fell's bright looks had been bestowed on him, on Christian never a whit. Sweyn's coxcombery was always frank, and most forgiveable, and not without fair colour.

"If you want an ally," continued Sweyn, "confide in old Trella. Out of her stores of wisdom, if her memory holds good, she can instruct you in the orthodox manner of tackling a werewolf. If I remember aright, you should watch the suspected person till midnight, when the beast's form must be resumed, and retained ever after if a human eye sees the change; or, better still, sprinkle hands and feet with holy water, which is certain death. Oh! never fear, but old Trella will be equal to the occasion."

Sweyn's contempt was no longer good-humoured; some touch of irritation or resentment rose at this monstrous doubt of White Fell. But Christian was too deeply distressed to take offence.

"You speak of them as old wives' tales; but if you had seen the proof I have seen, you would be ready at least to wish them true, if not also to put them to the test."

"Well," said Sweyn, with a laugh that had a little sneer in it, "put them to the test! I will not object to that, if you will only keep your notions to yourself. Now, Christian, give me your word for silence, and we will freeze here no longer."

Christian remained silent.

Sweyn put his hands on his shoulders again and vainly tried to see his face in the darkness.

"We have never quarrelled yet, Christian?"

"*I* have never quarrelled," returned the other, aware for the first time that his dictatorial brother had sometimes offered occasion for quarrel, had he been ready to take it.

"Well," said Sweyn emphatically, "if you speak against White Fell to any other, as tonight you have spoken to me—*we shall.*"

He delivered the words like an ultimatum, turned sharp round, and re-entered the house. Christian, more fearful and wretched than before, followed.

"Snow is falling fast: not a single light is to be seen."

White Fell's eyes passed over Christian without apparent notice, and turned bright and shining upon Sweyn.

"Nor any signal to be heard?" she queried. "Did you not hear the sound of a sea-horn?"

"I saw nothing, and heard nothing; and signal or no signal, the heavy snow would keep you here perforce."

She smiled her thanks beautifully. And Christian's heart sank like lead with a deadly foreboding, as he noted what a light was kindled in Sweyn's eyes by her smile.

That night, when all others slept, Christian, the weariest of all, watched outside the guest chamber till midnight was past. No sound, not the faintest, could be heard. Could the old tale be true of the midnight change? What was on the other side of the door, a woman or a beast? He would have given his right hand to know. Instinctively he laid his hand on the latch, and drew it softly, though believing that bolts fastened the inner side. The door yielded to his hand; he stood on the threshold; a keen gust of air cut at him; the window stood open; the room was empty.

So Christian could sleep with a somewhat lightened heart.

In the morning there was surprise and conjecture when White Fell's absence was discovered. Christian held his peace. Not even to his brother did he say how he knew that she had fled before midnight; and Sweyn, though evidently greatly chagrined, seemed to disdain reference to the subject of Christian's fears.

The elder brother alone joined the bear hunt; Christian found pretext to stay behind. Sweyn, being out of humour, manifested his contempt by uttering not a single expostulation.

All that day, and for many a day after, Christian would never go out of sight of his home. Sweyn alone noticed how he man-oeuvred for this, and was clearly annoyed by it. White Fell's name was never mentioned between them, though not seldom was it heard in general talk. Hardly a day passed but little Rol asked when White Fell would come again: pretty White Fell, who kissed like a snowflake. And if Sweyn answered, Christian would be quite sure that the light in his eyes, kindled by White Fell's smile, had not yet died out.

Little Rol! Naughty, merry, fair-haired little Rol. A day came when his feet raced over the threshold never to return; when his chatter and laugh were heard no more; when tears of anguish were wept by eyes that never would see his bright head again: never again, living or dead.

He was seen at dusk for the last time, escaping from the house with his puppy, in freakish rebellion against old Trella. Later, when his absence had begun to cause anxiety, his puppy crept back to the farm, cowed, whimpering, and yelping, a pitiful, dumb lump of terror, without intelligence or courage to guide the frightened search.

Rol was never found, nor any trace of him. Where he had perished was never known; how he had perished was known only by an awful guess—a wild beast had devoured him.

Christian heard the conjecture: "a wolf"; and a horrible cer-tainty flashed upon him that he knew what wolf it was. He tried to declare what he knew, but Sweyn saw him start at the words with white face and struggling lips; and, guessing his purpose, pulled him back, and kept him silent, hardly, by his imperious grip and wrathful eyes, and one low whisper.

That Christian should retain his most irrational suspicion against beautiful White Fell was, to Sweyn, evidence of a weak obstinacy of mind that would but thrive upon expostulation and argument. But this evident intention to direct the passions of grief and anguish to a hatred and fear of the fair stranger, such as his own, was intolerable, and Sweyn set his will against it. Again Christian yielded to his brother's stronger words and will, and against his own judgement consented to silence.

Repentance came before the new moon, the first of the year, was old. White Fell came again, smiling as she entered, as though assured of a glad and kindly welcome; and, in truth, there was only one who saw again her fair face and strange white garb without pleasure. Sweyn's face glowed with delight, while Christian's grew pale and rigid as death. He had given his word to keep silence; but he had not thought that she would dare to come again. Silence was impossible, face to face with that Thing, impossible. Irrepressibly he cried out:

"Where is Rol?"

Not a quiver disturbed White Fell's face. She heard, yet remained bright and tranquil. Sweyn's eyes flashed round at his brother dangerously. Among the women some tears fell at the poor child's name; but none caught alarm from its sudden utterance, for the thought of Rol rose naturally. Where was little Rol, who had nestled in the stranger's arms, kissing her; and watched for her since; and prattled of her daily?

Christian went out silently. One only thing there was that he could do, and he must not delay. His horror overmastered any curiosity to hear White Fell's smooth excuses and smiling apologies for her strange and uncourteous departure; or her easy tale of the circumstances of her return; or to watch her bearing as she heard the sad tale of little Rol.

The swiftest runner in the countryside had started on his hardest race: little less than three leagues and back, which he reckoned to accomplish in two hours, though the night was moonless and the way rugged. He rushed against the still cold air till it felt like a wind upon his face. The dim homestead sank below the ridges at his back, and fresh ridges of snowlands rose out of the obscure horizon level to drive past him as the stirless air drove, and sink away behind into obscure level again. He took no conscious heed of landmarks, not even when all sign of a path was gone under depths of snow. His will was set to reach his goal with unexampled speed; and thither by instinct his physical forces bore him, without one definite thought to guide.

And the idle brain lay passive, inert, receiving into its vacancy restless siftings of past sights and sounds; Rol, weeping, laughing, playing, coiled in the arms of that dreadful Thing: Tyr—O Tyr!—white fangs in the black jowl: the women who wept on the foolish puppy, precious for the child's last touch: footprints from pine wood to door: the smiling face among furs, of such womanly beauty—smiling—smiling: and Sweyn's face.

"Sweyn, Sweyn, O Sweyn, my brother!"

Sweyn's angry laugh possessed his ear within the sound of the wind of his speed; Sweyn's scorn assailed more quick and keen than the biting cold at his throat. And yet he was unimpressed by any thought of how Sweyn's anger and scorn would rise, if this errand were known.

Sweyn was a sceptic. His utter disbelief in Christian's testimony regarding the footprints was based upon positive scepticism. His reason refused to bend in accepting the possibility of the supernatural materialised. That a living beast could ever be other than palpably bestial—pawed, toothed, shagged, and eared as such, was to him incredible; far more that a human presence could be transformed from its god-like aspect, upright, freehanded, with brows, and speech, and laughter. The wild and fearful legends that he had known from childhood and then believed, he regarded now as built upon facts distorted, overlaid by imagination, and quickened by superstition. Even the strange summons at the threshold, that he himself had vainly answered, was, after the first shock of surprise, rationally explained by him as malicious foolery on the part of some clever trickster, who witheld the key to the enigma.

To the younger brother all life was a spiritual mystery, veiled from his clear knowledge by the density of flesh. Since he knew his own body to be linked to the complex and antagonistic forces that constitute one soul, it seemed to him not impossibly strange that one spiritual force should possess divers forms for widely various manifestation. Nor, to him, was it great effort to believe that as pure water washes away all natural foulness, so water, holy by consecration, must needs cleanse God's world from that supernatural evil Thing. Therefore, faster than ever man's foot had covered those leagues, he sped under the dark, still night, over the waste, trackless snow-ridges to the faraway church, where salvation lay in the holy-water stoup at the door. His faith was as firm as any that wrought miracles in days past, simple as a child's wish, strong as a man's will.

He was hardly missed during these hours, every second of which was by him fulfilled to its utmost extent by extremest effort that sinews and nerves could attain. Within the homestead the while, the easy moments went bright with words and looks of unwonted animation, for the kindly, hospitable instincts of the

inmates were roused into cordial expression of welcome and interest by the grace and beauty of the returned stranger.

But Sweyn was eager and earnest, with more than a host's
courteous warmth. The impression that at her first coming had
charmed him, that had lived since through memory, deepened
now in her actual presence. Sweyn, the matchless among men,
acknowledged in this fair White Fell a spirit high and bold as his
own, and a frame so firm and capable that only bulk was lacking
for equal strength. Yet the white skin was moulded most smoothly,
without such muscular swelling as made his might evident. Such
love as his frank self-love could concede was called forth by an
ardent admiration for this supreme stranger. More admiration than
love was in his passion, and therefore he was free from a lover's
hesitancy and delicate reserve and doubts. Frankly and boldly he
courted her favour by looks and tones, and an address that came
of natural ease, needless of skill by practice.

Nor was she a woman to be wooed otherwise. Tender whispers and sighs would never gain her ear; but her eyes would
brighten and shine if she heard of a brave feat, and her prompt
hand in sympathy fall swiftly on the axe-haft and clasp it hard.
That movement ever fired Sweyn's admiration anew; he watched
for it, strove to elicit it, and glowed when it came. Wonderful
and beautiful was that wrist, slender and steel-strong; also the
smooth shapely hand, that curved so fast and firm, ready to deal
instant death.

Desiring to feel the pressure of these hands, this bold lover
schemed with palpable directness, proposing that she should hear
how their hunting songs were sung, with a chorus that signalled
hands to be clasped. So his splendid voice gave the verses, and, as
the chorus was taken up, he claimed her hands, and, even through
the easy grip, felt, as he desired, the strength that was latent, and

the vigour that quickened the very fingertips, as the song fired her, and her voice was caught out of her by the rhythmic swell, and rang clear on the top of the closing surge.

Afterwards she sang alone. For contrast, or in the pride of sway-ing moods by her voice, she chose a mournful song that drifted along in a minor chant, sad as a wind that dirges:

> Oh, let me go!
> Around spin wreaths of snow;
> The dark earth sleeps below.

> Far up the plain
> Moans on a voice of pain:
> "Where shall my babe be lain?"

> In my white breast
> Lay the sweet life to rest!
> Lay, where it can lie best!

> "Hush! Hush its cries!
> Dense night is on the skies:
> Two stars are in thine eyes."

> Come, babe, away!
> But lie thou till dawn be grey,
> Who must be dead by day.

> This cannot last;
> But, ere the sickening blast,
> All sorrow shall be past;

And kings shall be
Low bending at thy knee,
Worshipping life from thee.

For men long sore
To hope of what's before—
To leave the things of yore.

Mine, and not thine,
How deep their jewels shine!
Peace laps thy head, not mine.

Old Trella came tottering from her corner, shaken to additional palsy by an aroused memory. She strained her dim eyes towards the singer, and then bent her head, that the one ear yet sensible to sound might avail of every note. At the close, groping forward, she murmured with the high-pitched quaver of old age:

"So she sang, my Thora; my last and brightest. What is she like, she whose voice is like my dead Thora's? Are her eyes blue?"

"Blue as the sky."

"So were my Thora's! Is her hair fair, and in plaits to the waist?"

"Even so," answered White Fell herself, and met the advancing hands with her own, and guided them to corroborate her words by touch.

"Like my dead Thora's," repeated the old woman; and then her trembling hands rested on the fur-clad shoulders, and she bent forward and kissed the smooth fair face that White Fell upturned, nothing loth, to receive and return the caress.

So Christian saw them as he entered.

He stood a moment. After the starless darkness and the icy night air, and the fierce silent two hours' race, his senses reeled on sudden entrance into warmth, and light, and the cheery hum of voices. A sudden unforeseen anguish assailed him, as now first he entertained the possibility of being overmatched by her wiles and her daring, if at the approach of pure death she should start up at bay transformed to a terrible beast, and achieve a savage glut at the last. He looked with horror and pity on the harmless, helpless folk, so unwitting of outrage to their comfort and security. The dreadful Thing in their midst, that was veiled from their knowledge by womanly beauty, was a centre of pleasant interest. There, before him, signally impressive, was poor old Trella, weakest and feeblest of all, in fond nearness. And a moment might bring about the revelation of a monstrous horror—a ghastly, deadly danger, set loose and at bay, in a circle of girls and women and careless defenceless men; so hideous and terrible a thing as might crack the brain, or curdle the heart stone dead.

And he alone of the throng prepared!

For one breathing space he faltered, no longer than that, while over him swept the agony of compunction that yet could not make him surrender his purpose.

He alone? Nay, but Tyr also; and he crossed to the dumb sole sharer of his knowledge.

So timeless is thought that a few seconds only lay between his lifting of the latch and his loosening of Tyr's collar; but in those few seconds succeeding his first glance, as lightning-swift had been the impulses of others, their motion as quick and sure. Sweyn's vigilant eye had darted upon him, and instantly his every fibre was alert with hostile instinct; and, half divining, half incredulous, of Christian's object in stooping to Tyr, he came hastily, wary, wrathful, resolute to oppose the malice of his wild-eyed brother.

But beyond Sweyn rose White Fell, blanching white as her furs, and with eyes grown fierce and wild. She leapt down the room to the door, whirling her long robe closely to her. "Hark!" she panted. "The signal horn! Hark, I must go!" as she snatched at the latch to be out and away.

For one precious moment Christian had hesitated on the half-loosened collar; for, except the womanly form were exchanged for the bestial, Tyr's jaws would gnash to rags his honour of manhood. Then he heard her voice, and turned—too late.

As she tugged at the door, he sprang across grasping his flask, but Sweyn dashed between, and caught him back irresistibly, so that a most frantic effort only availed to wrench one arm free. With that, on the impulse of sheer despair, he cast at her with all his force. The door swung behind her, and the flask flew into fragments against it. Then, as Sweyn's grasp slackened, and he met the questioning astonishment of surrounding faces, with a hoarse inarticulate cry: "God help us all!" he said. "She is a werewolf."

Sweyn turned upon him, "Liar, coward!" and his hands gripped his brother's throat with deadly force, as though the spoken word could be killed so; and as Christian struggled, lifted him clear off his feet and flung him crashing backward. So furious was he, that, as his brother lay motionless, he stirred him roughly with his foot, till their mother came between, crying shame; and yet then he stood by, his teeth set, his brows knit, his hands clenched, ready to enforce silence again violently, as Christian rose staggering and bewildered.

But utter silence and submission were more than he expected, and turned his anger into contempt for one so easily cowed and held in subjection by mere force. "He is mad!" he said, turning on his heel as he spoke, so that he lost his mother's look of pained reproach at this sudden free utterance of what was a lurking dread within her.

Christian was too spent for the effort of speech. His hard-drawn breath laboured in great sobs; his limbs were powerless and untrusting in utter relax after hard service. Failure in his endeavour induced a stupor of misery and despair. In addition was the wretched humiliation of open violence and strife with his brother, and the distress of hearing misjudging contempt expressed without reserve; for he was aware that Sweyn had turned to allay the scared excitement half by imperious mastery, half by explanation and argument, that showed painful disregard of brotherly consideration. All this unkindness of his twin he charged upon the fell Thing who had wrought this their first dissension, and, ah! most terrible thought, interposed between them so effectually, that Sweyn was wilfully blind and deaf on her account, resentful of interference, arbitrary beyond reason.

Dread and perplexity unfathomable darkened upon him; unshared, the burden was overwhelming: a foreboding of unspeakable calamity, based upon his ghastly discovery, bore down upon him, crushing out hope of power to withstand impending fate.

Sweyn the while was observant of his brother, despite the continual check of finding, turn and glance when he would, Christian's eyes always upon him, with a strange look of helpless distress, discomposing enough to the angry aggressor. "Like a beaten dog!" he said to himself, rallying contempt to withstand compunction. Observation set him wondering on Christian's exhausted condition. The heavy labouring breath and the slack inert fall of the limbs told surely of unusual and prolonged exertion. And then why had close upon two hours' absence been followed by open hostility against White Fell?

Suddenly, the fragments of the flask giving a clue, he guessed all, and faced about to stare at his brother in amaze. He forgot that the motive of the scheme was against White Fell, demanding derision and resentment from him; that was swept out of remembrance by astonishment and admiration for the feat of speed and endurance. In eagerness to question he inclined to attempt a generous part and frankly offer to heal the breach; but Christian's depression and sad following gaze provoked him to self-justification by recalling the offence of that outrageous utterance against White Fell; and the impulse passed. Then other considerations counselled silence; and afterwards a humour possessed him to wait and see how Christian would find opportunity to proclaim his performance and establish the fact, without exciting ridicule on account of the absurdity of the errand.

This expectation remained unfulfilled. Christian never attempted the proud avowal that would have placed his feat on record to be told to the next generation.

That night Sweyn and his mother talked long and late together, shaping into certainty the suspicion that Christian's mind had lost its balance, and discussing the evident cause. For Sweyn, declaring his own love for White Fell, suggested that his unfortunate brother, with a like passion, they being twins in loves as in birth, had through jealousy and despair turned from love to hate, until reason failed at the strain, and a craze developed, which the malice and treachery of madness made a serious and dangerous force.

So Sweyn theorised, convincing himself as he spoke; convincing afterwards others who advanced doubts against White Fell; fettering his judgement by his advocacy, and by his staunch defence of her hurried flight silencing his own inner consciousness of the unaccountability of her action.

But a little time and Sweyn lost his vantage in the shock of a fresh horror at the homestead. Trella was no more, and her end a mystery. The poor old woman crawled out in a bright gleam to visit a bed-ridden gossip living beyond the fir grove. Under the trees she was last seen, halting for her companion, sent back for a forgotten present. Quick alarm sprang, calling every man to the search. Her stick was found among the brushwood only a few paces from the path, but no track or stain, for a gusty wind was sifting the snow from the branches, and hid all sign of how she came by her death.

So panic-stricken were the farm folk that none dared go singly on the search. Known danger could be braced, but not this stealthy Death that walked by day invisible, that cut off alike the child in his play and the aged woman so near to her quiet grave.

"Rol she kissed; Trella she kissed!" So rang Christian's frantic cry again and again, till Sweyn dragged him away and strove to keep him apart, albeit in his agony of grief and remorse he accused himself wildly as answerable for the tragedy, and gave clear proof that the charge of madness was well founded, if strange looks and desperate, incoherent words were evidence enough.

But thenceforward all Sweyn's reasoning and mastery could not uphold White Fell above suspicion. He was not called upon to defend her from accusation when Christian had been brought to silence again; but he well knew the significance of this fact, that her name, formerly uttered freely and often, he never heard now: it was huddled away into whispers that he could not catch.

The passing of time did not sweep away the superstitious fears that Sweyn despised. He was angry and anxious; eager that White Fell should return, and, merely by her bright gracious presence, reinstate herself in favour: but doubtful if all his authority and example could keep from her notice an altered aspect of welcome; and he foresaw clearly that Christian would prove unmanageable, and might be capable of some dangerous outbreak.

For a time the twins' variance was marked, on Sweyn's part by an air of rigid indifference, on Christian's by heavy downcast silence, and a nervous apprehensive observation of his brother. Superadded to his remorse and foreboding, Sweyn's displeasure weighed upon him intolerably, and the remembrance of their violent rupture was a ceaseless misery. The elder brother, self-sufficient and insensitive, could little know how deeply his unkindness stabbed. A depth and force of affection such as Christian's was unknown to him. The loyal subservience that he could not appreciate had encouraged him to domineer; this strenuous opposition to his reason and will was accounted as furious malice, if not sheer insanity.

Christian's surveillance galled him incessantly, and embarrassment and danger he foresaw as the outcome. Therefore, that suspicion might be lulled, he judged it wise to make overtures for peace. Most easily done. A little kindliness, a few evidences of consideration, a slight return of the old brotherly imperiousness, and Christian replied by a gratefulness and relief that might have touched him had he understood all, but instead, increased his secret contempt.

So successful was this finesse, that when, late on a day, a message summoning Christian to a distance was transmitted by Sweyn, no doubt of its genuineness occurred. When, his errand proved useless, he set out to return, mistake or misapprehension was all that he surmised. Not till he sighted the homestead, lying low between the night-grey snow-ridges, did vivid recollection of the time when he had tracked that horror to the door rouse an intense dread, and with it a hardly defined suspicion.

His grasp tightened on the bear-spear that he carried as a staff; every sense was alert, every muscle strung; excitement urged him on, caution checked him, and the two governed his long stride, swiftly, noiselessly, to the climax he felt was at hand.

As he drew near to the outer gates, a light shadow stirred and went, as though the grey of the snow had taken detached motion. A darker shadow stayed and faced Christian, striking his life-blood chill with utmost despair.

Sweyn stood before him, and surely, the shadow that went was White Fell.

They had been together—close. Had she not been in his arms, near enough for lips to meet?

There was no moon, but the stars gave light enough to show that Sweyn's face was flushed and elate. The flush remained, though the expression changed quickly at sight of his brother. How, if Christian had seen all, should one of his frenzied outbursts be met and managed: by resolution? by indifference? He halted between the two, and as a result, he swaggered.

"White Fell?" questioned Christian, hoarse and breathless.

"Yes?"

Sweyn's answer was a query, with an intonation that implied he was clearing the ground for action.

From Christian came: "Have you kissed her?" like a bolt direct, staggering Sweyn by its sheer prompt temerity.

He flushed yet darker, and yet half-smiled over this earnest of success he had won. Had there been really between himself and Christian the rivalry that he imagined, his face had enough of the insolence of triumph to exasperate jealous rage.

"You dare ask this!"

"Sweyn, O Sweyn, I must know! You have!"

The ring of despair and anguish in his tone angered Sweyn, misconstruing it. Jealousy urging to such presumption was intolerable.

"Mad fool!" he said, constraining himself no longer. "Win for yourself a woman to kiss. Leave mine without question. Such an one as I should desire to kiss is such an one as shall never allow a kiss to you."

Then Christian fully understood his supposition.

"I—I!" he cried. "White Fell—that deadly Thing! Sweyn, are you blind, mad? I would save you from her: a werewolf!"

Sweyn maddened again at the accusation—a dastardly way of revenge, as he conceived; and instantly, for the second time, the brothers were at strife violently.

But Christian was now too desperate to be scrupulous; for a dim glimpse had shot a possibility into his mind, and to be free to follow it the striking of his brother was a necessity. Thank God! he was armed, and so Sweyn's equal.

Facing his assailant with the bear-spear, he struck up his arms, and with the butt end hit hard so that he fell. The matchless runner leapt away on the instant, to follow a forlorn hope.

Sweyn, on regaining his feet, was as amazed as angry at this unaccountable flight. He knew in his heart that his brother was no coward, and that it was unlike him to shrink from an encounter because defeat was certain, and cruel humiliation from a vindictive victor probable. Of the uselessness of pursuit he was well aware: he must abide his chagrin, content to know that his time for advantage would come. Since White Fell had parted to the right, Christian to the left, the event of a sequent encounter did not occur to him.

And now Christian, acting on the dim glimpse he had had, just as Sweyn turned upon him, of something that moved against the sky along the ridge behind the homestead, was staking his only hope on a chance, and his own superlative speed. If what he saw was really White Fell, he guessed she was bending her steps towards the open wastes; and there was just a possibility that, by a straight dash, and a desperate perilous leap over a sheer bluff, he might yet meet her or head her off. And then? He had no further thought.

It was past, the quick, fierce race, and the chance of death at the leap; and he halted in a hollow to fetch his breath and to look: did she come? Had she gone?

She came.

She came with a smooth, gliding, noiseless speed, that was neither walking nor running; her arms were folded in her furs that were drawn tight about her body; the white lappets from her head were wrapped and knotted closely beneath her face; her eyes were set on a far distance. So she went till the even sway of her going was startled to a pause by Christian.

"Fell!"

She drew a quick, sharp breath at the sound of her name thus mutilated, and faced Sweyn's brother. Her eyes glittered; her upper lip was lifted, and shewed the teeth. The half of her name, impressed with an ominous sense as uttered by him, warned her of the aspect of a deadly foe. Yet she cast loose her robes till they trailed ample, and spoke as a mild woman.

"What would you?"

Then Christian answered with his solemn dreadful accusation:

"You kissed Rol—and Rol is dead! You kissed Trella: she is dead! You have kissed Sweyn, my brother; but he shall not die!"

He added: "You may live till midnight."

The edge of the teeth and the glitter of the eyes stayed a moment, and her right hand also slid down to the axe haft. Then, without a word, she swerved from him, and sprang out and away swiftly over the snow.

And Christian sprang out and away, and followed her swiftly over the snow, keeping behind, but half a stride's length from her side.

So they went running together, silent, towards the vast wastes of snow, where no living thing but they two moved under the stars of night.

Never before had Christian so rejoiced in his powers. The gift of speed, and the training of use and endurance were priceless to him now. Though midnight was hours away, he was confident that, go where that Fell Thing would, hasten as she would, she could not outstrip him nor escape from him. Then, when came the time for transformation, when the woman's form made no longer a shield against a man's hand, he could slay or be slain to save Sweyn. He had struck his dear brother in dire extremity, but he could not, though reason urged, strike a woman.

For one mile, for two miles they ran: White Fell ever foremost, Christian ever at equal distance from her side, so near that, now and again, her out-flying furs touched him. She spoke no word; nor he. She never turned her head to look at him, nor swerved to evade him; but, with set face looking forward, sped straight on, over rough, over smooth, aware of his nearness by the regular beat of his feet, and the sound of his breath behind.

In a while she quickened her pace. From the first, Christian had judged of her speed as admirable, yet with exulting security in his own excelling and enduring whatever her efforts. But, when the pace increased, he found himself put to the test as never had he been before in any race. Her feet, indeed, flew faster than his; it was only by his length of stride that he kept his place at her side. But his heart was high and resolute, and he did not fear failure yet.

So the desperate race flew on. Their feet struck up the powdery snow, their breath smoked into the sharp clear air, and they were gone before the air was cleared of snow and vapour. Now and then Christian glanced up to judge, by the rising of the stars, of the coming of midnight. So long—so long!

White Fell held on without slack. She, it was evident, with confidence in her speed proving matchless, as resolute to outrun her pursuer as he to endure till midnight and fulfil his purpose. And Christian held on, still self-assured. He could not fail; he would not fail. To avenge Rol and Trella was motive enough for him to do what man could do; but for Sweyn more. She had kissed Sweyn, but he should not die too: with Sweyn to save he could not fail.

Never before was such a race as this; no, not when in old Greece man and maid raced together with two fates at stake; for the hard running was sustained unabated, while star after star rose and went wheeling up towards midnight, for one hour, for two hours.

Then Christian saw and heard what shot him through with fear. Where a fringe of trees hung round a slope he saw something dark moving, and heard a yelp, followed by a full horrid cry, and the dark spread out upon the snow, a pack of wolves in pursuit.

Of the beasts alone he had little cause for fear: at the pace he held he could distance them, four-footed though they were. But of White Fell's wiles he had infinite apprehension, for how might she not avail herself of the savage jaws of these wolves, akin as they were to half her nature. She vouchsafed to them nor look nor sign; but Christian, on an impulse to assure himself that she should not escape him, caught and held the back-flung edge of her furs, running still.

She turned like a flash with a beastly snarl, teeth and eyes gleaming again. Her axe shone, on the upstroke, on the downstroke, as she hacked at his hand. She had lopped it off at the wrist, but that he parried with the bear-spear. Even then, she shore through the shaft and shattered the bones of the hand at the same blow, so that he loosed perforce.

Then again they raced on as before, Christian not losing a pace, though his left hand swung useless, bleeding and broken.

The snarl, indubitable, though modified from a woman's organs, the vicious fury revealed in teeth and eyes, the sharp arrogant pain of her maiming blow, caught away Christian's heed of the beasts behind, by striking into him close vivid realisation of the infinitely greater danger that ran before him in that deadly Thing.

When he bethought him to look behind, lo! the pack had but reached their tracks, and instantly slunk aside, cowed; the yell of pursuit changing to yelps and whines, so abhorrent was that fell creature to beast as to man.

She had drawn her furs more closely to her, disposing them so that, instead of flying loose to her heels, no drapery hung lower than her knees, and this without a check to her wonderful speed, nor embarrassment by the cumbering of the folds. She held her head as before; her lips were firmly set, only the tense nostrils gave her breath; not a sign of distress witnessed to the long sustaining of that terrible speed.

But on Christian by now the strain was telling palpably. His head weighed heavy, and his breath came labouring in great sobs: the bear-spear would have been a burden now. His heart was beating like a hammer, but such a dullness oppressed his brain, that it was only by degrees he could realise his helpless state: wounded and weaponless, chasing that terrible Thing, that was a fierce, desperate, axe-armed woman, except she should assume the beast with fangs yet more formidable.

And still the far slow stars went lingering nearly an hour from midnight.

So far was his brain astray that an impression took him that she was fleeing from the midnight stars, whose gain was by such slow degrees that a time equalling days and days had gone in the race round the northern circle of the world, and days and days as long might last before the end—except she slackened, or except he failed.

But he would not fail yet.

How long had he been praying so? He had started with a self-confidence and reliance that had felt no need for that aid; and now it seemed the only means by which to restrain his heart from swelling beyond the compass of his body, by which to cherish his brain from dwindling and shrivelling quite away. Some sharp-toothed creature kept tearing and dragging on his maimed left hand; he never could see it, he could not shake it off; but he prayed it off at times.

The clear stars before him took to shuddering, and he knew why: they shuddered at sight of what was behind him. He had never divined before that strange things hid themselves from men under pretence of being snow-clad mounds or swaying trees; but now they came slipping out from their harmless covers to follow him, and mock at his impotence to make a kindred Thing resolve to truer form. He knew the air behind him was thronged; he heard the hum of innumerable murmurings together; but his eyes could never catch them, they were too swift and nimble. Yet he knew they were there, because, on a backward glance, he saw the snow mounds surge as they grovelled flatlings out of sight: he saw the trees reel as they screwed themselves rigid past recognition among the boughs.

And after such glance the stars for awhile returned to steadfastness, and an infinite stretch of silence froze upon the chill grey world, only deranged by the swift even beat of the flying feet, and his own—slower from the longer stride, and the sound of his breath. And for some clear moments he knew that his only concern was, to sustain his speed regardless of pain and distress, to deny with every nerve he had, her power to outstrip him or to widen the space between them, till the stars crept up to midnight. Then out again would come that crowd invisible, humming and hustling behind, dense and dark enough, he knew, to blot out the stars at his back, yet ever skipping and jerking from his sight.

A hideous check came to the race. White Fell swirled about and leapt to the right, and Christian, unprepared for so prompt a lurch, found close at his feet a deep pit yawning, and his own impetus past control. But he snatched at her as he bore past, clasping her right arm with his one whole hand, and the two swung together upon the brink.

And her straining away in self-preservation was vigorous enough to counterbalance his headlong impulse, and brought them reeling together to safety.

Then, before he was verily sure that they were not to perish so, crashing down, he saw her gnashing in wild pale fury as she wrenched to be free; and since her right hand was in his grasp, used her axe left-handed, striking back at him.

The blow was effectual enough even so; his right arm dropped powerless, gashed, and with the lesser bone broken, that jarred with horrid pain when he let it swing as he leaped out again, and ran to recover the few feet she had gained from his pause at the shock.

The near escape and this new quick pain made again every faculty alive and intense. He knew that what he followed was most surely Death animate: wounded and helpless, he was utterly at her mercy if so she should realise and take action. Hopeless to avenge, hopeless to save, his very despair for Sweyn swept him on to follow, and follow, and precede the kiss-doomed to death. Could he yet fail to hunt that Thing past midnight, out of the womanly form alluring and treacherous, into lasting restraint of the bestial, which was the last shred of hope left from the confident purpose of the outset?

"Sweyn, Sweyn, O Sweyn!" He thought he was praying, though his heart wrung out nothing but this: "Sweyn, Sweyn, O Sweyn!"

The last hour from midnight had lost half its quarters, and the stars went lifting up the great minutes; and again his greatening heart, and his shrinking brain, and the sickening agony that swung at either side, conspired to appal the will that had only seeming empire over his feet.

Now White Fell's body was so closely enveloped that not a lap nor an edge flew free. She stretched forward strangely aslant, leaning from the upright poise of a runner. She cleared the ground at times by long bounds, gaining an increase of speed that Christian agonised to equal.

Because the stars pointed that the end was nearing, the black brood came behind again, and followed, noising. Ah! If they could but be kept quiet and still, nor slip their usual harmless masks to encourage with their interest the last speed of their most deadly congener. What shape had they? Should he ever know? If it were not that he was bound to compel the fell Thing that ran before him into her truer form, he might face about and follow them. No—no—not so; if he might do anything but what he did—race, race, and racing bear this agony, he would just stand still and die, to be quit of the pain of breathing.

He grew bewildered, uncertain of his own identity, doubting of his own true form. He could not be really a man, no more than that running Thing was really a woman; his real form was only hidden under embodiment of a man, but what it was he did not know. And Sweyn's real form he did not know. Sweyn lay fallen at his feet, where he had struck him down—his own brother—he: he stumbled over him, and had to overleap him and race harder because she who had kissed Sweyn leapt so fast. "Sweyn, Sweyn, O Sweyn!"

Why did the stars stop to shudder? Midnight else had surely come!

The leaning, leaping Thing looked back at him with a wild, fierce look, and laughed in savage scorn and triumph. He saw in a flash why, for within a time measurable by seconds she would have escaped him utterly. As the land lay, a slope of ice sunk on the one hand; on the other hand a steep rose, shouldering forwards; between the two was space for a foot to be planted, but none for a body to stand; yet a juniper bough, thrusting out, gave a handhold secure enough for one with a resolute grasp to swing past the perilous place, and pass on safe.

Though the first seconds of the last moment were going, she dared to flash back a wicked look, and laugh at the pursuer who was impotent to grasp.

The crisis struck convulsive life into his last supreme effort; his will surged up indomitable, his speed proved matchless yet. He leapt with a rush, passed her before her laugh had time to go out, and turned short, barring the way, and braced to withstand her.

She came hurling desperate, with a feint to the right hand, and then launched herself upon him with a spring like a wild beast when it leaps to kill. And he, with one strong arm and a hand that could not hold, with one strong hand and an arm that could not guide and sustain, he caught and held her even so. And they fell together. And because he felt his whole arm slipping, and his whole hand loosing, to slack the dreadful agony of the wrenched bone above, he caught and held with his teeth the tunic at her knee, as she struggled up and wrung off his hands to overleap him victorious.

Like lightning she snatched her axe, and struck him on the neck, deep—once, twice—his lifeblood gushed out, staining her feet.

The stars touched midnight.

The death scream he heard was not his, for his teeth had hardly yet relaxed when it rang out; and the dreadful cry began with a woman's shriek, and changed and ended as the yell of a beast. And before the final blank overtook his dying eyes, he saw that She gave place to It; he saw more, that Life gave place to Death—causelessly, incomprehensibly.

For he did not presume that no holy water could be more holy, more potent to destroy an evil thing than the lifeblood of a pure heart poured out for another in free willing devotion.

His own true hidden reality that he had desired to know grew palpable, recognisable. It seemed to him just this: a great glad abounding hope that he had saved his brother; too expansive to be contained by the limited form of a sole man, it yearned for a new embodiment infinite as the stars.

What did it matter to that true reality that the man's brain shrank, shrank, till it was nothing; that the man's body could not retain the huge pain of his heart, and heaved it out through the red exit riven at the neck; that the black noise came again hurtling from behind, reinforced by that dissolved shape, and blotted out for ever the man's sight, hearing, sense.

In the early grey of day Sweyn chanced upon the footprints of a man—of a runner, as he saw by the shifted snow; and the direction they had taken aroused curiosity, since a little farther their line must be crossed by the edge of a sheer height. He turned to trace them. And so doing, the length of the stride struck his attention—a stride as long as his own if he ran. He knew he was following Christian.

In his anger he had hardened himself to be indifferent to the night-long absence of his brother; but now, seeing where the footsteps went, he was seized with compunction and dread. He had failed to give thought and care to his poor frantic twin, who might—was it possible?—have rushed to a frantic death.

His heart stood still when he came to the place where the leap had been taken. A piled edge of snow had fallen too, and nothing but snow lay below when he peered. Along the upper edge he ran for a furlong, till he came to a dip where he could slip and climb down, and then back again on the lower level to the pile of fallen snow. There he saw that the vigorous running had started afresh.

He stood pondering; vexed that any man should have taken that leap where he had not ventured to follow; vexed that he had been beguiled to such painful emotions; guessing vainly at Christian's object in this mad freak. He began sauntering along, half unconsciously following his brother's track; and so in a while he came to the place where the footprints were doubled.

Small prints were these others, small as a woman's, though the pace from one to another was longer than that which the skirts of women allow.

Did not White Fell tread so?

A dreadful guess appalled him, so dreadful that he recoiled from belief. Yet his face grew ashy white, and he gasped to fetch back motion to his checked heart. Unbelievable? Closer attention showed how the smaller footfall had altered for greater speed, striking into the snow with a deeper onset and a lighter pressure on the heels. Unbelievable? Could any woman but White Fell run so? Could any man but Christian run so? The guess became a certainty. He was following where alone in the dark night White Fell had fled from Christian pursuing.

Such villainy set heart and brain on fire with rage and indignation: such villainy in his own brother, till lately love-worthy, praise-worthy, though a fool for meekness. He would kill Christian; had he lives many as the footprints he had trodden, vengeance should demand them all. In a tempest of murderous hate he followed on in haste, for the track was plain enough, starting with such a burst of speed as could not be maintained, but brought him back soon to a plod for the spent, sobbing breath to be regulated. He cursed Christian aloud and called White Fell's name on high in a frenzied expense of passion. His grief itself was a rage, being such an intolerable anguish of pity and shame at the thought of his love, White Fell, who had parted from his kiss free and radiant, to be hounded straightway by his brother mad with jealousy, fleeing for more than life while her lover was housed at his ease. If he had but

known, he raved, in impotent rebellion at the cruelty of events,
if he had but known that his strength and love might have availed
in her defence; now the only service to her that he could render
was to kill Christian.

As a woman he knew she was matchless in speed, matchless
in strength; but Christian was matchless in speed among men,
nor easily to be matched in strength. Brave and swift and strong
though she were, what chance had she against a man of his strength
and inches, frantic, too, and intent on horrid revenge against his
brother, his successful rival?

Mile after mile he followed with a bursting heart; more piteous,
more tragic, seemed the case at this evidence of White Fell's splendid supremacy, holding her own so long against Christian's famous
speed. So long, so long that his love and admiration grew more
and more boundless, and his grief and indignation therewith also.
Whenever the track lay clear he ran, with such reckless prodigal-
ity of strength, that it soon was spent, and he dragged on heavily,
till, sometimes on the ice of a mere, sometimes on a wind-swept
place, all signs were lost; but, so undeviating had been their line
that a course straight on, and then short questing to either hand,
recovered them again.

Hour after hour had gone by through more than half that
winter day, before ever he came to the place where the trampled
snow showed that a scurry of feet had come—and gone! Wolves'
feet—and gone most amazingly! Only a little beyond he came to
the lopped point of Christian's bear-spear; farther on he would
see where the remnant of the useless shaft had been dropped.
The snow here was dashed with blood, and the footsteps of the
two had fallen closer together. Some hoarse sound of exultation
came from him that might have been a laugh had breath sufficed.
"O White Fell, my poor, brave love! Well struck!" he groaned, torn

by his pity and great admiration, as he guessed surely how she had turned and dealt a blow.

The sight of the blood inflamed him as it might a beast that ravens. He grew mad with a desire to have Christian by the throat once again, not to loose this time till he had crushed out his life, or beat out his life, or stabbed out his life; or all these, and torn him piecemeal likewise: and ah! then, not till then, bleed his heart with weeping, like a child, like a girl, over the piteous fate of his poor lost love.

On—on—on—through the aching time, toiling and straining in the track of those two superb runners, aware of the marvel of their endurance, but unaware of the marvel of their speed, that, in the three hours before midnight had overpassed all that vast distance that he could only traverse from twilight to twilight. For clear daylight was passing when he came to the edge of an old marl-pit, and saw how the two who had gone before had stamped and trampled together in desperate peril on the verge. And here fresh blood stains spoke to him of a valiant defence against his infamous brother; and he followed where the blood had dripped till the cold had staunched its flow, taking a savage gratification from this evidence that Christian had been gashed deeply, maddening afresh with desire to do likewise more excellently, and so slake his murderous hate. And he began to know that through all his despair he had entertained a germ of hope, that grew apace, rained upon by his brother's blood.

He strove on as best he might, wrung now by an access of hope, now of despair, in agony to reach the end, however terrible, sick with the aching of the toiled miles that deferred it.

And the light went lingering out of the sky, giving place to uncertain stars.

He came to the finish.

Two bodies lay in a narrow place. Christian's was one, but the other beyond not White Fell's. There where the footsteps ended lay a great white wolf.

At the sight Sweyn's strength was blasted; body and soul he was struck down grovelling.

The stars had grown sure and intense before he stirred from where he had dropped prone. Very feebly he crawled to his dead brother, and laid his hands upon him, and crouched so, afraid to look or stir farther.

Cold, stiff, hours dead. Yet the dead body was his only shelter and stay in that most dreadful hour. His soul, stripped bare of all sceptic comfort, cowered, shivering, naked, abject; and the living clung to the dead out of piteous need for grace from the soul that had passed away.

He rose to his knees, lifting the body. Christian had fallen face forward in the snow, with his arms flung up and wide, and so had the frost made him rigid: strange, ghastly, unyielding to Sweyn's lifting, so that he laid him down again and crouched above, with his arms fast round him, and a low heart-wrung groan.

When at last he found force to raise his brother's body and gather it in his arms, tight clasped to his breast, he tried to face the Thing that lay beyond. The sight set his limbs in a palsy with horror and dread. His senses had failed and fainted in utter cowardice, but for the strength that came from holding dead Christian in his arms, enabling him to compel his eyes to endure the sight, and take into the brain the complete aspect of the Thing. No wound, only blood stains on the feet. The great grim jaws had a savage grin, though dead-stiff. And his kiss: he could bear it no longer, and turned away, nor ever looked again.

And the dead man in his arms, knowing the full horror, had fol-lowed and faced it for his sake; had suffered agony and death for his sake; in the neck was the deep death gash, one arm and both hands were dark with frozen blood, for his sake! Dead he knew him, as in life he had not known him, to give the right meed of love and worship. Because the outward man lacked perfection and strength equal to his, he had taken the love and worship of that great pure heart as his due; he, so unworthy in the inner reality, so mean, so despicable, callous, and contemptuous towards the brother who had laid down his life to save him. He longed for utter annihilation, that so he might lose the agony of knowing himself so unworthy of such perfect love. The frozen calm of death on the face appalled him. He dared not touch it with lips that had cursed so lately, with lips fouled by kiss of the horror that had been Death.

He struggled to his feet, still clasping Christian. The dead man stood upright within his arm, frozen rigid. The eyes were not quite closed; the head had stiffened, bowed slightly to one side; the arms stayed straight and wide. It was the figure of one crucified, the bloodstained hands also conforming.

So living and dead went back along the track that one had passed in the deepest passion of love, and one in the deepest passion of hate. All that night Sweyn toiled through the snow, bearing the weight of dead Christian, treading back along the steps he before had trodden, when he was wronging with vilest thought, and cursing with murderous hatred, the brother who all the while lay dead for his sake.

Cold, silence, darkness encompassed the strong man bowed with the dolorous burden; and yet he knew surely that that night he entered Hell, and trod hell-fire along the homeward road, and endured through it only because Christian was with him. And he knew surely that to him Christian had been as Christ, and had suffered and died to save him from his sins.

A BALLAD OF THE WEREWOLF

Rosamund Marriott Watson

Published in *A Summer Night, and other Poems* (1891)

Rosamund Marriott Watson (1860–1911) was a poet, journalist, and nature writer. As well as publishing under her own name, she used the pseudonyms Graham R. Tomson and Rushworth Armytage (incorporating her husband, George Francis Armytage's, surname). Her first and second marriages ended in divorce, echoing her discussion of unsuccessful and serial marriages in her writings.

'A Ballad of the Werewolf' first appeared in *A Summer Night, and other Poems* (1891). The poem's Scottish dialect suggests that this ballad should be spoken aloud rather than silently read: in choosing to present the poem in this way, Watson evokes the long tradition of oral folkloric storytelling in which the figure of the werewolf flourished. The ballad begins with a husband returning to his wife who awaits him in their cabin while a storm rages outside. A wolf, we learn, has taken their two children, and the man has gone out in order to slaughter this animal. There are suggestions of marital aggression in this poem which resonate with Watson's own experiences of tempestuous relationships; here, this is entwined with more than a dash of the supernatural.

The gudewife sits i' the chimney-neuk,
    An' looks on the louping flame;
The rain fa's chill, and the win' ca's shrill,
    Ere the auld gudeman comes hame.

"Oh, why is your cheek sae wan, gudewife?
    An' why do ye glower on me?
Sae dour ye luik i' the chimney-neuk,
    Wi' the red licht in your e'e!

"Yet this nicht should ye welcome me,
    This ae nicht mair than a',
For I hae scotched yon great grey wolf
    That took our bairnies twa.

"'Twas a sair, sair strife for my very life,
    As I warstled there my lane;
But I'll hae her heart or e'er we part,
    Gin ever we meet again.

"An' 'twas ae sharp stroke o' my bonny knife
    That gar'd her haud awa';
Fu' fast she went out-owre the bent
    Wi'outen her right fore-paw.

"Gae tak' the foot, o' the drumlie brute,
    And hang it upo' the wa';
An' the next time that we meet, gudewife,
    The tane of us shall fa'."

He's flung his pouch on the gudewife's lap,
    I' the firelicht shinin' fair,
Yet naught they saw o' the grey wolf's paw,
    For a bluidy hand lay there.

O hooly, hooly rose she up,
    Wi' the red licht in her e'e,
Till she stude but a span frae the auld gudeman
    Whiles never a word spak' she.

But she stripped the claiths frae her lang richt arm,
    That were wrappit roun' and roun',
The first was white, an' the last was red;
    And the fresh bluid dreeped adown.

She stretchit him out her lang right arm,
    An' cauld as the deid stude he.
The flames louped bricht i' the gloamin' licht—
    There was nae hand there to see!

THE WEREWOLF

Eugene Field

Published in *The Second Book of Tales* (1896)

Eugene Field (1850–95) was an American writer and journalist, renowned for his humorous writings and children's poetry. A number of his short stories deal with religious themes, including his Faustian tale 'Daniel and the Devil'.

Influenced by Norse mythology, 'The Werewolf' was first published in a collection of stories entitled *The Second Book of Tales* (1896), which came out the year after Field's death. The archaic language spoken by the characters situates the monstrous in a superstitious past, far away from Field's native America. The tale concerns a beautiful maiden called Yseult, the man she loves, and a rival for her affection. Curses, magic, and bloodlines all play their part in this story of jealousy, secrecy, and misidentification. Elements of Field's tale, including the threat the werewolf poses to its human lover, can be traced through to werewolf films of the twentieth century, including *Werewolf of London* (1935), *The Wolf Man* (1941), and *An American Werewolf in London* (1981).

I N THE REIGN OF EGBERT THE SAXON THERE DWELT IN BRITAIN a maiden named Yseult, who was beloved of all, both for her goodness and for her beauty. But, though many a youth came wooing her, she loved Harold only, and to him she plighted her troth.

Among the other youth of whom Yseult was beloved was Alfred, and he was sore angered that Yseult showed favour to Harold, so that one day Alfred said to Harold: "Is it right that old Siegfried should come from his grave and have Yseult to wife?" Then added he, "Prithee, good sir, why do you turn so white when I speak your grandsire's name?"

Then Harold asked, "What know you of Siegfried that you taunt me? What memory of him should vex me now?"

"We know and we know," retorted Alfred. "There are some tales told us by our grandmas we have not forgot."

So ever after that Alfred's words and Alfred's bitter smile haunted Harold by day and night.

Harold's grandsire, Siegfried the Teuton, had been a man of cruel violence. The legend said that a curse rested upon him, and that at certain times he was possessed of an evil spirit that wreaked its fury on mankind. But Siegfried had been dead full many years, and there was naught to mind the world of him save the legend and a cunning-wrought spear which he had from Brunehilde, the witch. This spear was such a weapon that it never lost its brightness, nor had its point been blunted. It hung in Harold's chamber, and it was the marvel among weapons of that time.

Yseult knew that Alfred loved her, but she did not know of the bitter words which Alfred had spoken to Harold. Her love for Harold was perfect in its trust and gentleness. But Alfred had hit the truth: the curse of old Siegfried was upon Harold—slumbering a century, it had awakened in the blood of the grandson, and Harold knew the curse that was upon him, and it was this that seemed to stand between him and Yseult. But love is stronger than all else, and Harold loved.

Harold did not tell Yseult of the curse that was upon him, for he feared that she would not love him if she knew. Whensoever he felt the fire of the curse burning in his veins he would say to her, "Tomorrow I hunt the wild boar in the uttermost forest," or, "Next week I go stag-stalking among the distant northern hills." Even so it was that he ever made good excuse for his absence, and Yseult thought no evil things, for she was trustful; ay though he went many times away and was long gone, Yseult suspected no wrong. So none beheld Harold when the curse was upon him in its violence.

Alfred alone bethought himself of evil things. "'Tis passing strange," quoth he, "that ever and anon this gallant lover should quit our company and betake himself whither none knoweth. In sooth't will be well to have an eye on old Siegfried's grandson."

Harold knew that Alfred watched him zealously and he was tormented by a constant fear that Alfred would discover the curse that was on him; but what gave him greater anguish was the fear that mayhap at some moment when he was in Yseult's presence, the curse would seize upon him and cause him to do great evil unto her, whereby she would be destroyed or her love for him would be undone forever. So Harold lived in terror, feeling that his love was hopeless, yet knowing not how to combat it.

Now, it befell in those times that the country round about was ravaged of a werewolf, a creature that was feared by all men howe'er so valorous. This werewolf was by day a man, but by night a wolf given to ravage and to slaughter, and having a charmed life against which no human agency availed aught. Wheresoever he went he attacked and devoured mankind, spreading terror and desolation round about, and the dream-readers said that the earth would not be freed from the werewolf until some man offered himself a voluntary sacrifice to the monster's rage.

Now, although Harold was known far and wide as a mighty huntsman, he had never set forth to hunt the werewolf, and, strange enow, the werewolf never ravaged the domain while Harold was therein. Whereat Alfred marvelled much, and oftentimes he said: "Our Harold is a wondrous huntsman. Who is like unto him in stalking the timid doe and in crippling the fleeing boar? But how passing well doth he time his absence from the haunts of the werewolf. Such valour beseemeth our young Siegfried."

Which being brought to Harold, his heart flamed with anger, but he made no answer, lest he betray the truth he feared.

It happened so about that time that Yseult said to Harold, "Wilt thou go with me tomorrow even to the feast in the sacred grove?"

"That can I not do," answered Harold. "I am privily summoned hence to Normandy upon a mission of which I shall some time tell thee. And I pray thee, on thy love for me, go not to the feast in the sacred grove without me."

"What say'st thou?" cried Yseult. "Shall I not go to the feast of St Aelfreda? My father would be sore displeased were I not there with the other maidens. 'T were greatest pity that I should despite his love thus."

"But do not, I beseech thee," Harold implored. "Go not to the feast of St Aelfreda in the sacred grove! And thou would thus love me, go not—see, thou my life, on my two knees I ask it!"

"How pale thou art," said Yseult, "and trembling."

"Go not to the sacred grove upon the morrow night," he begged.

Yseult marvelled at his acts and at his speech. Then, for the first time, she thought him to be jealous—whereat she secretly rejoiced (being a woman).

"Ah," quoth she, "thou dost doubt my love," but when she saw a look of pain come on his face she added—as if she repented of the words she had spoken—"or dost thou fear the werewolf?"

Then Harold answered, fixing his eyes on hers, "Thou hast said it; it is the werewolf that I fear."

"Why dost thou look at me so strangely, Harold?" cried Yseult. "By the cruel light in thine eyes one might almost take thee to be the werewolf!"

"Come hither, sit beside me," said Harold tremblingly "and I will tell thee why I fear to have thee go to the feast of St Aelfreda tomorrow evening. Hear what I dreamed last night. I dreamed I was the werewolf—do not shudder, dear love, for 't was only a dream.

"A grizzled old man stood at my bedside and strove to pluck my soul from my bosom.

"'What would'st thou?' I cried.

"'Thy soul is mine,' he said, 'thou shalt live out my curse. Give me thy soul—hold back thy hands—give me thy soul, I say.'

"'Thy curse shall not be upon me,' I cried. 'What have I done that thy curse should rest upon me? Thou shalt not have my soul.'

"'For my offence shalt thou suffer, and in my curse thou shalt endure Hell—it is so decreed.'

"So spake the old man, and he strove with me, and he prevailed against me, and he plucked my soul from my bosom, and he said, 'Go, search and kill'—and—and lo, I was a wolf upon the moor.

"The dry grass crackled beneath my tread. The darkness of the night was heavy and it oppressed me. Strange horrors tortured my soul, and it groaned and groaned, jailed in that wolfish body. The wind whispered to me; with its myriad voices it spake to me and said, 'Go, search and kill.' And above these voices sounded the hideous laughter of an old man. I fled the moor—whither I knew not, nor knew I what motive lashed me on.

"I came to a river and I plunged in. A burning thirst consumed me, and I lapped the waters of the river—they were waves of flame, and they flashed around me and hissed, and what they said was, 'Go, search and kill,' and I heard the old man's laughter again.

"A forest lay before me with its gloomy thickets and its sombre shadows—with its ravens, its vampires, its serpents, its reptiles, and all its hideous brood of night. I darted among its thorns and crouched amid the leaves, the nettles, and the brambles. The owls hooted at me and the thorns pierced my flesh. 'Go, search and kill,' said everything. The hares sprang from my pathway; the other beasts ran bellowing away; every form of life shrieked in my ears—the curse was on me—I was the werewolf.

"On, on I went with the fleetness of the wind, and my soul groaned in its wolfish prison, and the winds and the waters and the trees bade me, 'Go, search and kill, thou accursed brute; go, search and kill.'

"Nowhere was there pity for the wolf; what mercy, thus, should I, the werewolf, show? The curse was on me and it filled me with hunger and a thirst for blood. Skulking on my way within myself I cried, 'Let me have blood, oh, let me have human blood, that this wrath may be appeased, that this curse may be removed.'

"At last I came to the sacred grove. Sombre loomed the poplars, the oaks frowned upon me. Before me stood an old man—'twas he, grizzled and taunting, whose curse I bore. He feared me not. All other living things fled before me, but the old man feared me not. A maiden stood beside him. She did not see me, for she was blind.

"'Kill, kill,' cried the old man, and he pointed at the girl beside him.

"Hell raged within me—the curse impelled me—I sprang at her throat. I heard the old man's laughter once more, and then—then I awoke, trembling, cold, horrified."

Scarce was this dream told when Alfred strode the way.

"Now, by'r Lady," quoth he, "I bethink me never to have seen a sorrier twain."

Then Yseult told him of Harold's going away and how that Harold had besought her not to venture to the feast of St Aelfreda in the sacred grove.

"These fears are childish," cried Alfred boastfully. "And thou sufferest me, sweet lady, I will bear thee company to the feast, and a score of my lusty yeoman with their good yew-bows and honest spears, they shall attend me. There be no werewolf, I trow, will chance about with us."

Whereat Yseult laughed merrily, and Harold said: "'Tis well; thou shalt go to the sacred grove, and may my love and Heaven's grace forefend all evil."

Then Harold went to his abode, and he fetched old Siegfried's spear back unto Yseult, and he gave it into her two hands, saying, "Take this spear with thee to the feast tomorrow night. It is old Siegfried's spear, possessing mighty virtue and marvellous."

And Harold took Yseult to his heart and blessed her, and he kissed her upon her brow and upon her lips, saying, "Farewell, oh, my beloved. How wilt thou love me when thou know'st my sacrifice. Farewell, farewell, forever, oh, alder-liefest mine."

So Harold went his way, and Yseult was lost in wonderment.

On the morrow night came Yseult to the sacred grove wherein the feast was spread, and she bore old Siegfried's spear with her in her girdle. Alfred attended her, and a score of lusty yeomen were with him. In the grove there was great merriment, and with singing and dancing and games withal did the honest folk celebrate the feast of the fair St Aelfreda.

But suddenly a mighty tumult arose, and there were cries of "The werewolf!" "The werewolf!" Terror seized upon all—stout hearts were frozen with fear. Out from the further forest rushed the werewolf, wood wroth, bellowing hoarsely, gnashing his fangs and tossing hither and thither the yellow foam from his snapping jaws. He sought Yseult straight, as if an evil power drew him to the spot where she stood. But Yseult was not afeared; like a marble statue she stood and saw the werewolf's coming. The yeomen, dropping their torches and casting aside their bows, had fled; Alfred alone abided there to do the monster battle.

At the approaching wolf he hurled his heavy lance, but as it struck the werewolf's bristling back the weapon was all to-shivered.

Then the werewolf, fixing his eyes upon Yseult, skulked for a moment in the shadow of the yews and thinking then of Harold's words, Yseult plucked old Siegfried's spear from her girdle, raised it on high, and with the strength of despair sent it hurtling through the air.

The werewolf saw the shining weapon, and a cry burst from his gaping throat—a cry of human agony. And Yseult saw in the werewolf's eyes the eyes of someone she had seen and known, but 't was for an instant only, and then the eyes were no longer human, but wolfish in their ferocity.

A supernatural force seemed to speed the spear in its flight. With fearful precision the weapon smote home and buried itself by half its length in the werewolf's shaggy breast just above the heart, and then, with a monstrous sigh—as if he yielded up his life without regret—the werewolf fell dead in the shadow of the yews.

Then, ah, then in very truth there was great joy, and loud were the acclaims, while, beautiful in her trembling pallor, Yseult was led unto her home, where the people set about to give a great feast to do her homage, for the werewolf was dead, and she it was that had slain him.

But Yseult cried out: "Go, search for Harold—go, bring him to me. Nor eat, nor sleep till he be found."

"Good my lady," quoth Alfred, "how can that be, since he hath betaken himself to Normandy?"

"I care not where he be," she cried. "My heart stands still until I look into his eyes again."

"Surely he hath not gone to Normandy," outspake Hubert. "This very eventide I saw him enter his abode."

They hastened thither—a vast company. His chamber door was barred.

"Harold, Harold, come forth!" they cried, as they beat upon the door, but no answer came to their calls and knockings. Afeared, they battered down the door, and when it fell they saw that Harold lay upon his bed.

"He sleeps," said one. "See, he holds a portrait in his hand—and it is her portrait. How fair he is and how tranquilly he sleeps."

But no, Harold was not asleep. His face was calm and beautiful, as if he dreamed of his beloved, but his raiment was red with the blood that streamed from a wound in his breast—a gaping, ghastly spear wound just above his heart.

WHERE THERE IS NOTHING, THERE IS GOD

William Butler Yeats

Published in the magazine *Sketch* (1896)

William Butler Yeats (1865–1939) was an Irish writer and poet, and one of the most celebrated literary figures of the twentieth century. He was fascinated by occultism and, in particular, Irish mythologies. He was awarded the Nobel Prize in Literature in 1923.

'Where There Is Nothing, There Is God' was originally published in the magazine *Sketch* in 1896, and reproduced in Yeats's collection *The Secret Rose* (1897). This story reveals Yeats's twin interests in the supernatural and Irish folklore: the setting is an Irish monastery, and in this tale the magical is closely entwined with Christianity. A child, Olioll, grows increasingly intelligent after the arrival of a mysterious stranger who approaches the monastery accompanied by a number of wolves. Might this affinity be the result of a religious connection to nature, or something more sinister?

THE LITTLE WICKER HOUSES AT TULLAGH, WHERE THE
Brothers were accustomed to pray, or bend over many
handicrafts, when twilight had driven them from the fields, were
empty, for the hardness of the winter had brought the brotherhood together in the little wooden house under the shadow of
the wooden chapel; and Abbot Malathgeneus, Brother Dove,
Brother Bald Fox, Brother Peter, Brother Patrick, Brother Bittern,
Brother Fair-Brows, and many too young to have won names in
the great battle, sat about the fire with ruddy faces, one mending lines to lay in the river for eels, one fashioning a snare for
birds, one mending the broken handle of a spade, one writing in
a large book, and one shaping a jewelled box to hold the book;
and among the rushes at their feet lay the scholars, who would
one day be Brothers, and whose school-house it was, and for the
succour of whose tender years the great fire was supposed to leap
and flicker. One of these, a child of eight or nine years, called
Olioll, lay upon his back looking up through the hole in the roof,
through which the smoke went, and watching the stars appearing
and disappearing in the smoke with mild eyes, like the eyes of a
beast of the field. He turned presently to the Brother who wrote
in the big book, and whose duty was to teach the children, and
said, "Brother Dove, to what are the stars fastened?" The Brother,
rejoicing to see so much curiosity in the stupidest of his scholars,
laid down the pen and said, "There are nine crystalline spheres,

and on the first the Moon is fastened, on the second the planet Mercury, on the third the planet Venus, on the fourth the Sun, on the fifth the planet Mars, on the sixth the planet Jupiter, on the seventh the planet Saturn; these are the wandering stars; and on the eighth are fastened the fixed stars; but the ninth sphere is a sphere of the substance on which the breath of God moved in the beginning."

"What is beyond that?" said the child.

"There is nothing beyond that; there is God."

And then the child's eyes strayed to the jewelled box, where one great ruby was gleaming in the light of the fire, and he said, "Why has Brother Peter put a great ruby on the side of the box?"

"The ruby is a symbol of the love of God."

"Why is the ruby a symbol of the love of God?"

"Because it is red, like fire, and fire burns up everything, and where there is nothing, there is God."

The child sank into silence, but presently sat up and said, "There is somebody outside."

"No," replied the Brother. "It is only the wolves; I have heard them moving about in the snow for some time. They are growing very wild, now that the winter drives them from the mountains. They broke into a fold last night and carried off many sheep, and if we are not careful they will devour everything."

"No, it is the footstep of a man, for it is heavy; but I can hear the footsteps of the wolves also."

He had no sooner done speaking than somebody rapped three times, but with no great loudness.

"I will go and open, for he must be very cold."

"Do not open, for it may be a man-wolf, and he may devour us all."

But the boy had already drawn back the heavy wooden bolt,

and all the faces, most of them a little pale, turned towards the slowly opening door.

"He has beads and a cross, he cannot be a man-wolf," said the child, as a man with the snow heavy on his long, ragged beard, and on the matted hair that fell over his shoulders and nearly to his waist, and dropping from the tattered cloak that but half-covered his withered brown body, came in and looked from face to face with mild, ecstatic eyes. Standing some way from the fire, and with eyes that had rested at last upon the Abbot Malathgeneus, he cried out, "O blessed abbot, let me come to the fire and warm myself and dry the snow from my beard and my hair and my cloak; that I may not die of the cold of the mountains and anger the Lord with a wilful martyrdom."

"Come to the fire," said the abbot, "and warm yourself, and eat the food the boy Olioll will bring you. It is sad indeed that any for whom Christ has died should be as poor as you."

The man sat over the fire, and Olioll took away his now dripping cloak and laid meat and bread and wine before him; but he would eat only of the bread, and he put away the wine, asking for water. When his beard and hair had begun to dry a little and his limbs had ceased to shiver with the cold, he spoke again.

"O blessed abbot, have pity on the poor, have pity on a beggar who has trodden the bare world this many a year, and give me some labour to do, the hardest there is, for I am the poorest of God's poor."

Then the Brothers discussed together what work they could put him to, and at first to little purpose, for there was no labour that had not found its labourer in that busy community; but at last one remembered that Brother Bald Fox, whose business it was to turn the great quern in the quern-house, for he was too stupid for anything else, was getting old for so heavy a labour; and so the beggar was put to the quern from the morrow.

The cold passed away, and the spring grew to summer, and the quern was never idle, nor was it turned with grudging labour, for when any passed the beggar was heard singing as he drove the handle round. The last gloom, too, had passed from that happy community, for Olioll, who had always been stupid and unteachable, grew clever, and this was the more miraculous because it had come of a sudden. One day he had been even duller than usual, and was beaten and told to know his lesson better on the morrow or be sent into a lower class among little boys who would make a joke of him. He had gone out in tears, and when he came the next day, although his stupidity, born of a mind that would listen to every wandering sound and brood upon every wandering light, had so long been the byword of the school, he knew his lesson so well that he passed to the head of the class, and from that day was the best of scholars. At first Brother Dove thought this was an answer to his own prayers to the Virgin, and took it for a great proof of the love she bore him; but when many far more fervid prayers had failed to add a single wheatsheaf to the harvest, he began to think that the child was trafficking with bards, or druids, or witches, and resolved to follow and watch. He had told his thought to the abbot, who bid him come to him the moment he hit the truth; and the next day, which was a Sunday, he stood in the path when the abbot and the Brothers were coming from vespers, with their white habits upon them, and took the abbot by the habit and said, "The beggar is of the greatest of saints and of the workers of miracle. I followed Olioll but now, and by his slow steps and his bent head I saw that the weariness of his stupidity was over him, and when he came to the little wood by the quern-house I knew by the path broken in the underwood and by the footmarks in the muddy places that he had gone that way many times. I hid behind a bush where the path doubled upon itself at a sloping place, and understood by the tears in his eyes that his stupidity was too old and his wisdom too new to save him from terror of the rod. When he was in the quern-house I went to the window and looked in, and the birds came down and perched upon my head and my shoulders, for they are not timid in that holy place; and a wolf passed by, his right side shaking my habit, his left the leaves of a bush. Olioll opened his book and turned to the page I had told him to learn, and began to cry, and the beggar sat beside him and comforted him until he fell asleep. When his sleep was of the deepest the beggar knelt down and prayed aloud, and said, 'O Thou Who dwellest beyond the stars, show forth Thy power as at the beginning, and let knowledge sent from Thee awaken in his mind, wherein is nothing from the world, that the nine orders of angels may glorify Thy name'; and then a light broke out of the air and wrapped Olioll, and I smelt the breath of roses. I stirred a little in my wonder, and the beggar turned and saw me, and, bending low, said, 'O Brother Dove, if I have done wrong, forgive me, and I will do penance. It was my pity moved me'; but I was afraid and I ran away, and did not stop running until I came here."

Then all the Brothers began talking together, one saying it was such and such a saint, and one that it was not he but another; and one that it was none of these, for they were still in their brother-hoods, but that it was such and such a one; and the talk was as near to quarrelling as might be in that gentle community, for each would claim so great a saint for his native province. At last the abbot said, "He is none that you have named, for at Easter I had greeting from all, and each was in his brotherhood; but he is Aengus the Lover of God, and the first of those who have gone to live in the wild places and among the wild beasts. Ten years ago he felt the burden of many labours in a brotherhood under the Hill of Patrick and went into the forest that he might labour only with song to the Lord; but the fame of his holiness brought many thousands to his cell, so that a little pride clung to a soul from which all else had been driven. Nine years ago he dressed himself in rags, and from that day none has seen him, unless, indeed, it be true that he has been seen living among the wolves on the mountains and eating the grass of the fields. Let us go to him and bow down before him; for at last, after long seeking, he has found the nothing that is God; and bid him lead us in the pathway he has trodden."

They passed in their white habits along the beaten path in the wood, the acolytes swinging their censers before them, and the abbot, with his crozier studded with precious stones, in the midst of the incense; and came before the quern-house and knelt down and began to pray, awaiting the moment when the child would wake, and the Saint cease from his watch and come to look at the sun going down into the unknown darkness, as his way was.

THE WEREWOLVES

Henry Beaugrand

Published in the *Century Magazine* (1898)

Henry Beaugrand (1855–1929) was born in Montreal, Canada. While he devoted much time to producing fiction, he does not appear to have been particularly successful in his literary endeavours. 'The Werewolves' was the only tale of his that met with much favour.

'The Werewolves' was first published in the *Century Magazine*. Set in Canada in 1706, this tale draws upon all of the mysticism associated with the native Iroquois people. In a French settlement, with a sentry on the lookout for Iroquois attackers, one man offers up a supernatural story of Native American werewolves. Beaugrand's treatment of the Native Americans can seem jarringly prejudiced to modern readers, yet it is significant that werewolves in Beaugrand's tale can be of any racial background. A Canadian film adaptation entitled *The Werewolf* (now lost) followed in 1913, purportedly the first moving picture to feature a werewolf.

A MOTLEY AND PICTURESQUE-LOOKING CROWD HAD GATH-ered within the walls of Fort Richelieu to attend the annual distribution of powder and lead, to take part in the winter drills and target practice, and to join in the Christmas festivities, that would last until the fast-approaching New Year.

Coureurs des bois from the Western country, scouts, hunters, trappers, militiamen, and habitants from the surrounding settlements, Indian warriors from the neighbouring tribe of friendly Abenakis, were all placed under the military instruction of the company of regular marine infantry that garrisoned the fort constructed in 1665, by M. de Saurel, at the mouth of the Richelieu River, where it flows into the waters of the St Lawrence, forty-five miles below Montreal.

It was on Christmas Eve of the year 1706, and the dreaded Iroquois were committing depredations in the surrounding country, burning farmhouses, stealing cattle and horses, and killing every man, woman, and child whom they could not carry away to their own villages to torture at the stake.

The Richelieu River was the natural highway to the Iroquois country during the open season, but now that its waters were ice-bound, it was hard to tell whence the attacks from those terrible savages could be expected.

The distribution of arms and ammunition having been made, under the joint supervision of the notary royal and the commandant of the fort, the men had retired to the barracks, where they were drinking, singing, and telling stories.

Tales of the most extraordinary adventures were being unfolded by some of the hunters, who were vying with one another in their attempts at relating some unheard-of and fantastic incidents that would create a sensation among their superstitious and wonder-loving comrades.

A sharp lookout was kept outside on the bastions, where four sentries were pacing up and down, repeating every half hour the familiar watch-cry:

"Sentinelles! Prenez garde... vous!"

Old Sergeant Bellehumeur of the regulars, who had seen forty years of service in Canada, and who had come over with the regiment of Carignan-Salieres, was quietly sitting in a corner of the guard-room, smoking his Indian calumet, and watching over and keeping order among the men who were inclined to become boisterous over the oft-repeated libations.

One of the men, who had accompanied La Salle in his first expedition in search of the mouths of the Mississippi, was in the act of reciting his adventures with the hostile tribes that they had met in that far-off country, when the crack of a musket was heard from the outside, through the battlements. A second report immediately followed the first one, and the cry, *"Aux armes!"* was soon heard, with two more shots following close on each other.

The four sentries had evidently fired their muskets at some enemy or enemies, and the guard tumbled out in a hurry, followed by all the men, who had seized their arms, ready for an emergency.

The officer on duty was already on the spot when Sergeant Bellehumeur arrived to inquire into the cause of all this turmoil.

The sentry who had fired the first shot declared excitedly that all at once, on turning round on his beat, he had seen a party of red devils dancing around a bush fire, a couple of hundred yards away, right across the river from the fort, on the point covered with tall pine trees. He had fired his musket in their direction, more with the intention of giving alarm than in the hope of hitting any of them at that distance.

The second, third, and fourth shots had been successively fired by the other sentries, who had not seen anything of the Indians, but who had joined in the firing with the idea of calling the guard to the spot, and scaring away the enemy who might be prowling around.

"But where are the Indians now?" inquired the officer, who had climbed on the parapet, "and where is the fire of which you speak?"

"They seem to have disappeared as by enchantment, sir," answered the soldier, in astonishment; "but they were there a few moments ago, when I fired my musket at them."

"Well, we will see"; and, turning to Bellehumeur: "Sergeant, take ten men with you, and proceed over there cautiously, to see whether you can discover any signs of the presence of Indians on the point. Meanwhile, see to it that the guard is kept under arms until your return, to prevent any surprise."

Bellehumeur did as he was ordered, picking ten of his best men to accompany him. The gate of the fort was opened, and the draw-bridge was lowered to give passage to the party, who proceeded to cross the river, over the ice, marching at first in Indian file. When nearing the opposite shore, near the edge of the wood, the men were seen to scatter, and to advance carefully, taking advantage of every tree to protect themselves against a possible ambush.

The night was a bright one, and any dark object could be plainly seen on the white snow, in the clearing that surrounded the fort.

The men disappeared for a short time, but were soon seen again, coming back in the same order and by the same route.

"Nothing, sir," said the sergeant, in saluting the officer. "Not a sign of fire of any kind, and not a single Indian track, in the snow, over the point."

"Well, that is curious, I declare! Had the sentry been drinking, sergeant, before going on post?"

"No more than the rest of the men, sir; and I could see no sign of liquor on him when the relief was sent out, an hour ago."

"Well, the man must be a fool or a poltroon to raise such an alarm without any cause whatever. See that he is immediately relieved from his post, sergeant, and have him confined in the guard house until he appears before the commandant in the morning."

The sentry was duly relieved, and calm was restored among the garrison. The men went back to their quarters, and the conversation naturally fell on the peculiar circumstances that had just taken place.

An old weather-beaten trapper who had just returned from the Great Lakes volunteered the remark that, for his part, he was not so very sure that the sentry had not acted in perfect good faith, and had not been deceived by a band of loups-garous—werwolves—who came and went, appeared and disappeared, just as they pleased, under the protection of old Nick himself.

"I have seen them more than once in my travels," continued the trapper; "and only last year I had occasion to fire at just such a band of miscreants, up on the Ottawa River, above the portage of the Grandes-Chaudieres."

"Tell us about it!" chimed in the crowd of superstitious adventurers, whose credulous curiosity was instantly awakened by the promise of a story that would appeal to their love of the supernatural.

And everyone gathered about the old trapper, who was evidently proud to have the occasion to recite his exploits before as

distinguished an assemblage of daredevils as one could find anywhere, from Quebec to Michilimackinac.

"We had left Lachine, twenty-four of us, in three war-canoes,
bound for the Illinois country, by way of the Ottawa River and
the Upper Lakes; and in four days we had reached the portage of
the Grandes-Chaudieres, where we rested for one day to renew
our stock of meat, which was getting exhausted. Along with one
of my companions, I had followed some deer-tracks, which led
us several miles up the river, and we soon succeeded in killing a
splendid animal. We divided the meat so as to make it easier for us
to carry, and it was getting on toward nightfall when we began to
retrace our steps in the direction of the camp. Darkness overtook
us on the way, and as we were heavily burdened, we had stopped
to rest and to smoke a pipe in a clump of maple trees on the edge
of the river. All at once, and without warning of any kind, we saw
a bright fire of balsam boughs burning on a small island in the
middle of the river. Ten or twelve renegades, half human and half
beasts, with heads and tails like wolves, arms, legs, and bodies like
men, and eyes glaring like burning coals, were dancing around
the fire and barking a sort of outlandish chant that was now and
then changed to peals of infernal laughter. We could also vaguely
perceive, lying on the ground, the body of a human being that
two of the imps were engaged in cutting up, probably getting it
ready for the horrible meal that the miscreants would make when
the dance would be over. Although we were sitting in the shadow
of the trees, partly concealed by the underbrush, we were at once
discovered by the dancers, who beckoned to us to go and join
them in their disgusting feast. That is the way they entrap unwary
hunters for their bloody sacrifices. Our first impulse was to fly
toward the woods; but we soon realised that we had to deal with
loups-garous; and as we had both been to confession and taken

holy communion before embarking at Lachine, we knew we had nothing to fear from them. White loups-garous are bad enough at anytime, and you all know that only those who have remained seven years without performing their Easter duties are liable to be changed into wolves, condemned to prowl about at night until they are delivered by some Christian drawing blood from them by inflicting a wound on their forehead in the form of a cross. But we had to deal with Indian renegades, who had accepted the sacraments only in mockery, and who had never since performed any of the duties commanded by the Church. They are the worst loups-garous that one can meet, because they are constantly intent on capturing some misguided Christian, to drink his blood and to eat his flesh in their horrible *fricots*. Had we been in possession of holy water to sprinkle at them, or of a four-leaved clover to make wadding for our muskets, we might have exterminated the whole crowd, after having cut crosses on the lead of our bullets. But we were powerless to interfere with them, knowing full well that ordinary ammunition was useless, and that bullets would flatten out on their tough and impenetrable hides. Wolves at night, those devils would assume again, during the day, the appearance of ordinary Indians; but their hide is only turned inside out, with the hair growing inward. We were about to proceed on our way to the camp, leaving the loups-garous to continue their witchcraft unmolested, when a thought struck me that we might at least try to give them a couple of parting shots. We both withdrew the bullets from our muskets, cut crosses on them with our hunting-knives, placed them back in the barrels, along with two dizaines [a score] of beads from the blessed rosary which I carried in my pocket. That would surely make the renegades sick, if it did not kill them outright.

"We took good aim, and fired together. Such unearthly howling and yelling I have never heard before or since. Whether we killed any of them I could not say; but the fire instantly disappeared, and the island was left in darkness, while the howls grew fainter and fainter as the loups-garous seemed to be scampering in the distance. We returned to camp, where our companions were beginning to be anxious about our safety.

"We found that one man, a hard character who bragged of his misdeeds, had disappeared during the day, and when we left on the following morning he had not yet returned to camp, neither did we ever hear of him afterward. In paddling up the river in our canoes, we passed close to the island where we had seen the loups-garous the night before. We landed, and searched around for some time; but we could find no traces of fire, or any signs of the passage of werewolves or of any other animals. I knew that it would turn out just so, because it is a well-known fact that those accursed brutes never leave any tracks behind them. My opinion was then, and has never changed to this day, that the man who strayed from our camp, and never returned, was captured by the loups-garous, and was being eaten up by them when we disturbed their horrible feast."

"Well, is that all?" inquired Sergeant Bellehumeur, with an ill-concealed contempt.

"Yes, that is all; but is it not enough to make one think that the sentry who has just been confined in the guardhouse by the lieutenant for causing a false alarm has been deceived by a band of loups-garous who were picnicking on the point, and who disappeared in a twinkle when they found out that they were discovered?"

GABRIEL-ERNEST

Saki

Published in the *Westminster Gazette* (1909)

Saki was the pseudonym of Hector Hugh Munro (1870–1916), a Scottish writer born in Burma, known for his wit as well as his interest in the macabre. His work is often compared to that of his Victorian predecessors, Oscar Wilde and Lewis Carroll. He was killed by a German sniper at the Battle of the Ancre during the First World War, and his body was never identified.

A number of Saki's stories deal with animals, and wolves (and werewolves) recur across his body of work: Saki's tales that integrate wolves and werewolves include the chilling 'The Interlopers' (1909), and the more humorous tales 'She-Wolf' (1912) and 'The Storyteller' (1914). The following story, 'Gabriel-Ernest', first published in the *Westminster Gazette* in 1909 and later reproduced in the collection *Reginald in Russia* (1910), demonstrates Saki's characteristic morbid streak. The protagonist, Van Cheele, learns that there is a predator stalking his land, and killing livestock. But this hunter, we learn, is not a fox, as Van Cheele first suspects, but something altogether more astonishing.

"THERE IS A WILD BEAST IN YOUR WOODS," SAID THE artist Cunningham, as he was being driven to the station. It was the only remark he had made during the drive, but as Van Cheele had talked incessantly, his companion's silence had not been noticeable.

"A stray fox or two and some resident weasels. Nothing more formidable," said Van Cheele. The artist said nothing.

"What did you mean about a wild beast?" said Van Cheele later, when they were on the platform.

"Nothing. My imagination. Here is the train," said Cunningham.

That afternoon, Van Cheele went for one of his frequent rambles through his woodland property. He had a stuffed bittern in his study, and knew the names of quite a number of wild flowers, so his aunt had possibly some justification in describing him as a great naturalist. At any rate, he was a great walker. It was his custom to take mental notes of everything he saw during his walks, not so much for the purpose of assisting contemporary science as to provide topics for conversation afterwards. When the bluebells began to show themselves in flower, he made a point of informing everyone of the fact; the season of the year might have warned his hearers of the likelihood of such an occurrence, but at least they felt that he was being absolutely frank with them.

What Van Cheele saw on this particular afternoon was, however, something far removed from his ordinary range of experience.

On a shelf of smooth stone overhanging a deep pool in the hollow of an oak coppice, a boy of about sixteen lay asprawl, drying his wet brown limbs luxuriously in the sun. His wet hair, parted by a recent dive, lay close to his head, and his light-brown eyes, so light that there was an almost tigerish gleam in them, were turned towards Van Cheele with a certain lazy watchfulness. It was an unexpected apparition, and Van Cheele found himself engaged in the novel process of thinking before he spoke. Where on earth could this wild-looking boy hail from? The miller's wife had lost a child some two months ago, supposed to have been swept away by the mill race, but that had been a mere baby, not a half-grown lad.

"What are you doing there?" he demanded.

"Obviously, sunning myself," replied the boy.

"Where do you live?"

"Here, in these woods."

"You can't live in the woods," said Van Cheele.

"They are very nice woods," said the boy, with a touch of patronage in his voice.

"But where do you sleep at night?"

"I don't sleep at night: that's my busiest time."

Van Cheele began to have an irritated feeling that he was grappling with a problem that was eluding him.

"What do you feed on?" he asked.

"Flesh," said the boy, and he pronounced the word with slow relish, as though he were tasting it.

"Flesh! What flesh?"

"Since it interests you, rabbits, wild fowl, hares, poultry, lambs in their season, children when I can get any—they're usually too well locked in at night, when I do most of my hunting. It's quite two months since I tasted child flesh."

Ignoring the chaffing nature of the last remark, Van Cheele tried to draw the boy on the subject of possible poaching operations.

"You're talking rather through your hat when you speak of feeding on hares." Considering the nature of the boy's toilet, the simile was hardly an apt one. "Our hillside hares aren't easily caught."

"At night I hunt on four feet," was the somewhat cryptic response.

"I suppose you mean that you hunt with a dog?" hazarded Van Cheele.

The boy rolled slowly over onto his back and laughed a weird low laugh that was pleasantly like a chuckle and disagreeably like a snarl.

"I don't fancy any dog would be very anxious for my company, especially at night."

Van Cheele began to feel that there was something positively uncanny about the strange-eyed, strange-tongued youngster.

"I can't have you staying in these woods," he declared authoritatively.

"I fancy you'd rather have me here than in your house," said the boy.

The prospect of this wild, nude animal in Van Cheele's primly ordered house was certainly an alarming one.

"If you don't go, I shall have to make you," said Van Cheele.

The boy turned like a flash, plunged into the pool and in a moment had flung his wet and glistening body halfway up the bank where Van Cheele was standing. In an otter the movement would not have been remarkable; in a boy, Van Cheele found it sufficiently startling. His foot slipped as he made an involuntary backward movement, and he found himself almost prostrate on the slippery weed-grown bank, with those tigerish yellow eyes not very far from his own. Almost instinctively he half-raised his hand to his throat. The boy laughed again, a laugh in which the snarl had nearly driven out the chuckle, and then, with another of his astonishing lightning movements, plunged out of view into a yielding tangle of weed and fern.

"What an extraordinary wild animal!" said Van Cheele as he picked himself up. And then he recalled Cunningham's remark: "There is a wild beast in your woods."

Walking slowly homeward, Van Cheele began to turn over in his mind various local occurrences which might be traceable to the existence of this astonishing young savage.

Something had been thinning the game in the woods lately, poultry had been missing from the farms, hares were growing unaccountably scarcer, and complaints had reached him of lambs being carried off bodily from the hills. Was it possible that this wild boy was really hunting the countryside in company with some clever poacher dog? He had spoken of hunting "four-footed" by night—but then again, he had hinted strangely at no dog caring to come near him, "especially at night". It was certainly puzzling. And then, as Van Cheele ran his mind over the various depredations that had been committed during the last month or two, he came suddenly to a dead stop, alike in his walk and his speculations. The child missing from the mill two months ago—the accepted theory was that it had tumbled into the mill race and been swept away, but the mother had always declared she had heard a shriek on the hill side of the house, in the opposite direction from the water. It was unthinkable, of course, but he wished that the boy had not made that uncanny remark about child flesh eaten two months ago. Such dreadful things should not be said even in fun.

Van Cheek, contrary to his usual wont, did not feel disposed to be communicative about his discovery in the wood. His position as a parish councillor and justice of the peace seemed somehow compromised by the fact that he was harbouring a personality of such doubtful repute on his property: there was even a possibility that a heavy bill of damages for raided lambs and poultry might be laid at his door. At dinner that night he was quite unusually silent.

"Where's your voice gone to?" said his aunt. "One would think you had seen a wolf."

Van Cheele, who was not familiar with the old saying, thought the remark rather foolish: if he *had* seen a wolf on his property, his tongue would have been extraordinarily busy with the subject.

At breakfast next morning Van Cheele was conscious that his feeling of uneasiness regarding yesterday's episode had not wholly disappeared, and he resolved to go by train to the neighbouring cathedral town, hunt up Cunningham and learn from him what he had really seen that had prompted the remark about a wild beast in the woods. With this resolution taken, his usual cheerfulness partially returned, and he hummed a bright little melody as he sauntered to the morning room for his customary cigarette. As he entered the room, the melody made way abruptly for a pious invocation. Gracefully asprawl on the ottoman, in an attitude of almost exaggerated repose, was the boy of the woods. He was drier than when Van Cheele had last seen him, but no other alteration was noticeable in his toilet.

"How dare you come here?" asked Van Cheele furiously.

"You told me I was not to stay in the woods," said the boy calmly.

"But not to come here. Supposing my aunt should see you!"

And with a view to minimising that catastrophe, Van Cheele hastily obscured as much of his unwelcome guest as possible under the folds of a *Morning Post*. At that moment his aunt entered the room.

"This is a poor boy who has lost his way—and lost his memory. He doesn't know who he is or where he comes from," explained Van Cheele desperately, glancing apprehensively at the waif's face to see whether he was going to add inconvenient candour to his other savage propensities.

Miss Van Cheele was enormously interested.

"Perhaps his underlinen is marked," she suggested.

"He seems to have lost most of that, too," said Van Cheele, making frantic little grabs at the *Morning Post* to keep it in its place.

A naked homeless child appealed to Miss Van Cheele as warmly as a stray kitten or derelict puppy would have done.

"We must do all we can for him," she decided, and in a very short time a messenger, dispatched to the rectory, where a page boy was kept, had returned with a suit of pantry clothes and the necessary accessories of shirt, shoes, collar, etc. Clothed, clean, and groomed, the boy lost none of his uncanniness in Van Cheele's eyes, but his aunt found him sweet.

"We must call him something till we know who he really is," she said. "Gabriel-Ernest, I think: those are nice suitable names."

Van Cheele agreed, but he privately doubted whether they were being grafted onto a nice, suitable child. His misgivings were not diminished by the fact that his staid and elderly spaniel had bolted out of the house at the first incoming of the boy, and now obstinately remained shivering and yapping at the farther end of the orchard, while the canary, usually as vocally industrious as Van Cheele himself, had put itself on an allowance of frightened cheeps. More than ever he was resolved to consult Cunningham without loss of time.

As he drove off to the station, his aunt was arranging that Gabriel-Ernest should help her to entertain the infant members of her Sunday-school class at tea that afternoon.

Cunningham was not at first disposed to be communicative.

"My mother died of some brain trouble," he explained, "so you will understand why I am averse to dwelling on anything of an impossibly fantastic nature that I may see or think that I have seen."

"But what *did* you see?" persisted Van Cheele.

"What I thought I saw was something so extraordinary that no really sane man could dignify it with the credit of having actually happened. I was standing, the last evening I was with you, half-hidden in the hedge-growth by the orchard gate, watching the dying glow of the sunset. Suddenly I became aware of a naked boy, a bather from some neighbouring pool, I took him to be, who was standing out on the bare hillside also watching the sunset. His pose was so suggestive of some wild faun of pagan myth that I instantly wanted to engage him as a model, and in another moment I think I should have hailed him. But just then the sun dipped out of view, and all the orange and pink slid out of the landscape, leaving it cold and grey. And at the same moment an astounding thing happened—the boy vanished too!"

"What! Vanished away into nothing?" asked Van Cheele excitedly.

"No: that is the dreadful part of it," answered the artist. "On the open hillside where the boy had been standing a second ago, stood a large wolf, blackish in colour, with gleaming fangs and cruel, yellow eyes. You may think—"

But Van Cheele did not stop for anything as futile as thought. Already he was tearing at top speed towards the station. He dismissed the idea of a telegram. "Gabriel-Ernest is a werewolf" was a hopelessly inadequate effort at conveying the situation, and his aunt would think it was a code message to which he had omitted to give her the key. His one hope was that he might reach home before sundown. The cab which he chartered at the other end of the railway journey bore him with what seemed exasperating slowness along the country roads, which were pink and mauve with the flush of the sinking sun. His aunt was putting away some unfinished jams and cake when he arrived.

"Where is Gabriel-Ernest?" he almost screamed.

"He is taking the little Toop child home," said his aunt. "It was getting so late, I thought it wasn't safe to let it go back alone. What a lovely sunset, isn't it?"

But Van Cheele, although not oblivious of the glow in the western sky, did not stay to discuss its beauties. At a speed for which he was scarcely geared, he raced along the narrow lane that led to the home of the Toops. On one side ran the swift current of the mill stream, on the other rose the stretch of bare hillside. A dwindling rim of red sun showed still on the skyline, and the next turning must bring him in view of the ill-assorted couple he was pursuing. Then the colour went suddenly out of things, and a grey light settled itself with a quick shiver over the landscape. Van Cheele heard a shrill wail of fear and stopped running.

Nothing was ever seen again of the Toop child or Gabriel-Ernest, but the latter's discarded garments were found lying in the road, so it was assumed that the child had fallen into the water, and that the boy had stripped and jumped in, in a vain endeavour to save it. Van Cheele and some workmen who were nearby at the time testified to having heard a child scream loudly just near the spot where the clothes were found. Mrs Toop, who had eleven other children, was decently resigned to her bereavement, but Miss Van Cheele sincerely mourned her lost foundling. It was on her initiative that a memorial brass was put up in the parish church to "Gabriel-Ernest, an unknown boy, who bravely sacrificed his life for another".

Van Cheele gave way to his aunt in most things, but he flatly refused to subscribe to the Gabriel-Ernest memorial.

THE THING IN THE FOREST

Bernard Capes

Published in *The Fabulists* (1915)

Bernard Capes (1854–1918) was an English writer and journalist, whose fictional work spanned historical romances, detective fiction, ghost stories, and poetry. He was a prolific author, producing over forty volumes across a thirty-year literary career. A number of his stories were forgotten before being rediscovered in the 1970s.

'The Thing in the Forest' appeared in *The Fabulists* (1915), a collection of poems and short stories published by Mills and Boon. The tale is written in a mode evocative of the fairy tale, featuring a woodsman's wife as its main character. The woodsman's wife encounters a wolf which she recognises as a human soul consigned to a wolf's body by night, rather than a wild animal. 'The Thing in the Forest' is noteworthy for its religious imagery: this werewolf is not an unfortunate who has been bitten and infected, but an individual condemned for his sins. Lycanthropy, in this tale, is religious punishment.

INTO THE SNOW-LOCKED FORESTS OF UPPER HUNGARY STEAL wolves in winter; but there is a footfall worse than theirs to knock upon the heart of the lonely traveller.

One December evening Elspet, the young, newly wedded wife of the woodman Stefan, came hurrying over the lower slopes of the White Mountains from the town where she had been all day marketing. She carried a basket with provisions on her arm; her plump cheeks were like a couple of cold apples; her breath spoke short, but more from nervousness than exhaustion. It was nearing dusk, and she was glad to see the little lonely church in the hollow below, the hub, as it were, of many radiating paths through the trees, one of which was the road to her own warm cottage yet a half-mile away.

She paused a moment at the foot of the slope, undecided about entering the little chill, silent building and making her plea for protection to the great battered stone image of Our Lady of Succour which stood within by the confessional box; but the stillness and the growing darkness decided her, and she went on. A spark of fire glowing through the presbytery window seemed to repel rather than attract her, and she was glad when the convolutions of the path hid it from her sight. Being new to the district, she had seen very little of Father Ruhl as yet, and somehow the penetrating knowledge and burning eyes of the pastor made her feel uncomfortable.

The soft drift, the lane of tall, motionless pines, stretched on in a quiet like death. Somewhere the sun, like a dead fire, had fallen into opalescent embers faintly luminous: they were enough only to touch the shadows with a ghastlier pallor. It was so still that the light crunch in the snow of the girl's own footfalls trod on her heart like a desecration.

Suddenly there was something near her that had not been before. It had come like a shadow, without more sound or warning. It was here—there—behind her. She turned, in mortal panic, and saw a wolf. With a strangled cry and trembling limbs she strove to hurry on her way; and always she knew, though there was no whisper of pursuit, that the gliding shadow followed in her wake. Desperate in her terror, she stopped once more and faced it.

A wolf!—was it a wolf? O who could doubt it! Yet the wild expression in those famished eyes, so lost, so pitiful, so mingled of insatiable hunger and human need! Condemned, for its unspeakable sins, to take this form with sunset, and so howl and snuffle about the doors of men until the blessed day released it. A were-wolf—not a wolf.

That terrific realisation of the truth smote the girl as with a knife out of darkness: for an instant she came near fainting. And then a low moan broke into her heart and flooded it with pity. So lost, so infinitely hopeless. And so pitiful—yes, in spite of all, so pitiful. It had sinned, beyond any sinning that her innocence knew or her experience could gauge; but she was a woman, very blest, very happy, in her store of comforts and her surety of love. She knew that it was forbidden to succour these damned and nameless outcasts, to help or sympathise with them in any way.

But— There was good store of meat in her basket, and who need ever know or tell? With shaking hands she found and threw a sop to the desolate brute—then, turning, sped upon her way.

But at home her secret sin stood up before her, and, interposing between her husband and herself, threw its shadow upon both their faces. What had she dared—what done? By her own act forfeited her birthright of innocence; by her own act placed herself in the power of the evil to which she had ministered. All that night she lay in shame and horror, and all the next day, until Stefan had come about his dinner and gone again, she moved in a dumb agony. Then, driven unendurably by the memory of his troubled, bewildered face, as twilight threatened she put on her cloak and went down to the little church in the hollow to confess her sin.

"Mother, forgive, and save me," she whispered, as she passed the statue.

After ringing the bell for the confessor, she had not knelt long at the confessional box in the dim chapel, cold and empty as a waiting vault, when the chancel rail clicked, and the footsteps of Father Ruhl were heard rustling over the stones. He came, he took his seat behind the grating; and, with many sighs and falterings, Elspet avowed her guilt. And as, with bowed head, she ended, a strange sound answered her—it was like a little laugh, and yet not so much like a laugh as a snarl. With a shock as of death she raised her face. It was Father Ruhl who sat there— and yet it was not Father Ruhl. In that time of twilight his face was already changing, narrowing, becoming wolfish—the eyes rounded and the jaw slavered. She gasped, and shrunk back; and at that, barking and snapping at the grating, with a wicked look he dropped—and she heard him coming. Sheer horror lent her wings. With a scream she sprang to her feet and fled. Her cloak caught in something—there was a wrench and crash and, like a flood, oblivion overswept her.

It was the old deaf and near senile sacristan who found them lying there, the woman unhurt but insensible, the priest crushed out of life by the fall of the ancient statue, long tottering to its collapse. She recovered, for her part: for his, no one knows where he lies buried. But there were dark stories of a baying pack that night, and of an empty, bloodstained pavement when they came to seek for the body.

RUNNING WOLF

Algernon Blackwood

Published in the *Century Magazine* (1920)

Algernon Blackwood (1869–1951) was a prolific writer of novels and short stories, renowned not only for his supernatural fiction, but for his genuine interest in occultism, spanning from theosophy to psychical research. He was also particularly interested in psychology, especially the works of Sigmund Freud.

'Running Wolf' first appeared in the *Century Magazine* in 1920, two decades after Henry Beaugrand's 'The Werewolves' and in the same publication. This is only one of a number of Blackwood's tales with a lycanthropic element: others include 'The Strange Adventures of a Private Secretary in New York' (1906), 'The Camp of the Dog' (1908), and 'The Man-Eater' (1937). 'Running Wolf' features a hotel clerk, Malcolm Hyde, who seeks the peace of a fishing holiday in Canada. He is not alone, however, and the sensation that he is being watched is followed by the appearance of a wolf. Hyde's name is undoubtedly influenced by Robert Louis Stevenson's famous novella, *Strange Case of Dr Jekyll and Mr Hyde* (1886), with its splitting of the self into two, as well as a range of meanings of the homonym 'hide': an animal pelt, or else to conceal oneself or something, a concept central to much werewolf fiction.

T HE MAN WHO ENJOYS AN ADVENTURE OUTSIDE THE GENERAL
experience of the race, and imparts it to others, must not be
surprised if he is taken for either a liar or a fool, as Malcolm Hyde,
hotel clerk on a holiday, discovered in due course. Nor is "enjoy"
the word to use in describing his emotions; the word he chose was
probably "survive".

When he first set eyes on Medicine Lake he was struck by its
still, sparkling beauty, lying there in the vast Canadian backwoods;
next, by its extreme loneliness; and, lastly—a good deal later, this—
by its combination of beauty, loneliness, and singular atmosphere,
due to the fact that it was the scene of adventure.

"It's fairly stiff with big fish," said Morton of the Montreal
Sporting Club. "Spend your holidays there up Mattawa way,
some fifteen miles west of Stony Creek. You'll have it all yourself
except for an old Indian who's got a shack there. Camp on the
east side—if you'll take a tip from me." He then talked for half
an hour about the wonderful sport; yet he was not otherwise
very communicative, and did not suffer questions gladly, Hyde
noticed. Nor had he stayed there very long himself. If it was such
a paradise as Morton, its discoverer and the most experienced rod
in the province, claimed, why had he himself spent only three
days there?

"Ran short of grub," was the explanation offered; but to another
friend he had mentioned briefly "flies", and to a third, so Hyde

learned later, he gave the excuse that his half-breed "took sick", necessitating a quick return to civilisation.

Hyde, however, cared little for the explanations; his interest in these came later. "Stiff with fish" was the phrase he liked. He took the Canadian Pacific train to Mattawa, laid in his outfit at Stony Creek, and set off thence for the fifteen-mile canoe-trip without a care in the world.

Travelling light, the portages did not trouble him; the water was swift and easy, the rapids negotiable; everything came his way, as the saying is. Occasionally he saw big fish making for the deeper pools, and was sorely tempted to stop; but he resisted. He pushed on between the immense world of forests that stretched for hundreds of miles, known to deer, bear, moose, and wolf, but strange to any echo of human tread, a deserted and primeval wilderness. The autumn day was calm, the water sang and sparkled, the blue sky hung cloudless over all, ablaze with light. Toward evening he passed an old beaver-dam, rounded a little point, and had his first sight of Medicine Lake. He lifted his dripping paddle; the canoe shot with silent glide into calm water.

He gave an exclamation of delight, for the loveliness caught his breath away.

Though primarily a sportsman, he was not insensible to beauty. The lake formed a crescent, perhaps four miles long, its width between a mile and half a mile. The slanting gold of sunset flooded it. No wind stirred its crystal surface. Here it had lain since the redskins' god first made it; here it would lie until he dried it up again. Towering spruce and hemlock trooped to its very edge, majestic cedars leaned down as if to drink, crimson sumachs shone in fiery patches, and maples gleamed orange and red beyond belief. The air was like wine, with the silence of a dream.

It was here the red men formerly "made medicine", with all the wild ritual and tribal ceremony of an ancient day. But it was of Morton, rather than of Indians, that Hyde thought. If this lonely, hidden paradise was really stiff with big fish, he owed a lot to Morton for the information. Peace invaded him, but the excitement of the hunter lay below.

He looked about him with quick, practised eye for a camping-place before the sun sank below the forests and the half-lights came. The Indian's shack, lying in full sunshine on the eastern shore, he found at once; but the trees lay too thick about it for comfort, nor did he wish to be so close to its inhabitant. Upon the opposite side, however, an ideal clearing offered. This lay already in shadow, the huge forest darkening it toward evening; but the open space attracted. He paddled over and quickly examined it. The ground was hard and dry, he found, and a little brook ran tinkling down one side of it into the lake. This outfall, too, would be a good fishing spot.

Also it was sheltered. A few low willows marked the mouth.

An experienced camper soon makes up his mind. It was a perfect site, and some charred logs, with traces of former fires, proved that he was not the first to think so. Hyde was delighted.

Then, suddenly, disappointment came to tinge his pleasure. His kit was landed, and preparations for putting up the tent were begun, when he recalled a detail that excitement had so far kept in the background of his mind—Morton's advice. But not Morton's only, for the storekeeper at Stony Creek reinforced it. The big fellow with straggling moustache and stooping shoulders, dressed in shirt and trousers, had handed him out a final sentence with the bacon, flour, condensed milk, and sugar. He had repeated Morton's half-forgotten words:

"Put yer tent on the east shore, I should," he had said at parting.

He remembered Morton, too, apparently. "A shortish fellow, brown as an Indian and fairly smelling of the woods. Travelling with Jake, the half-breed." That assuredly was Morton. "Didn't stay long, now, did he," he added to himself in a reflective tone.

"Going Windy Lake way, are yer? Or Ten Mile Water maybe?" he had first inquired of Hyde.

"Medicine Lake."

"Is that so?" the man said, as though he doubted it for some obscure reason. He pulled at his ragged moustache a moment. "Is that so, now?" he repeated. And the final words followed him down-stream after a considerable pause—the advice about the best shore on which to put his tent. All this now suddenly flashed back upon Hyde's mind with a tinge of disappointment and annoyance, for when two experienced men agreed, their opinion was nor to be lightly disregarded. He wished he had asked the storekeeper for more details. He looked about him, he reflected, he hesitated, His ideal camping-ground lay certainly on the forbidden shore. What in the world, he wondered, could be the objection to it?

But the light was fading; he must decide quickly one way or the other. After staring at his unpacked dunnage, and the tent, already half erected, he made up his mind with a muttered expression that consigned both Morton and the storekeeper to less pleasant places. "They must have some reason," he growled to himself; "fellows like that usually know what they're talking about. I guess I'd better shift over to the other side—for tonight at any rate."

He glanced across the water before actually reloading. No smoke rose from the Indian's shack.

He had seen no sign of a canoe. The man, he decided, was away. Reluctantly, then, he left the good camping-ground and paddled across the lake, and half an hour later his tent was up, firewood collected, and two small trout were already caught for supper. But the bigger fish, he knew, lay waiting for him on the other side by the little out-fall, and he fell asleep at length on his bed of balsam boughs, annoyed and disappointed, yet wondering how a mere sentence could have persuaded him so easily against his own better judgement. He slept like the dead; the sun was well up before he stirred.

But his morning mood was a very different one. The brilliant light, the peace, the intoxicating air, all this was too exhilarating for the mind to harbour foolish fancies, and he marvelled that he could have been so weak the night before. No hesitation lay in him anywhere. He struck camp immediately after breakfast, paddled back across the strip of shining water, and quickly settled in upon the forbidden shore, as he now called it, with a contemptuous grin. And the more he saw of the spot, the better he liked it. There was plenty of wood, running water to drink, an open space about the tent, and there were no flies. The fishing, moreover, was magnificent. Morton's description was fully justified, and "stiff with big fish" for once was not an exaggeration.

The useless hours of the early afternoon he passed dozing in the sun, or wandering through the underbrush beyond the camp. He found no sign of anything unusual. He bathed in a cool deep pool; he revelled in the lonely little paradise. Lonely it certainly was, but the loneliness was part of its charm; the stillness, the peace, the isolation of this beautiful backwoods lake delighted him.

The silence was divine. He was entirely satisfied.

After a brew of tea, he strolled toward evening along the shore, looking for the first sign of a rising fish. A faint ripple on the water, with the lengthening shadows, made good conditions.

Plop followed plop, as the big fellows rose, snatched at their food, and vanished into the depths.

He hurried back. Ten minute later he had taken his rods and was gliding cautiously in the canoe through the quiet water.

So good was the sport, indeed, and so quickly did the big trout pile up in the bottom of the canoe, that despite the growing lateness, he found it hard to tear himself away. "One more," he said, "and then I really will go." He landed that "one more", and was in the act of taking off the hook, when the deep silence of the evening was curiously disturbed. He became abruptly aware that someone watched him. A pair of eyes, it seemed, were fixed upon him from some point in the surrounding shadows.

Thus, at least, he interpreted the odd disturbance in his happy mood; for thus he felt it. The feeling stole over him without the slightest warning. He was not alone. The slippery big trout dropped from his fingers. He sat motionless, and stared about him.

Nothing stirred; the ripple on the lake had died away; there was no wind; the forest lay a single purple mass of shadow; the yellow sky, fast fading, threw reflections that troubled the eye and made distances uncertain. But there was no sound, no movement; he saw no figure anywhere.

Yet he knew that someone watched him, and a wave of quite unreasoning terror gripped him.

The nose of the canoe was against the bank. In a moment, and instinctively, he shoved it off and paddled into deeper water. The watcher, it came to him also instinctively, was quite close to him upon that bank. But where? And who? Was it the Indian?

Here, in deeper water, and some twenty yards from the shore, he paused and strained both sight and hearing to find some possible clue. He felt half ashamed, now that the first strange feeling passed a little. But the certainty remained. Absurd as it was, he felt positive that someone watched him with concentrated and intent regard. Every fibre in his being told him so; and though he could discover no figure, no new outline on the shore, he could even have sworn in which clump of willow bushes the hidden person crouched and stared. His attention seemed drawn to that particular clump.

The water dripped slowly from his paddle, now lying across the thwarts. There was no other sound. The canvas of his tent gleamed dimly. A star or two were out. He waited. Nothing happened.

Then, as suddenly as it had come, the feeling passed, and he knew that the person who had been watching him intently had gone. It was as if a current had been turned off; the normal world flowed back; the landscape emptied as if someone had left a room. The disagreeable feeling left him at the same time, so that he instantly turned the canoe in to the shore again, landed, and, paddle in hand, went over to examine the clump of willows he had singled out as the place of concealment. There was no one there, of course, nor any trace of recent human occupancy. No leaves, no branches stirred, nor was a single twig displaced; his keen and practised sight detected no sign of tracks upon the ground. Yet, for all that, he felt positive that a little time ago someone had crouched among these very leaves and watched him. He remained absolutely convinced of it.

The watcher, whether Indian hunter, stray lumberman, or wandering half-breed, had now withdrawn, a search was useless, and dusk was falling. He returned to his little camp, more disturbed perhaps than he cared to acknowledge. He cooked his supper, hung up his catch on a string, so that no prowling animal could get at it during the night, and prepared to make himself comfortable until bedtime. Unconsciously, he built a bigger fire than usual and found himself peering over his pipe into the deep shadows beyond the firelight, straining his ears to catch the slightest sound. He remained generally on the alert in a way that was new to him.

A man under such conditions and in such a place need not know discomfort until the sense of loneliness strikes him as too vivid a reality. Loneliness in a backwoods camp brings charm, pleasure, and a happy sense of calm until, and unless, it comes too near. It should remain an ingredient only among other conditions; it should not be directly, vividly noticed. Once it has crept within short range, however, it may easily cross the narrow line between comfort and discomfort, and darkness is an undesirable time for the transition. A curious dread may easily follow—the dread lest the loneliness suddenly be disturbed, and the solitary human feel himself open to attack.

For Hyde, now, this transition had been already accomplished; the too intimate sense of his loneliness had shifted abruptly into the worst condition of no longer being quite alone. It was an awkward moment, and the hotel clerk realised his position exactly. He did not quite like it. He sat there, with his back to the blazing logs, a very visible object in the light, while all about him the darkness of the forest lay like an impenetrable wall. He could not see a yard beyond the small circle of his camp-fire; the silence about him was like the silence of the dead. No leaf rustled, no wave lapped; he himself sat motionless as a log.

Then again he became suddenly aware that the person who watched him had returned, and that same intent and concentrated gaze as before was fixed upon him where he lay. There was no warning; he heard no stealthy tread or snapping of dry twigs, yet the owner of those steady eyes was very close to him, probably not a dozen feet away. This sense of proximity was overwhelming.

It is unquestionable that a shiver ran down his spine. This time, moreover, he felt positive that the man crouched just beyond the firelight, the distance he himself could see being nicely calculated, and straight in front of him. For some minutes he sat without stirring a single muscle, yet with each muscle ready and alert, straining his eyes in vain to pierce the darkness, but only succeeding in dazzling his sight with the reflected light. Then, as he shifted his position slowly, cautiously, to obtain another angle of vision, his heart gave two big thumps against his ribs and the hair seemed to rise on his scalp with the sense of cold that gave him goose-flesh. In the darkness facing him he saw two small and greenish circles that were certainly a pair of eyes, yet not the eyes of an Indian hunter, or of any human being. It was a pair of animal eyes that stared so fixedly at him out of the night. And this certainty had an immediate and natural effect upon him.

For, at the menace of those eyes, the fears of millions of long-dead hunters since the dawn of time woke in him. Hotel clerk though he was, heredity surged through him in an automatic wave of instinct. His hand groped for a weapon. His fingers fell on the iron head of his small camp axe, and at once he was himself again. Confidence returned; the vague, superstitious dread was gone. This was a bear or wolf that smelt his catch and came to steal it. With beings of that sort he knew instinctively how to deal, yet admitting, by this very instinct, that his original dread had been of quite another kind.

"I'll damned quick find out what it is," he exclaimed aloud, and snatching a burning brand from the fire, he hurled it with good aim straight at the eyes of the beast before him.

The bit of pitch-pine fell in a shower of sparks that lit the dry grass this side of the animal, flared up a moment, then died quickly down again. But in that instant of bright illumination he saw clearly what his unwelcome visitor was. A big timber wolf sat on its hindquarters, staring steadily at him through the firelight. He saw its legs and shoulders, he saw its hair, he saw also the big hemlock trunks lit up behind it, and the willow scrub on each side. It formed a vivid, clear-cut picture shown in clear detail by the momentary blaze. To his amazement, however, the wolf did not turn and bolt away from the burning log, but withdrew a few yards only, and sat there again on its haunches, staring, staring as before. Heavens, how it stared! He "shoo-ed" it, but without effect; it did not budge. He did not waste another good log on it, for his fear was dissipated now; a timber wolf was a timber wolf, and it might sit there as long as it pleased, provided it did not try to steal his catch. No alarm was in him any more. He knew that wolves were harmless in the summer and autumn, and even when "packed" in the winter they would attack a man only when suffering desperate hunger. So he lay and watched the beast, threw bits of stick in its direction, even talked to it, wondering only that it never moved. "You can stay there for ever, if you like," he remarked to it aloud, "for you cannot get at my fish, and the rest of the grub I shall take into the tent with me!"

The creature blinked its bright green eyes, but made no move. Why, then, if his fear was gone, did he think of certain things as he rolled himself in the Hudson Bay blankets before going sleep? The immobility of the animal was strange, its refusal to turn and bolt was still stranger.

Never before had he known a wild creature that was not afraid of fire. Why did it sit and watch him, as if with purpose in its gleaming eyes? How had he felt its presence earlier and instantly? A timber wolf, especially a solitary wolf, was a timid thing, yet this one feared neither man nor fire.

Now, as he lay there wrapped in his blankets inside the cosy tent, it sat outside beneath the stars, beside the fading embers, the wind chilly in its fur, the ground cooling beneath its planted paws, watching him, steadily watching him, perhaps until the dawn.

It was unusual, it was strange. Having neither imagination nor tradition, he called upon no store of racial visions. Matter of fact, a hotel clerk on a fishing holiday, he lay there in blankets, merely wondering and puzzled. A timber wolf was a timber wolf and nothing more. Yet this timber wolf—the idea haunted him—was different. In a word, the deeper part, his original uneasiness, remained. He tossed about, he shivered sometimes in his broken sleep; he did not go out to see, but he woke early and unrefreshed.

Again with the sunshine and the morning wind, however, the incident of the night before was forgotten, almost unreal. His hunting zeal was uppermost. The tea and fish were delicious, his pipe had never tasted so good, the glory of this lonely lake amid primeval forests went to his head a little; he was a hunter before the Lord, and nothing else. He tried the edge of the lake, and in the excitement of playing a big fish, knew suddenly that it, the wolf, was there. He paused with the rod, exactly as if struck. He looked about him, he looked in a definite direction. The brilliant sunshine made every smallest detail clear and sharp—boulders of granite, burned stems, crimson sumach, pebbles along the shore in neat, separate detail—without revealing where the watcher hid. Then, his sight wandering farther inshore among the tangled undergrowth, he suddenly picked up the familiar, half-expected outline. The wolf was lying behind a granite boulder, so that only the head, the muzzle, and the eyes were visible. It merged in its background. Had he not known it was a wolf, he could never have separated it from the landscape. The eyes shone in the sunlight.

There it lay. He looked straight at it. Their eyes, in fact, actually met full and square. "Great Scott!" he exclaimed aloud, "why, it's like looking at a human being!"

From that moment, unwittingly, he established a singular personal relation with the beast. And what followed confirmed this undesirable impression, for the animal rose instantly and came down in leisurely fashion to the shore, where it stood looking back at him. It stood and stared into his eyes like some great wild dog, so that he was aware of a new and almost incredible sensation—that it courted recognition.

"Well! Well!" he exclaimed again, relieving his feelings by addressing it aloud, "if this doesn't beat everything I ever saw! What d'you want, anyway?"

He examined it now more carefully. He had never seen a wolf so big before; it was a tremendous beast, a nasty customer to tackle, he reflected, if it ever came to that. It stood there absolutely fearless, and full of confidence. In the clear sunlight he took in every detail of it—a huge, shaggy, lean-flanked timber wolf, its wicked eyes staring straight into his own, almost with a kind of purpose in them. He saw its great jaws, its teeth, and its tongue hung out, dropping saliva a little. And yet the idea of its savagery, its fierceness, was very little in him.

He was amazed and puzzled beyond belief. He wished the Indian would come back. He did not understand this strange behaviour in an animal. Its eyes, the odd expression in them, gave him a queer, unusual, difficult feeling. Had his nerves gone wrong, he almost wondered.

The beast stood on the shore and looked at him. He wished for the first time that he had brought a rifle. With a resounding smack he brought his paddle down flat upon the water, using all his strength, till the echoes rang as from a pistol-shot that was audible from one end of the lake to the other. The wolf never stirred. He shouted, but the beast remained unmoved. He blinked his eyes, speaking as to a dog, a domestic animal, a creature accustomed to human ways.

It blinked its eyes in return.

At length, increasing his distance from the shore, he continued fishing, and the excitement of the marvellous sport held his attention—his surface attention, at any rate. At times he almost forgot the attendant beast; yet whenever he looked up, he saw it there. And worse; when he slowly paddled home again, he observed it trotting along the shore as though to keep him company.

Crossing a little bay, he spurted, hoping to reach the other point before his undesired and undesirable attendant. Instantly the brute broke into that rapid, tireless lope that, except on ice, can run down anything on four legs in the woods. When he reached the distant point, the wolf was waiting for him. He raised his paddle from the water, pausing a moment for reflection; for his very close attention—there were dusk and night yet to come—he certainly did not relish. His camp was near; he had to land; he felt uncomfortable even in the sunshine of broad day, when, to his keen relief, about half a mile from the tent, he saw the creature suddenly stop and sit down in the open. He waited a moment, then paddled on. It did not follow. There was no attempt to move; it merely sat and watched him. After a few hundred yards, he looked back. It was still sitting where he left it. And the absurd, yet significant, feeling came to him that the beast divined his thought, his anxiety, his dread, and was now showing him, as well as it could, that it entertained no hostile feeling and did not meditate attack.

He turned the canoe toward the shore; he landed; he cooked his supper in the dusk; the animal made no sign. Not far away it certainly lay and watched, but it did not advance. And to Hyde, observant now in a new way, came one sharp, vivid reminder of the strange atmosphere into which his commonplace personality had strayed: he suddenly recalled that his relations with the beast, already established, had progressed distinctly a stage further. This startled him, yet without the accompanying alarm he must

certainly have felt twenty-four hours before. He had an understand-
ing with the wolf. He was aware of friendly thoughts toward it.
He even went so far as to set out a few big fish on the spot where
he had first seen it sitting the previous night. "If he comes," he
thought, "he is welcome to them, I've got plenty, anyway." He
thought of it now as "he".

Yet the wolf made no appearance until he was in the act of
entering his tent a good deal later. It was close on ten o'clock,
whereas nine was his hour, and late at that, for turning in. He had,
therefore, unconsciously been waiting for him. Then, as he was
closing the flap, he saw the eyes close to where he had placed the
fish. He waited, hiding himself, and expecting to hear sounds of
munching jaws; but all was silence. Only the eyes glowed steadily
out of the background of pitch darkness. He closed the flap. He
had no slightest fear. In ten minutes he was sound asleep.

He could not have slept very long, for when he woke up he
could see the shine of a faint red light through the canvas, and the
fire had not died down completely. He rose and cautiously peeped
out. The air was very cold, he saw his breath. But he also saw the
wolf, for it had come in, and was sitting by the dying embers, not
two yards away from where he crouched behind the flap. And
this time, at these very close quarters, there was something in the
attitude of the big wild thing that caught his attention with a vivid
thrill of startled surprise and a sudden shock of cold that held him
spellbound. He stared, unable to believe his eyes; for the wolf's
attitude conveyed to him something familiar that at first he was
unable to explain. Its pose reached him in the terms of another
thing with which he was entirely at home. What was it? Did his
senses betray him? Was he still asleep and dreaming?

Then, suddenly, with a start of uncanny recognition, he knew.
Its attitude was that of a dog.

Having found the clue, his mind then made an awful leap. For it was, after all, no dog its appearance aped, but something nearer to himself, and more familiar still. Good heavens! It sat there with the pose, the attitude, the gesture in repose of something almost human. And then, with a second shock of biting wonder, it came to him like a revelation. The wolf sat beside that camp-fire as a man might sit.

Before he could weigh his extraordinary discovery, before he could examine it in detail or with care, the animal, sitting in this ghastly fashion, seemed to feel his eyes fixed on it. It slowly turned and looked him in the face, and for the first time Hyde felt a full-blooded superstitious fear flood through his entire being. He seemed transfixed with that nameless terror that is said to attack human beings who suddenly face the dead, finding themselves bereft of speech and movement. This moment of paralysis certainly occurred. Its passing, however, was as singular as its advent. For almost at once he was aware of something beyond and above this mockery of human attitude and pose, something that ran along unaccustomed nerves and reached his feeling, even perhaps his heart. The revulsion was extraordinary, its result still more extraordinary and unexpected. Yet the fact remains. He was aware of another thing that had the effect of stilling his terror as soon as it was born. He was aware of appeal, silent, half expressed, yet vastly pathetic.

He saw in the savage eyes beseeching, even a yearning, expression that changed his mood as if by magic from dread to natural sympathy. The great grey brute, symbol of cruel ferocity, sat there beside his dying fire and appealed for help.

The gulf betwixt animal and human seemed in that instant bridged. It was, of course, incredible. Hyde, sleep still possibly clinging to his inner being with the shades and half shapes of dream yet about his soul, acknowledged, how he knew not, the amazing fact. He found himself nodding to the brute in half consent, and instantly, without more ado, the lean grey shape rose like a wraith and trotted off swiftly, but with stealthy tread, into the background of the night.

When Hyde woke in the morning his first impression was that he must have dreamed the entire incident. His practical nature asserted itself. There was a bite in the fresh autumn air; the bright sun allowed no half lights anywhere; he felt brisk in mind and body. Reviewing what had happened, he came to the conclusion that it was utterly vain to speculate; no possible explanation of the animal's behaviour occurred to him: he was dealing with something entirely outside his experience. His fear, however, had completely left him. The odd sense of friendliness remained.

The beast had a definite purpose, and he himself was included in that purpose. His sympathy held good.

But with the sympathy there was also an intense curiosity. "If it shows itself again," he told himself, "I'll go up close and find out what it wants." The fish laid out the night before had not been touched.

It must have been a full hour after breakfast when he next saw the brute; it was standing on the edge of the clearing, looking at him in the way now become familiar. Hyde immediately picked up his axe and advanced toward it boldly, keeping his eyes fixed straight upon its own. There was nervousness in him, but kept well under; nothing betrayed it; step by step he drew nearer until some ten yards separated them. The wolf had not stirred a muscle as yet. Its jaws hung open, its eyes observed him intently; it allowed him to approach without a sign of what its mood might be. Then, with these ten yards between them, it turned abruptly and moved slowly off, looking back first over one shoulder and then over the other, exactly as a dog might do, to see if he was following.

A singular journey it was they then made together, animal and man. The trees surrounded them at once, for they left the lake behind them, entering the tangled bush beyond. The beast, Hyde noticed, obviously picked the easiest track for him to follow; for obstacles that meant nothing to the four-legged expert, yet were difficult for a man, were carefully avoided with an almost uncanny skill, while yet the general direction was accurately kept. Occasionally there were windfalls to be surmounted; but though the wolf bounded over these with ease it was always waiting for the man on the other side after he had laboriously climbed over. Deeper and deeper into the heart of the lonely forest they penetrated in this singular fashion, cutting across the arc of the lake's crescent, it seemed to Hyde; for after two miles or so, he recognised the big rocky bluff that overhung the water at its northern end. This outstanding bluff he had seen from his camp, one side of it falling sheer into the water; it was probably the spot, he imagined, where the Indians held their medicine-making ceremonies, for it stood out in isolated fashion, and its top formed a private plateau not easy of access. And it was here, close to a big spruce at the foot of the bluff upon the forest side, that the wolf stopped suddenly and for the first time since its appearance gave audible expression to its feelings. It sat down on its haunches, lifted its muzzle with open jaws, and gave vent to a subdued and long-drawn howl that was more like the wail of a dog than the fierce barking cry associated with a wolf, By this time Hyde had lost not only fear, but caution too; nor, oddly enough, did this warning howl revive a sign of unwelcome emotion in him. In that curious sound he detected the same message that the eyes conveyed—appeal for help. He paused, nevertheless, a little startled, and while the wolf sat waiting for him, he looked about him quickly. There was young timber here; it had once been a small clearing, evidently. Axe and fire had done their work, but

there was evidence to an experienced eye that it was Indians and
not white men who had once been busy here. Some part of the
medicine ritual, doubtless, took place in the little clearing, thought
the man, as he advanced again towards his patient leader. The end
of their queer journey, he felt, was close at hand.

He had not taken two steps before the animal got up and moved
very slowly in the direction of some low bushes that formed a
clump just beyond. It entered these, first looking back to make
sure that its companion watched. The bushes hid it; a moment
later it emerged again. Twice it performed this pantomime, each
time, as it reappeared, standing still and staring at the man with
as distinct an expression of appeal in the eyes as an animal may
compass, probably. Its excitement, meanwhile, certainly increased,
and this excitement was, with equal certainty, communicated to
the man. Hyde made up his mind quickly. Gripping his axe tightly,
and ready to use it at the first hint of malice, he moved slowly
nearer to the bushes, wondering with something of a tremor what
would happen.

If he expected to be startled, his expectation was at once fulfilled; but it was the behaviour of the beast that made him jump.
It positively frisked about him like a happy dog. It frisked for joy.

Its excitement was intense, yet from its open mouth no sound
was audible. With a sudden leap, then, it bounded past him into
the clump of bushes, against whose very edge he stood, and began
scraping vigorously at the ground. Hyde stood and stared, amazement and interest now banishing all his nervousness, even when
the beast, in its violent scraping, actually touched his body with
its own. He had, perhaps, the feeling that he was in a dream, one
of those fantastic dreams in which things may happen without
involving an adequate surprise; for otherwise the manner of scraping and scratching at the ground must have seemed an impossible

phenomenon. No wolf, no dog certainly, used its paws in the way those paws were working. Hyde had the odd, distressing sensation that it was hands, not paws, he watched. And yet, somehow, the natural, adequate surprise he should have felt was absent. The strange action seemed not entirely unnatural. In his heart some deep hidden spring of sympathy and pity stirred instead. He was aware of pathos.

The wolf stopped in its task and looked up into his face. Hyde acted without hesitation then.

Afterwards he was wholly at a loss to explain his own conduct. It seemed he knew what to do, divined what was asked, expected of him. Between his mind and the dumb desire yearning through the savage animal there was intelligent and intelligible communication. He cut a stake and sharpened it, for the stones would blunt his axe-edge. He entered the clump of bushes to complete the digging his four-legged companion had begun. And while he worked, though he did not forget the close proximity of the wolf, he paid no attention to it; often his back was turned as he stooped over the laborious clearing away of the hard earth; no uneasiness or sense of danger was in him any more. The wolf sat outside the clump and watched the operations. Its concentrated attention, its patience, its intense eagerness, the gentleness and docility of the grey, fierce, and probably hungry brute, its obvious pleasure and satisfaction, too, at having won the human to its mysterious purpose—these were colours in the strange picture that Hyde thought of later when dealing with the human herd in his hotel again. At the moment he was aware chiefly of pathos and affection. The whole business was, of course, not to be believed, but that discovery came later, too, when telling it to others.

The digging continued for fully half an hour before his labour was rewarded by the discovery of a small whitish object. He picked

it up and examined it—the finger-bone of a man. Other discover
ies then followed quickly and in quantity. The cache was laid bare.
He collected nearly the complete skeleton. The skull however, he
found last, and might not have found at all but for the guidance of
his strangely alert companion. It lay some few yards away from the
central hole now dug, and the wolf stood nuzzling the ground with
its nose before Hyde understood that he was meant to dig exactly
in that spot for it. Between the beast's very paws his stake struck
hard upon it. He scraped the earth from the bone and examined it
carefully. It was perfect, save for the fact that some wild animal had
gnawed it, the teeth-marks being still plainly visible. Close beside it
lay the rusty iron head of a tomahawk. This and the smallness of
the bones confirmed him in his judgement that it was the skeleton
not of a white man, but of an Indian.

During the excitement of the discovery of the bones one by
one, and finally of the skull, but, more especially, during the period
of intense interest while Hyde was examining them, he had paid
little if any attention to the wolf. He was aware that it sat and
watched him, never moving its keen eyes for a single moment
from the actual operations, but sign or movement it made none
at all. He knew that it was pleased and satisfied, he knew also that
he had now fulfilled its purpose in a great measure. The further
intuition that now came to him, derived, he felt positive, from his
companion's dumb desire, was perhaps the cream of the entire
experience to him.

Gathering the bones together in his coat, he carried them,
together with the tomahawk, to the foot of the big spruce where
the animal had first stopped. His leg actually touched the creature's
muzzle as he passed. It turned its head to watch, but did not follow,
nor did it move a muscle while he prepared the platform of boughs
upon which he then laid the poor worn bones of an Indian who had

been killed, doubtless, in sudden attack or ambush, and to whose remains had been denied the last grace of proper tribal burial. He wrapped the bones in bark; he laid the tomahawk beside the skull; he lit the circular fire round the pyre, and the blue smoke rose upward into the clear bright sunshine of the Canadian autumn morning till it was lost among the mighty trees far overhead.

In the moment before actually lighting the little fire he had turned to note what his companion did. It sat five yards away, he saw, gazing intently, and one of its front paws was raised a little from the ground. It made no sign of any kind. He finished the work, becoming so absorbed in it that he had eyes for nothing but the tending and guarding of his careful ceremonial fire. It was only when the platform of boughs collapsed, laying their charred burden gently on the fragrant earth among the soft wood ashes, that he turned again, as though to show the wolf what he had done, and seek, perhaps, some look of satisfaction in its curiously expressive eyes. But the place he searched was empty. The wolf had gone.

He did not see it again; it gave no sign of its presence there; he was not watched. He fished as before, wandered through the bush about his camp, sat smoking round his fire after dark, and slept peacefully in his cosy little tent. He was not disturbed. No howl was ever audible in the distant forest, no twig snapped beneath a stealthy tread, he saw no eyes. The wolf that behaved like a man had gone for ever.

It was the day before he left that Hyde, noticing smoke rising from the shack across the lake, paddled over to exchange a word or two with the Indian, who had evidently now returned. The Redskin came down to meet him as he landed, but it was soon plain that he spoke very little English. He emitted the familiar grunts at first; then bit by bit Hyde stirred his limited vocabulary

into action. The net result, however, was slight enough, though it
was certainly direct:

"You camp there?" the man asked, pointing to the other side.

"Yes."

"Wolf come?"

"Yes."

"You see wolf?"

"Yes." The Indian stared at him fixedly a moment, a keen,
wondering look upon his coppery, creased face.

"You 'fraid wolf?" he asked after a moment's pause.

"No," replied Hyde, truthfully. He knew it was useless to ask
questions of his own, though he was eager for information. The
other would have told him nothing. It was sheer luck that the man
had touched on the subject at all, and Hyde realised that his own
best role was merely to answer, but to ask no questions. Then,
suddenly, the Indian became comparatively voluble. There was
awe in his voice and manner.

"Him no wolf. Him big medicine wolf. Him spirit wolf."

Whereupon he drank the tea the other had brewed for him,
closed his lips tightly, and said no more. His outline was discern-
ible on the shore, rigid and motionless, an hour later, when Hyde's
canoe turned the corner of the lake three miles away, and landed
to make the portages up the first rapid of his homeward stream.

It was Morton who, after some persuasion, supplied further
details of what he called the legend. Some hundred years before,
the tribe that lived in the territory beyond the lake began their
annual medicine-making ceremonies on the big rocky bluff at the
northern end; but no medicine could be made. The spirits, declared
the chief medicine man, would not answer. They were offended.
An investigation followed. It was discovered that a young brave had
recently killed a wolf, a thing strictly forbidden, since the wolf was

the totem animal of the tribe. To make matters worse, the name of the guilty man was Running Wolf. The offence being unpardonable, the man was cursed and driven from the tribe:

"Go out. Wander alone among the woods, and if we see you, we slay you. Your bones shall be scattered in the forest, and your spirit shall not enter the Happy Hunting Grounds till one of another race shall find and bury them."

"Which meant," explained Morton laconically, his only comment on the story, "probably for ever."